PRAISE FOR
THE HEIRLOOM

"It's no secret that kids love to read about magic. But instead of serving up another scoop of the fanciful, good-versus-evil flavor of magic that saturates contemporary kid-lit, Alexandra Folz delivers something entirely different. Lucky young readers of *The Heirloom* will discover the true potential they have for creating real magic in their lives. While sharing Indigo's journey, they'll absorb the message that their own magical powers are within reach as well, and everyday magic is available to us all."

—Lisa McCourt, bestselling author of *I Love You Stinky Face*
and dozens of other books for kids and adults

"In this heartwarming story, Alexandra turns the spotlight on the inner journey of the child's soul, teaching children how to be fearless in their authentic state. A wonderful tribute to the voice of clarity and wisdom we all carry within us! This book's profound messages will nourish the mindful nature of every child. It's a must-read!"

—Dr. Shefali Tsabary, *New York Times* bestselling author
and clinical psychologist

"*The Heirloom* is a beautifully crafted story that takes the reader on an amazing journey of self-discovery. Your child will enjoy the captivating story line and illustrations that make this book very special. The journey that the main character, Indigo, goes through will inspire your child to find and tap into their own inner wisdom—what a gift!"

—Nicki Paulan, Life Coach and author of *Unlock Your Parenting: The Key to More Joy, Peace and Connection*

"*The Heirloom* is a beautiful and insightful book, the perfect self-discovery tool to ignite deep reflection and discussion. It opens the door to powerful conversations about compassion and inner wisdom, and allows the reader to feel normalized on the journey of self-understanding. Children and parents will find valuable guidance in this book, an opportunity to practice self-acceptance and expand what it means to be conscious and human."

—Cathy Adams, Zen Parenting Radio

"The Heirloom lovingly creates a space for me, the reader, to hear my own true pure inner voice in the safety of living with Indigo in hers. I only wish I had had such a knowing refuge, a voicing of the unspoken inner world when I was young. What a gift Alexandra Folz has provided to young and old alike—for our souls are timeless."

—Sheryl Stoller, PCI Certified Parent Coach at Stoller Parent Coaching; and at The Center for Identity Potential, serving parents of the gifted and twice-exceptional children

"*The Heirloom* will awaken your child's inner curiosity. It can't help but teach them how to trust their own intuition, be in the present moment, and be aware of their surroundings at all times."

—Carol Lawrence and Stacy Toten, authors of *10 Ways to Parent Consciously*, www.intentionalconsciousparenting.com

"Beautifully written in an engaging way that enables the reader to reflect on themselves while be deeply immersed in the unfolding story. The lead character, Indigo, effortlessly connects the reader to their natural inner guidance and the mysteries of crystals, symbols, dreams, intuition, and more. This story empowers readers to recognize and overcome their internal judgments and self-doubts that are common to all of us, but so seldom taught or discussed."

—Andrew Newman, founder of The Conscious Bedtime Story Club, www.consciousstories.com

"We live in a time when children need to feel empowered by their own gifts and have the courage to believe in them. Alexandra provides a beautiful, exciting, and unpredictable roadmap for each reader to access their gifts and inner voice. Thank you for letting me read about Indigo and her inner magic . . . which like for all of us, lies in the every day, and when looked at deeper, can be so mysteriously wonderful."

—Christina Fletcher, Spiritually Aware Parent Coach and author at www.spirituallyawareparenting.com

"*The Heirloom* is a beautiful and enchanting story that resonates deeply with me, even as an adult. I look forward to sharing it with my children."

—Renee Jain, Chief Storyteller, GoZen.com

"Alexandra Folz tells a wonderful tale in *The Heirloom* of a young girl who is a bit different than her peers. It is a story of Indigo coming to understand her gifts and the power that she has in them. In *The Heirloom*, Alexandra has created lovable, relatable characters. My 5th grade daughter and I read the book together, and we could not wait to turn each page to find out what would happen next. We were both sad when we finished the book, as we were not ready to say goodbye to Indigo, Caroline, Jake, Mom, Dad and all the rest of the characters. This book is a wonderful gift for a child, especially a young girl, who may feel a bit different than the rest of her peers and is trying to find her unique way in the world."

—Erin Taylor, MA, therapist, parent coach, consulting business co-owner, mom of 4, author of *Connection and Kindness: The Key to Changing the World Through Parenting*

"I really like this book because I feel sometimes I can relate to Indigo and I love animals too. I would recommend this book to any girl who likes books with a cool plot. When I read, I felt myself smiling with joy, sighing with sadness, and gasping with surprise. This book will leave you begging for more. If you're in the mood for an easy, fun, family-friendly novel, this is the one for you. Enjoy!"

—Faith Taylor, EP (Epic Person), 5th grader, lover of books, daughter of Erin Taylor, author of school assignments

THE
HEIRLOOM

ALEXANDRA FOLZ

ILLUSTRATIONS BY CAROL ANN JOHNSON

FEATHER INSIGHT
PRESS
SEATTLE, WA

Feather Insight Press
Seattle, WA

ISBN-13 (Softcover): 978-0-9982769-0-8
ISBN-13 (Hardcover): 978-0-9982769-1-5

Library of Congress Control Number: 2016920447

To contact the author: alexandrafolz@gmail.com
or call 906-361-1047

Edited by
Carol Killman Rosenberg • www.carolkillmanrosenberg.com

Cover and interior design by
Gary A. Rosenberg • www.thebookcouple.com

Printed in the United States of America

A portion of the proceeds from the sale of *The Heirloom* will be donated to Zazu's House Parrot Sanctuary. To learn more, please visit **www.zazushouse.org** and **www.alexandrafolz.com**.

To the rising seeker who asks, "Who am I?"
May you have the strength to unveil
what you've always been
and the courage to *be* what you discover.

And to Sophia Delaney and Emma Louise . . .
May you soar through the Worlds
with courage, joy, and discernment.

CONTENTS

STOP

You must read the following pages before you enter.
I want you to have what I didn't have . . .
the very first clue.

This is Indigo Monroe here, and I must tell you a few really personal things before you read *any* further. I'm sharing these details because, well, because you deserve to know the *whole* truth upfront. By the end of my story, what I have to say here won't seem so strange to you—well, maybe not *as* strange.

When I was five, I saw a girl my age other people didn't see. When she first appeared in my room, I clenched my doll, Stella, and stared right through the girl as if she were glass. Like a shimmering mirage, she stood before me barefooted, wearing a flowy yellow dress with spaghetti straps. She knelt down beside me and asked all kinds of questions about Stella. I showed her my doll, and we laughed and played together like we'd know each other forever.

Somewhere during that time, I asked her name.

"Sienna," she said.

Since she didn't mention a last name, I asked if I could call her Sienna Glass.

She giggled yes.

We played together for days before Mom started getting curious about my "imaginary friend." Even though Mom seems to know things other people don't know and spooky-psychic-ghostly things don't scare her, she couldn't see or hear Sienna. From the doorway of my bedroom, she watched as I kept trying to wrap my pink feather boa around Sienna's shoulders. Sienna kept disappearing, and the fluffy boa would drop to the carpet.

Mom came in and sat beside me on the bed. When she asked what I was doing, I told her I was playing dress up with Sienna Glass; Mom's eyes got this faraway look. "Human clothes aren't fitting for spirits from the stars," she'd said with a smile. Sienna, who had reappeared, nodded in agreement, and from that day forward, I never tried to get her to wear my silly boa again.

The next week, I started kindergarten. Sienna was also eager to learn, so I invited her along. I introduced her to all my new classmates. Having a friend none of my classmates could see caused quite a stir. The other kids laughed when I reserved a seat for Sienna Glass at our table, and during recess, they pointed when I pushed her on the playground swings. It took my teacher only two days to call Mom up to the school.

Mom listened calmly as my teacher told her about my unusual behavior. Then, Mom walked Sienna and me out to our car. She looked really frustrated, and that's how I felt. The kids at school couldn't see Sienna Glass, so I wanted nothing to do with them . . . or with kindergarten.

That night Mom, Dad, Sienna Glass, and I snuggled

up in my parents' bed to read *The Bear Snores On.* When the book was done, Mom asked me some questions about Sienna. I told her she looked a lot like me: my height and size, and she even had long red curly hair like mine. "I wish Sienna was my sister," I said.

Dad's jaw dropped, and Mom gasped.

"When people die, their spirits live on," Mom said, tears welling up in her eyes. "I wasn't sure how or when to talk about this with you, Indigo, but now seems like a perfect time. You see, you had a twin—her name was Vienna." She hesitated and then went on in a low voice, "On the day of your birth, when your sister came out—right after you did—she had trouble breathing. And even though the doctors and nurses did *everything* they could to save her, she . . ." Mom's voice cracked.

"She died?" I asked.

Mom squeezed her eyes shut for a second, then looked at me. "Yes, Indigo, she did. Just two days after you two were born."

Mom didn't have to say it; I knew she believed that Sienna was my sister's spirit. Mom smiled even while tears trickled down her face, but Dad, on the other hand, squirmed off the bed and left the room without a word.

The next day, my parents told me kindergarten could wait until next year. I felt relieved. Mom left her job as a nurse to spend the days with Sienna Glass and me. Of course Sienna Glass and Mom couldn't talk to each other directly, so I would tell Mom everything Sienna said and did. Meanwhile, Dad's job kept him super busy. He even started to sleep on the couch in his city office during the week. When he was home, my parents argued a lot. Mom would cry, and sometimes Dad would storm out of the house and take a drive to "cool off."

I don't remember everything about that year, but I can recall the day Sienna Glass left like it was yesterday. The new school year was about to start, and she told me angels were calling her home. She told me to do my very best in kindergarten and she would go follow the light, which was the very best *she* could do. Then, with a feeling of loss and wonder, I watched her float up and away. I imagined her with humongous white wings soaring through space to her very own star. When I blinked away my tears, Sienna Glass was gone.

That night, Mom lit four white candles in her bedroom, pulled out a tray of crystals from under her bed, and organized them in a circular grid on top of her homemade quilt. Mom said a blessing, and together, we said goodbye to Sienna Glass. Dad didn't join us for the blessing that night. All our talk about Sienna Glass seemed to zip his lips—permanently.

Within a few years, my parents got a divorce. Dad moved to Tacoma, a big, busy city, and we stayed here on Fox Island, in the house and on the land that had been in our family for generations. Even though Mom said that the reason for the divorce was complicated, I couldn't help but wonder if that year with Sienna had something do with it. Dad just wasn't the same after she'd started coming around. Deep down I felt responsible for the divorce, as if my ability to see Sienna Glass had made Dad stop wanting to see me.

Anyway, when I restarted kindergarten, I still felt like the other kids didn't "get" me, even without Sienna at my side. Mom told me I'd have to make the best of it, and so I tried. Even now, as an eighth grader, I don't exactly "fit in," but with the help of the heirloom, my tools, and my gifts (all of which I'm going to tell you about), I've come to realize . . . and accept . . . that I see the world differently than most people do. It's just part of who I am.

The story of Sienna Glass might seem like it has nothing to do with the heirloom, but my connection with her was my first clue that there is *a lot* more to the ordinary world than most people think—and there's a lot more to each of us than we realize. Sometimes I wonder if that's how all mysteries are solved: by realizing that the answers are within us from the very beginning. So, let's go back to the beginning—well, at least back to fifth grade—and I'll share the story of the heirloom and all the mystical things that happened and how I discovered the answer to the greatest mystery of all: Who am I?

PART ONE

LISTEN

CHAPTER 1

THE RESCUE

I clenched the chain links and pulled the fence toward me. The sun's rays pierced my eyes. Determined to see Waffle and Mr. Adams approach, I squinted through the pain. When I blinked for relief, tears trickled down my cheek. It was bad enough that the kids on the soccer field thought I was a total fifth-grade weirdo. The last thing I needed was for them to think I was crying, too.

I smooshed away the tears with the back of my hand, and I felt a sudden, sharp pain in my scalp. My leather bracelet had gotten snagged in my hair. My long red tentacles wouldn't let it go. So there I was, tear-faced and all snagged up. I tried my best to pretend everything was normal. With my head tilted to one side and my elbow aimed at the sky, I watched the players on the field, as if I always watched soccer that way.

Then Waffle, the cutest, most wrinkly basset hound ever, and Mr. Adams stopped on the other side of the fence. I'd met them at the start of the school year in this very spot since this was not the first day I had been left *un*-picked by the team captains.

"Good day, Indigo," greeted Mr. Adams, tugging on the brim of his old-fashioned railroad hat.

I smiled. "Hi, guys. I thought you would *never* come."

I quickly squeezed my free hand through the fence. If I moved really fast, maybe Mr. Adams would focus on the hand that petted Waffle and not on the arm that dangled from my hair.

Mr. Adams nodded and smiled, his messy white beard spreading out even farther around his face. Sporting his white undershirt and faded denim overalls, he reminded me of how Santa Claus might look on his day off.

And then, of course, there was Waffle. His wet nose, droopy eyelids, and stubby legs were beyond adorable. And who could ignore those Dumbo ears? Every time I petted them, I imagined my smooth, old, yellow blankie between my fingertips, the one Mom had "taken care of" years ago.

"Looks like you're hung up," Mr. Adams observed. "Need some help?"

"Nope, I'll be just fine," I replied, feeling my cheeks turn cherry red. To save face, I yanked my hand back through the fence and turned all my attention back to the field. I felt bad about giving Mr. Adams the cold shoulder, but I didn't look back as I called out, "Have a good day!"

As the players got into position, I saw Jake point at me and laugh from center field. It didn't take long for that brat Simone to join in, jumping around and pretending her hand was caught in her perfect, blond, snag-proof hair. I suddenly felt exposed, like I'd just stepped onto the school bus naked. I gasped at my stupidity. Clearly, acting like my arm wasn't dangling from a wad of tangled hair hadn't worked.

Then there was Luke, too busy scheming to be bothered with me. Prepping to pull a fast one on Jake, he grabbed his red baseball cap and rotated it, plunking it down backward on his head. Then he ran up to the ball and nailed it with his purple, high-top Converse shoe.

The ball soared in the air, past Jake, and Luke and his teammates chased it downfield. Watching it bounce a few feet from the goal, I caught a glimpse of something in the grass. I peered harder. Oh no! It was a bird—a robin, to be exact—and the poor thing was flapping helplessly in the grass just inches behind the ball. No question; if I didn't act fast, it would find itself splattered on the sole of someone's shoe.

"Stop!" I yelled, dashing into a sprint. "Watch out for the bird!"

But nobody paid me any mind. Unbelievable! Frustration exploded within, so I ripped my bracelet free—taking a large clump of red, curly hair out of my head in the process—and waved my arms like flashing ambulance lights as I ran.

"Get out of my way!" I screamed.

All the other kids, except for Jake, stopped and turned in my direction. My long, hand-sewn skirt slapped and yanked my legs, tripping me and launching me headlong into Jake just as he was about to kick the ball and squash the robin. As I crash-landed in front of the ball, I made a little tent with my hands and cupped them over the frightened bird.

"You crazy lion-haired girl!" Jake yelled, struggling to crawl out from under me. "You could've broken my leg! That's it! I'm telling Mrs. Harris."

A few kids gathered around and peered over my shoulder. Together, we peeked through the small opening between my thumbs. The wide-eyed robin shook with fear, so I scooped her up and cupped her in my hands. While Jake limped off the field to find our teacher, I walked to the school entrance and sat down on the concrete steps. Even though I could tell a few kids cared about the bird, nobody joined me.

A few minutes later, Mrs. Harris came over to the steps to discuss my "reckless interruption of the game." She wore a long skirt, too, which she straightened along her backside before taking a seat beside me. Pushing her antique, metal-framed glasses up onto the bridge of her nose, she asked, "Did you apologize to Jake?"

"Nope," I replied quietly, looking down at the robin so I didn't have to meet her eyes. "He stormed off before I could say anything."

"Oh, I see," she replied, folding her hands together on her lap. "Well, it's important to apologize to him so he knows you understand how *he* felt in that scary moment on the field."

"Oh. All right then. I can do that," I mumbled. Then I showed Mrs. Harris the bird. "I was just trying to protect this tiny thing. Jake's a monster in comparison, don't you think?"

Mrs. Harris patted my cupped hands as she listened to my side of the story. The backs of her soft hands displayed worm-sized veins, the kind my grandma used to have. I didn't think Mrs. Harris was a grandma, but with all her gray hair, I believed she could be one soon.

After she comforted me, Mrs. Harris stared far out at the playground, like she was thinking really hard. As we sat in uncomfortable silence, I readjusted my hands into a new cupping position and stared down at my skirt. It was something I'd created by sewing lots of red and blue bandanas together. Mom had been my assistant; she'd helped me perfect the drawstring closure at the waistband.

Finally Mrs. Harris bumped my shoulder with hers and grinned. "You have such heart when it comes to animals, don't you?"

I glanced up at her, then bashfully returned my gaze to the bandanas. The truth was, I didn't know how to answer her. I'd never really thought about myself like that. I mean, I was just *me,* you know?

"Next time, just remember that safety for yourself and others takes priority, okay? And just so you know, I told Jake the same thing: Animals need protection, too." Mrs. Harris gave me a wink. "In the meantime, why don't we put the robin in a box, and you can take it home and care for it there? I know your Mom would approve."

I sighed with relief as the bell rang.

Once back inside, Mrs. Harris motioned for me to follow her to the school office, where we found an empty shoebox in the utility closet. I punched small holes in the lid for airflow and gently placed the robin inside. While I settled the bird down, Mrs. Harris arranged for me to leave her in the office where she'd be safe. The secretary assured me she would watch over the box until I came for it after school.

On the way back to the classroom, I lagged behind my teacher. I did not want to apologize to Jake. By the time we arrived, the other kids were already in their seats. Even Caroline, my best friend since first grade who preferred to spend her free time as a library helper, had beaten us back. After every recess, I'd usually wait for Caroline in the hallway outside the library, where we'd steal a few moments to chat about the new books that hit the shelves or about my time with Waffle. She loved reading and the smell of books like I loved animals and the feeling of Waffle's soft ears.

Mrs. Harris tapped my shoulder. That was my cue. I cleared my throat with a nervous cough, and then shuffled over to Jake's desk.

"What now, Indigo Monroe?!" Jake exclaimed, throwing his hands in the air.

"I'm sorry, Jake," I sputtered, twirling a strand of my hair around my finger. "I made a quick decision to save that bird on the soccer field, but I know I could have seriously hurt you. I didn't mean to."

Jake sat back in his chair, pulled at the fish-like creature printed across the chest of his blue T-shirt, and let out a sigh. Then he looked up and gave me a quick nod, his shaggy blond hair falling over his eyes. I guessed that was his way of accepting my apology, so I shakily walked back to my desk.

It felt like every kid was staring me down, scrutinizing me from head to toe, exchanging barely concealed, mean remarks behind their hands. And how could I miss Simone in her florescent pink hoody, mimicking me by twirling her blond hair around her index finger? She flashed me a gruesome grin and whispered something to Caroline. My breath caught in my throat. Of course, Mrs. Harris had her back turned, which was always the case when Simone struck. Thankfully, Caroline ignored Simone. She smiled at me until I made it to my seat, her eyes like lifelines that, once again, pulled me to safety.

As I sat down, I thought about how most of the other kids seemed at home in the classroom, but not me. School and I just didn't fit. For one, I wasn't very coordinated. That meant that anything that required me to run or jump became a reason for others to laugh. For another, I loved sewing, so most of my clothes were handmade. I'd never understood fashion trends—how clothes were popular one day, then unpopular the next. I preferred to wear my "artsy originals," which most of the other kids poked fun at. And then there was my undying passion for all things animal. If I wasn't caring for my own pets, I was riding Silvy, my horse, or playing outdoors in the hopes of encountering a squirrel or a friendly beetle.

That got me thinking about the robin. I imagined the secretary peeking in the box every so often to check on the bird, and maybe even finding a small water dish to place inside. That's what I would have done if I had had the time.

The robin was my third animal rescue of the year. Marigold, my dog, had been the first. She was a yellow-coated mutt who'd found me ten months ago at the Looking Pond. Silvy and I rode to the pond every weekend. On that particular day, Marigold had limped out of the woods, her ribs clearly visible beneath her matted fur, and I knew it had been forever since she'd had a meal. I'd whistled to her, and her ears had perked up.

"Here, girl!" I'd encouraged, and she'd hobbled in my direction.

When she'd plopped herself down at my feet, she carefully crossed her left paw over her right front leg, drawing my attention to a red sore on her footpad. It looked infected and painful, so rather than ride Silvy home, I'd walked alongside him and our new friend.

As soon as we got home, Mom had jumped right in to help and made a huge bowl of rice and boiled chicken, which Marigold scarfed down in seconds. After she'd eaten, she seemed pretty calm, so I tended to her foot.

Mom had insisted that if Marigold was going to stay with us until the animal shelter found her owners, she had to sleep in the barn overnight.

"But, Mom," I'd cried, "look at her bones! See? There's not a single blob of fat anywhere! You're going to make her stay out here in the cold?"

"Honey," Mom had replied gently, "it looks like she's been sleeping outside a long time. The barn is an upgrade."

Bummed that she couldn't sleep with me in my room, I'd made her a special bed with two fleece blankets and a bunch of pillows from our linen closet (which Mom wasn't too happy about). Within seconds, Marigold had climbed up and collapsed in the heap.

"Good night," I'd said, rubbing her ears. "And don't you worry—before you know it, you'll be healthy and strong, shining bright just like those marigolds in our garden." That's when I knew that Marigold was the name for her.

The next day, we'd notified the shelter and posted pictures of Marigold on the bulletin board at the grocery store and the library. Mom warned me not to get too attached, but of course I did. I had a strong feeling that she was meant to be with us. After four weeks, no one claimed her. The night Mom finally said we could keep her is etched into my memory for all eternity: I stumbled into the kitchen for dinner that evening, and there sat Marigold, a real live present with a red bow on her head.

My second animal rescue was Scarlett, a wild dove. I found her about two weeks ago in the grass trying to take flight after she failed to fly *through* the glass of our kitchen window. Her right wing was broken, but she was doing much better now. I figured she'd still have to spend a couple more weeks in the "hospital cage" in my room until her injured wing was fully healed.

And, in an hour, I'd be bringing home a robin. That would make this one my third animal rescue in less than a year.

CHAPTER 2

CRAZY LION-HAIRED GIRL

"**H**and it over, Indigo," insisted Caroline as she reached for my school bag. "I'll hold this while you get the bird."

"Thanks," I said, as the secretary waved me into the office. "How'd she do?" I asked.

"Well, she tweeted a bunch," she replied cheerfully. "And occasionally, I'd hear her little feet stumble across the cardboard. That's when I sang to her—it seemed to calm her nerves. I hope you can help her, Indigo."

Caroline poked her head into the office, her perfectly straight, wonderfully brown hair swishing across her shoulders. "If anyone can help that bird, it's Indigo!" she announced. She pulled my arm. "C'mon, Dr. Doolittle! We don't want the buses to leave us behind."

When the secretary handed me the shoebox, I grabbed my skirt and curtsied. A spontaneous curtsy isn't really my style, and I'm not sure what came over me, except that I felt really grateful that she'd comforted the robin.

"Thanks a lot! I'll sing, too," I declared. "And I'll let you know if I find anything wrong with her." That was all I could say before Caroline yanked me into the hall.

It was a good thing Caroline had rushed us. She flung my bag over my shoulder and sprinted down the row to her bus, barely getting her whole body inside before the door closed shut. Once I knew she was safely on board, I scrambled up the steps of my bus. The driver stared me down, looking annoyed that I had held up the works.

I apologized, then hurried past Jake and Simone with lowered eyes to find an empty seat. I rode the whole way home with the shoebox on my lap, and I didn't feel the robin move once.

After our bus coasted down the hill and came to our stop, the door opened. A bundle of nerves, I followed Jake cautiously down the aisle. When he leaped off, I took it slow, one step at a time, to the sidewalk. To my surprise, when I landed safely, the robin peeped three times.

"Are you kidding me?" Jake exclaimed, looking back at me in total disbelief.

We had only gone a few paces on the sidewalk when he made a squeal-like tweet from deep in his throat, flapped his arms like an injured bird, and dropped to his knees at my feet. His dramatic performance startled me backward a smidge, and a second later, I'd thrown my bag in the air, as I tried to keep from falling. When I crash-landed, my bag and books had scattered all over the neighbor's lawn. Miraculously, the shoebox remained safely in my hand.

Jake looked worried for a second, but then he laughed,

flung his "so-long-it's-a-crime" bangs off his forehead, and then turned toward home. "See ya tomorrow, crazy lion-haired girl!"

Even though we'd been neighbors for years, Jake and I had never developed a friendship. Instead, he always seemed to find ways to either annoy or avoid me. His nickname for me—crazy lion-haired girl—had come about in kindergarten. It still made my blood boil.

I watched him turn up his driveway as I sat in the grass. Maybe Jake was right. Maybe I *was* a crazy lion-haired girl. With that thought, my mind became a jumble of disapproving voices. There was Simone's and Jake's and a bunch of my other classmates' mean-spirited comments replaying over and over in my mind.

I began to wipe the dirt from my skirt as if I could wipe away their disapproval and disgust. As I pushed stray strands of hair from my face, my eyes fell on my bare wrist. My heart dropped. "Oh no!" I cried. "My bracelet!"

Mom had given me the bracelet just two days earlier. It had all started when I'd told her how Simone had made fun of my outfit again the day before and how bad it made me feel and that maybe we should go shopping for "real" clothes. Then Dad had called to cancel our weekend together because he had to go out of town for work. It had felt like the billionth time he had canceled on me. And even though he had told me a trillion times what it was he did for a living, I still didn't understand what a "business consultant" was or why he needed to travel so much. All I knew was that he'd ditched me once again.

I'd felt so "blah" that morning that I couldn't even finish my favorite breakfast—soggy cinnamon French toast with raspberry jam. So off Mom had gone to her room. When she returned to the kitchen, she'd asked me to hold out my hand and close my eyes. When I did, she placed something in my hand.

"Open your eyes," she'd whispered.

In my palm was the bracelet. It was made of thin strips of leather, braided to make a tight strand, and the ends were held together by an antique silver clasp in the shape of an infinity symbol.

Mom had pressed my fingers closed over the bracelet. "This is our family's most treasured heirloom, Indigo," she'd explained softly. "It has been passed down from generation to generation. You can tell, right? See how worn out the leather is?"

I opened my hand to study the treasure.

"My mom gave it to me when I was about your age," she'd continued, "and now, I give it to you, Indigo Monroe. When I wore the bracelet, I became aware of the valuable gifts inside me. So look and listen carefully. That might happen for you, too."

Gifts? I'd wondered. It all felt a little strange, and Mom was acting all mysterious. I did feel very drawn to the bracelet, though. She must have noticed me thinking real hard because, a second later, she pulled me into a tight hug. We clung to each other long enough for me to smell the sweet fragrance of lavender shampoo lingering in her smooth reddish-brown hair. When we had finally let go, she'd pulled a tissue from her back jean pocket and quickly wiped it across her face.

"Are you sad, Mom?" I'd blurted.

"Oh no, honey," she'd giggled.

"Oh, so it's one of *those* cries, huh?" I'd asked, wanting to confirm that her tears were sweet, not salty.

Mom had sniffled and then smiled to reassure me. She pulled her white, long-sleeve shirt down past her waist and readjusted the bell sleeves that flared to just past her wrists.

Once Mom had fastened the bracelet around my wrist, I hadn't taken it off. Even though it was old and plain, I'd felt special wearing something my mom had worn . . . and now it was gone.

Shaking, I frantically combed my fingers through the grass. There was no sign of the leather bracelet, and once it hit me that I'd lost our family heirloom—my most precious gift—my eyes filled with tears, and not the ones that taste like cotton candy.

With each salty droplet that splattered on my face, I thought, *The other kids are right. I'm such a loser. A weirdo, crazy lion-haired girl who dresses like a circus clown, just like Simone said. I hang out alone during recess to talk to dogs on their afternoon walks because I'm too strange to talk to people. I'm a total klutz. And, worst of all, I can't be good enough, whatever that takes, to keep our family heirloom safe.*

I gasped. My *own* mean voice had become the loudest of them all. Disgusted with myself, I put the shoebox on the lawn and fell back into angel pose. And then there I was with my arms and legs desperately swishing in and out, waiting for a feeling of being so good to rise up inside me. It didn't happen.

∽

After a few minutes, I collected my books and bag from the lawn, picked up the shoebox, and walked home. Since Mom had the day off work and wasn't in the kitchen or the garden, I went straight to the den and stood in the doorway until she felt my stare. When she saw my face, she stopped typing on her laptop and puckered her lower lip to match mine. Somehow, she always seemed to know exactly how I felt. And honestly, this time, it was a relief.

"Mom, I had the worst day ever." I leaned my body up against the doorway for support and explained, "I got in trouble at school and had to apologize to Jake in front of the whole class. Besides being the one who everyone laughs at and makes fun of, Jake still thinks it's cool to call me 'crazy lion-haired girl,' which he did twice today, which only made me feel a million times worse. And"—I took a deep breath—"I lost the bracelet."

"Indigo," Mom gasped, "you mean you lost *the* bracelet?"

I gulped, and when I tried to take a breath, I couldn't. My throat got all tight, and I could feel my eyes drowning in tears. Mom immediately stood up from her chair and hurried forward. "It'll be all right, sweetheart," she said, leading me over to the couch where she stroked my

23

hair. When she saw the shoebox in my hands, she asked, "Whatcha got there?"

I sucked a glob of slippery snot back into my nose and wiped a few stray tears off my right ear. "Oh, that's . . ." and then I waited for the robin's name to come to me. I remembered holding the bird like a precious gem, my hands her shell of protection. "That's Pearl," I said finally. "She's a robin I rescued off the soccer field, which is part of the reason I'm in this mess. I think there's something wrong with her foot."

"Pearl," Mom repeated. Then she smiled. "What a strong name!" She reached into her back jeans pocket, this time handing *me* the tissue. "Well, Pearl's lucky she has you to care for her."

"Yeah," I grumbled, "but I'm not so sure saving her was worth all the embarrassment."

"Oh, Indigo, you're a natural when it comes to caring for animals. That's a gift. Now, go on, tend to your pets, and take care of Pearl. You'll just have to look for the bracelet at the bus stop and school tomorrow. Believe it or not, I'm not worried. Things always have a way of working out."

I let out a loud sigh and kissed Mom on the cheek. Then I walked to the kitchen, set Pearl—safe in her shoebox—on the table and headed out to the barn. The second Silvy saw me crossing the backyard, he trotted to the fence. "I'm comin'," I announced.

I ducked under the wooden rail, and Silvy greeted me with a friendly snort. Then I grabbed his harness, pulled myself up just a little, and kissed him on the neck, right where a patch of white hair meets a patch of brown. Even though I didn't have my boots on, I led him through the pasture to the barn, making sure not step in you-know-what along the way.

Once inside, I replaced my tennis shoes with barn boots and mucked out Silvy's stall. Using a plastic-tined pitchfork, I sifted through soiled wood shaving for manure and dumped the poop into the wheelbarrow beside me. Then I looked for the darker-colored shavings that indicated pee spots that had to be removed, too. Once I raked them up and dumped those shavings into the barrel, I poured armfuls of new wood shavings over the bald spots on the dirt floor.

Silvy waited, all calm and still in the hallway, for ten minutes until I was done, then quickly entered when I left to gather his dinner. When I returned, his nose followed my bucket all the way to his feed trough, but never once did he try to steal a bite. Only when I walked away with an empty pail did he gobble up his meal.

Marigold met me in the barn, tail all a-wag; she knew what came next. I put my tennis shoes back on while Marigold turned around in circles at my side. We left the barn and she ran past me, making a beeline for the back door. Once I let her in, she zoomed straight to her bowl.

"I know," I reassured her. "I'm coming, girl."

Once Marigold was fed, I greeted our yellow finches and my parakeet, Mr. Magoo. Their separate cages hung from our big kitchen window that overlooked the backyard. I put fresh food and water in each of them.

A few years ago, on the day Dad had moved out of

our home, he had gifted me Mr. Magoo. I think he'd felt really bad about the divorce, just like I did, and he knew the beautiful blue Mr. Magoo would cheer me up. Still, I would have preferred to have Dad around.

My chores done, I picked up Pearl's box and headed upstairs. As I pushed through the strings of multicolored beads that served as my bedroom door, I noticed Scarlett sitting quietly on the floor of her "hospital" cage.

I placed Pearl's box on the window seat and took Scarlett out of the cage to inspect her injured wing. Even though she was a wild bird, she always rested easily in my hands, which seemed to surprise Mom, but it just seemed right to me.

Still weak, Scarlett couldn't even muster an "I still have pain" coo, so I held her gently and whispered healthy wing wishes into her soft body. "Don't you worry, Scarlett," I assured her as I placed her back in the cage. "You'll be better in no time. Trust me, pretty bird."

I opened the lid to Pearl's shoebox very slowly and peeked in. She was tucked in the left corner, shaking, so I petted her and sang softly until she relaxed. Then I picked her up and noticed small fragments of dirty pink gum stuck to her left foot. *You gotta be kidding me,* I thought. *How'd I miss this earlier?*

"It's okay, Pearl," I assured her. "I'm sorry you got yourself into this mess. Someone else's chewed gum is best in the trash, not on the soccer field. We'll fix this right up."

I carried Pearl to my bathroom sink and gently rubbed the gum off with a soapy washcloth, holding her tight up against my white button-down shirt with one hand. I was thankful she didn't struggle either. When she was all clean, I touched the silky feathers on her back with my thumbs. "You're all better now," I whispered. "Are you ready to fly?"

At last, Pearl wiggled like she'd had enough of me, so I hurried to my bedroom window, opened it up, and held her outside. When I opened my hands, the robin hesitated for a moment, cocked her head at me, and then took off. I watched her fly toward the trees and then up and over them until she was just a speck in the sky.

"Phew," I whispered. "That's one problem solved."

CHAPTER 3

UP A TREE
AND BEYOND

I woke up the next morning with a pit in my stomach. Every second without the bracelet around my wrist made the hole inside me deeper and deeper. I wrestled the curly monster on top of my head into a ponytail in record time. Most days I didn't bother to brush it, since doing so would make it grow to twice its size, which made me despise it even more.

I grabbed my denim shirt and the "moon and stars" skirt Mom and I had made out of old bedroom curtains we'd found at the thrift store a few weekends back when Dad had canceled our weekend plans—again. (The skirt had a white moon and stars scattered around the dark gray fabric.) Mom wasn't too sure about making the curtains into a skirt, but I convinced her they'd make a smashing Monroe Original.

I hurried downstairs, feeling the soft curtain-skirt on my legs, and found Mom sitting at the kitchen table, wrapped in her fluffy white robe and sipping her morning coffee. Spread out before her were three different skirt patterns. "I was thinking about your spring concert," she said. "It's a week from this Friday. How about a new skirt? Want to go fabric shopping after school today? We could start sewing this weekend."

"This weekend?" I asked. "But Dad and I . . ." my voice trailed off. I guessed that Dad had canceled our plans for this weekend, too, and Mom thought that sewing a new skirt would take my mind off it. "That's a great idea, Mom."

Following breakfast, we hovered over the skirt patterns, and I became so immersed in choosing one that I forgot all about Dad, the lost heirloom, and the fact that I'd have to face Jake at the bus stop in minutes. When the oven clock beamed that time was slipping by, I quickly fed the indoor crew and then gave Mom a kiss before I hurried to the barn to feed Silvy—slipping in and out of my barn boots in record time.

As soon as my tennis shoes were back on my feet, I hurried toward the dreaded bus stop.

"Help!" I heard Jake shouting. "Dad, help! Ed's stuck in the tree!"

Jake's voice gave me goose bumps. He didn't live far, just two doors down on our curved block, but the distance between his backyard pasture and our backyard pasture made it seem like we lived a whole block away. Standing at the top of our driveway now, I could see him beneath the oak tree in his front yard, looking up into its branches.

"Dad!" he shouted again.

Then it hit me. I sprinted to Jake's front yard, brushed past him—and miraculously didn't trip or knock him down. I hauled myself up onto the lowest branch and then climbed several feet up into the tree to reach Jake's cat.

Eddy meowed at me as if begging to be saved, so I wrapped my arms around her trembling body. (And, yes, Eddy was a girl. Why Jake chose a boy name for his girl cat is something that had perplexed me since we were in kindergarten.) The cat clung to me, and I rubbed her pretty calico fur until she relaxed.

"Indigo!" Jake yelled. "Ya got her? Don't move! My dad's on his way."

"She's all right," I called down. "Don't worry, I'll bring her to you."

I adjusted my footing to start the climb down, but hesitated when a robin landed in the tree just inches from my face. The moment froze.

"Pearl?" I whispered. Thinking I'd gone to that insane place beyond mad, I squeezed my eyes shut. When I reopened them, Pearl was still there. "Is . . . is it really you?"

Pearl's head bobbed.

I felt lightheaded, and my heart beat loudly in my chest. Below Jake and his dad were engaged in a heated discussion. With them preoccupied and Eddy safely pressed against my chest, I whispered, "What's that under your foot?" I leaned in even closer and gasped. *My bracelet!*

Eddy squirmed, so I clenched down gently with one

arm and leaned back into the tree trunk. Pearl stepped toward me, leaving the heirloom hanging precariously on the branch. Instantly, I reached for the bracelet, and when I felt the leather braid safely between my fingertips, I whispered, "Thank you, thank you, thank you."

Seemingly satisfied, Pearl fluttered her wings, and one of her orange feathers came loose and floated onto my knee. I scooped it up, and she chirped once and flew away.

With Ed still tucked safely under my arm, I dropped the bracelet and feather into my shirt pocket. I called out short orders to Jake. "I need help. Grab my foot. Please!"

"Don't worry, Indigo, we've got you!" Mr. Peterson called up through the branches.

Jake positioned himself below me, while his dad held up his hand and steadied me as I made my way down. Once on solid ground, I handed Eddy over to Jake. As he took her into his arms, he flipped those shaggy bangs out of his eyes. "I've never seen a girl climb a tree so fast in a skirt like that," he breathed.

"Ah . . . thanks," I replied, brushing and slapping the stars and moon straight.

"Oh crap, we'd better get going!" Jake exclaimed, pointing up the road at our bus barreling down the hill.

Mr. Peterson took Ed from Jake's arms and thanked me for rescuing her. "You'd make a great fire-woman," he announced.

Seriously? I thought. But I knew better than to question a compliment from our town's fire marshal. "Thank you, Mr. Peterson."

∽

I plopped down in a seat in the middle of the bus and dug the bracelet and feather out of my shirt pocket. Stuck to the feather was a strand of thread probably left over from one of my sewing projects. *Curious,* I thought, feeling compelled to tie the feather to my bracelet with the string.

As I did so, a chill rushed up my spine, and I heard a soft voice whisper in my left ear: *"The feather will remind you of your gift. You're a natural when it comes to helping animals."*

I looked around. The bus still hadn't filled up, so no one was sitting in front of me or in back of me . . . and certainly not beside me. For a moment, I thought of Sienna Glass. *Had she just whispered in my ear?*

My heart swelled for a moment and then shriveled back to normal when Sienna didn't appear. I placed the hand holding the bracelet over my chest. My broken heart was still beating, so I held my hand there until the pieces of my heart mended themselves back together. As much as I missed Sienna Glass, I also knew she was just a memory away. And then came the thought that maybe I'd gone see-through, too. I scratched my head, pinched my arm and felt the sting, then picked my nose with my pinky finger, just a little. I had to do something really human just to be sure *I* hadn't turned into a spirit from the stars.

Reassured that I was a solid, I began to wonder about the source of the whisper and Pearl's reappearance. My eyes locked on the bracelet clamped between my fingers. I was holding on to something very real. *I've been given another chance with the heirloom,* I thought.

I clasped the bracelet, feather and all, securely around my wrist and stared out the window as the scenery whizzed by.

"Hey, Indigo," I heard behind me and I jumped. It wasn't the whisper; it was Jake. "Do you want to play on my team at recess today?"

I turned to gape at him, unsure if he was being sincere. He was leaning forward in his seat so he could look over mine. That's when Simone, who sat across from him, cleared her throat. She looked wide-eyed at Jake for speaking to me, and he flipped his bangs casually as if he was just readjusting his position.

Looking down, I touched the silky feather on my bracelet and recalled the moment I freed Pearl from my hands. . . . *I have a natural gift for caring for animals.* That is one gift I was more than happy to have.

Not sure if Jake was even listening, I replied, "No thanks."

∽

I somehow managed to survive the rest of that day and the week that followed unscathed. At recess, I still hung around the sidelines with Waffle despite Jake's sort-of invitation, and Simone all but ignored me, which I preferred over her nasty comments. I did notice, though, that she'd called Caroline "Library Nerd" a couple times in class when Mrs. Harris wasn't watching, and Caroline was left speechless. She usually wasn't on the receiving end of Simone's barbs, and I felt bad for her. They seemed to shake her up.

Meanwhile, we all practiced for the spring concert every day during music, and everyone in my class—in fact, the whole school—buzzed with excitement. Mom and I had worked nonstop on my skirt over the weekend, and I didn't even miss Dad . . . not really.

The morning of the concert arrived quickly. Streams of orange and purple light danced on the sequins of my new knee-length skirt, which hung over the purple lounge chair across from my bedroom window, a magnet for the sun's rays. Still cuddled in bed, I stared in wonder at the kaleidoscope of color. Mom and I had really combined our magic on this one. We had created a real work of art out of the fabric and the trinkets we'd gathered.

Excitement bubbled inside me, so I jumped out of bed, followed the sunlit path to my chair, lifted up the clear plastic bag, and examined the skirt. The orange taffeta crinkled between my fingers as I inspected the magenta felt flowers, the yellow felt sun, and the purple butterfly made of fabric, ribbons, beads, and sequins.

Because the concert was in the afternoon and the skirt was so delicate, I decided I would change into it right before the performance. I jumped up and down, danced, and clapped. Scarlett observed my performance and gave three coos, all in a row. Even though they were quiet coos, it was a sign that she was feeling better.

As I made my bed, I hummed the concert songs.

Then I dressed in a white button-down shirt and the long tie-dyed skirt that Mom and I had made out of a white vintage tablecloth we'd bought for twenty-five cents. Although I'd never been a fan of dress-up shoes, I slipped into my black patent leather flats. Something about my new skirt radiated sophistication to me, so my usual tennis shoes just wouldn't do.

All dressed, I examined my bracelet. Yes, there it was—the feather was securely attached even after all this time. My double-check delivered an image into my head of Pearl resting in my hand for a moment, then flying away. I stopped humming. My feet froze, and I smiled from ear to ear.

In a flash I thought: *Silvy. The barn. My chores.* I only had nine minutes before the bus rolled down the hill. I dashed to the chair, snatched up the hanger, blew Scarlett a kiss, and ran downstairs to the kitchen. Mom wasn't down yet, so I yelled back up the stairs. "Mom, I'm headed to the barn!"

"Okay!" Mom shouted from her room. "Remember, I won't be able to stop home before the concert, so bring everything you need!"

I imagined my mom on the edge of her bed putting on her blue scrub pants, which she had to wear every time she went to work at the hospital. Where was the artsy-smartsy style in a nurse's uniform?

"You got it!" I called back. "I'll see you and Dad at the concert!"

I heard Mom fumbling around, and then she stuck her head out from the landing at the top of the stairs.

"Oh, Indigo, I'm so sorry, but your dad can't make it. He said he'd call you tonight."

All of the excitement I'd been feeling suddenly evaporated. I made some sort of comment before I ran out the back door. *Of course he won't be there*, I thought. *He's always avoiding me.*

With slumped shoulders, I hung my skirt on the barn door and removed my dress shoes, placing them on a clean pile of hay and my school bag and lunch on another. I pulled up my barn boots.

"Good morning, Silvy," I mumbled as I entered his stall with a fresh pail of water and food for the day. When I'd set the bucket down, I reached back around the door and grabbed a few apples from the treat bag. "Today I get to wear that skirt I told you about," I said, trying to cheer myself up. "I'll give you a fashion show after school."

Silvy gobbled the apples from my palm, and I gave him a quick kiss on the coarse hair between his eyes. My horse was a whole lot of goodness to me. He always brightened my day.

Marigold ran in and barked twice at my feet. Another day-brightener.

"The bus is coming, right? Good girl, Marigold."

I darted out of the barn, grabbed my lunch, school bag, and skirt, and stumbled down the driveway toward the bus stop. "Wait up!" I yelled, waving to the bus driver as the skirt's plastic bag flapped in my face.

The bus door was still open when I reached it, and I staggered up the steps. Right away, I saw Simone, her straight blond hair tied back neatly with a white bow. She put her hand over her mouth and whispered to the girl next to her. So much for being ignored. I turned my eyes away and felt myself shrinking.

As I hurried down the aisle with quick little steps, she stood up and called out, "Did you and your *mom* make another one of your stupid skirts for the concert today?"

"Well, Simone . . ." I began, trying to puff myself up, but then I fell silent and stunned like I'd swallowed a tennis ball.

Simone placed her hands on her hips, smiled, and watched me struggle. "I'm waiting, Princess Weirdo."

My life force burst forward, dislodging the ball and growing me back to size. I lifted my finger and practically pointed it up Simone's nose. "It's a good thing I'm wearing it and not you!" I belted out.

"That's for sure!" she snapped. "I wouldn't be caught dead in one of your hideous skirts. Honestly, didn't anyone ever teach you how to dress?"

Just as I was about to go all "warrior priestess" on her—at least that was what I imagined would happen if I had the nerve—the bus started to move, so I turned away and plunked myself down in the farthest possible seat from her. Once I'd caught my breath, comebacks flashed one after the other inside my mind, getting louder and louder with each burst.

I never realized someone had to teach you how to dress. Was it Barbie's evil twin? Come to think of it, maybe you'd have an ounce of style if you sewed some of your own clothes! Oh, but wait, you probably don't even know how to use a needle and thread because no one ever taught you!

It was then I remembered that Simone's mom had died in a car crash when we were in second grade. I felt relieved that I hadn't spoken any of my comebacks aloud. I had a brief flicker of a thought that maybe Simone was jealous of my skirts because I'd made them with my mom, but did that give her the right to be so nasty? I sank into the green plastic seat, deflated.

As I crossed my legs to get comfy, I felt a strange heaviness on my feet. I lifted the hem of my skirt and gasped: My horse-poop-and-hay-encrusted barn boots mocked me: *We're not your dress shoes!* And they were right: I'd left my shoes back at the barn.

I turned to look out the window and watched my house disappear over the hill.

CHAPTER 4
BARN BOOTS

My plastic-wrapped skirt just wouldn't hang perfectly in my cubby, so I snuck behind the coats and backpacks to reposition the hanger like a hundred times. I waited for Mrs. Harris to begin our first lesson. Once everyone focused on the morning worksheet, I sped over to my desk, only to stare at the blank paper before me. *What a hot mess I've gotten myself into.*

At ten o'clock—current events time—Mrs. Harris asked us to join her on the orange shag carpet in the corner of the classroom. Gathering around on the floor like we were first graders always made me chuckle, but I didn't find it so amusing this time. Gingerly lowering myself down, I sat crooked on my heels, my boots covered by my long tie-dyed skirt.

As Mrs. Harris announced the new recycling program, my eyes locked on a clump of dirt and hay lying on the floor right next to Jake. My body stiffened. I snuck my hand across my body, reaching for the barn boot evidence like I was trying to catch a frog before it jumped away. But when I stretched forward, my creeping finger-tips caught Jake's attention.

"Yuck, Indigo!" he said out loud. "I wouldn't touch that if I were you."

Now all the students turned to look at me.

"Yeah," Luke agreed, "it looks like something you'd find in a pigpen."

Across the circle, Simone shook her head. The look of disgust on her face made me feel like the dirtiest girl on the planet. "Ew," she cried, as she held her nose with her thumb and index finger. "Can anyone smell what I smell?"

"That's enough!" commanded Mrs. Harris.

But it was too late; the entire class was already sniffing and snorting. My heart pounded so loudly I was sure everyone could hear it. Still squatting with my boots tucked under my skirt, I decided to snatch the clump of dirt anyway and pretend like it was harmless. But as I leaned toward it, I lost my balance, fell forward, and poof! My boots popped into view for all to see.

"Indigo," Luke exclaimed, "look at your boots! They're soooo gross! Oh man, so *you're* the one who dragged this in?"

Mrs. Harris hurried over, lifted the hem of her skirt, and bent down to inspect the cause of distraction. "It's just a clump of dirt, guys," she said, winking at me. She picked it up with a paper towel and threw it in the trash. "Now hush, everyone, please."

Instead of that being the end of it, everyone stood up and stared at my boots, shouting, "Eeew! Gross! Nasty!"

Soon the entire class was a chorus of screams and laughter—except Caroline, who glared at everyone on my behalf. As for me, I sat frozen on the floor, still as a statue for fear that, if I moved, I'd crack and fluorescent green goo would ooze everywhere.

Mrs. Harris put two fingers in her mouth and blew the most hideous whistle ever. The kids slammed their hands over their ears, and the room went silent. She pointed to the desks, and everyone walked to their chairs like zombies. Mrs. Harris whispered to me, "Are you okay?"

Still seated on the carpet, I lifted my arm, pretend-inspected myself for battle scars, then exhaled, and waited to breathe again so I could feel my body crave another breath. Yep, I was still alive. However, half-wishing I were dead, I answered Mrs. Harris, "Nope, I'm not okay. You've gotta believe me, it was an accident! I forgot to take my boots off outside the barn this morning, and my mom's coming straight from work, so I can't even call her for help. Or my dad, for that matter; he's totally useless."

Mrs. Harris knelt down and placed her hand on my shoulder. "Why don't you take your boots outside and knock off the mud so you don't track more barn dirt into the class," she suggested gently. "While you're out there, try to relax and take deep breaths. By lunchtime, the kids will have forgotten all about your boots."

Mrs. Harris motioned me in the direction of the side door. Ashamed of all the commotion I'd caused, I exited the class without a fight. Once outside, I squatted down on the pavement and banged my boots on the concrete as hard as I could. Then I took one boot at a time and swept the muck under a nearby bush. My head throbbed with anger and disgust. "There's no way I'm going onstage in these boots," I vowed.

Exhausted, I sat down on the pavement and slammed my palm into my forehead. There, before my eyes, the orange feather dangled from my bracelet. Even though I wanted to shrivel up and blow away, something inside me willed me to put my boots back on and break the spell. With my head down, I walked back into the classroom and sat down at my desk.

I didn't touch my classwork. Instead, I devised an escape plan for getting out of the concert. When it was time for my class to head to the auditorium, I'd ask to use the bathroom and stay in a stall until after the concert. Then, when everyone gathered in the lobby, I'd join the crowd, find my mom, grab her arm, and escort us both off the premises.

When I finally mustered the courage to look at the clock, it read 1:50 p.m.

"Okay, everybody, it's time to head to the auditorium. I'm excited for the performance!"

That was my cue. I shuffled to Mrs. Harris's desk, pulled my long red curls forward so they covered the side of my face that faced the classroom, then leaned in and whispered, "May I please go to the restroom?"

I could feel the kids staring at me; my body felt pierced and punctured. When I tucked my hair behind my ear and checked over my shoulder, there was Simone, her nostrils flared, laughing so loud I thought she might fall out of her chair. Now *that* would've been funny.

"Simone!" Mrs. Harris barked. Simone choked on her own breath. Mrs. Harris turned back to me. "Hurry up, Indigo. And when you're done, meet us in the auditorium."

Before I exited the room, I looked back over my shoulder and saw my teacher giving Simone what for. It was about time.

⌒

I stood at one of the bathroom sinks and stared into the mirror. My face had turned an angry red and almost matched my hair. I tilted my head and moved in closer to my reflection. "You *are* a stupid, ugly, crazy lion-haired girl!"

Hypnotized by the eyes of a monster, I felt my heart skip a beat and sputter, like it was running out of gas. In shock, I crept away from the mirror until my back touched the bathroom wall and slid down until my butt hit the tile floor. I folded my hands over my knees, and the robin feather on my bracelet caught my eye.

I flicked the feather with my finger. As it came to rest in the palm of my hand, an image of Pearl appeared in my head, followed by the image of my orange taffeta skirt, sparkling with sequins. My heart began to thump with a strong rhythm, and to my surprise, I felt what I could only describe as love begin to flow through me, like hot chocolate on a winter's day.

Out of nowhere, I heard that whisper: *"Believe the love you feel inside, not the fear that makes you hide."*

I searched the bathroom in the silence that followed,

but there was no one in sight. The whisper spoke again: *"You are an artsy seamstress who sews fabulous skirts. That's one of your gifts. Don't let dirty barn boots keep you from wearing your masterpiece."*

My eyes grew wide with curiosity, and I stood up, feeling taller. Maybe I should have felt frightened, too, but I wasn't trembling. I turned and studied myself in the mirror. This time, my lips parted into a smile. Once again I felt hopeful and excited about the skirt I'd made, just like I'd felt that morning.

"Oh my goodness, what am I doing?" I burst out. "I *love* that skirt!"

In a flash, I scampered to the sink and yanked off my boots. I quickly washed them with soapy water. When the saturated paper towels shredded in my hands, I reached for more, polishing the leather of my boots until it was not only clean, but shiny. Then I shimmied back into my beautiful boots and fled the bathroom. I hurried to my empty classroom. I retrieved my skirt from the coatroom, put in on, and then ran as fast as I could to the auditorium.

The other fifth-grade classes were already in position on the risers. My class was about to proceed to the steps, and I slipped into the only available space in line— between Jake and Simone.

"I can't believe you are actually going onstage in *those* boots!" Simone exclaimed.

Expecting gasps of horror to travel up the line, I was surprised to hear only the footsteps of my classmates as we moved toward the front-row riser.

Jake turned his head and did his Peterson bang flip so he could, well . . . see. "Hey, Indigo," he whispered. "Those boots actually look pretty cool now."

Did Jake Peterson really just pay me a compliment?

"Indigo, great skirt!" said Caroline. She was standing down the row, a few places from me. "I've never seen anything like it."

"Thanks, Caroline. It's the skirt Mom and I made especially for this concert."

"Oh, *please,* Indigo," sighed Simone. "Who takes these concerts seriously anyway?"

"I do," said Caroline with a quiver in her voice.

"Me, too," whispered another girl from behind us.

At that moment, the music teacher walked toward me with a white note card in her hand. *Oh no,* I thought with dismay, *it's the boots! She's going to make me stand in the back row for a dress-code violation or something.*

I grabbed my bracelet, held on tight, and bravely awaited my punishment.

She stopped in front of me and announced, "Indigo, Julie was going to read this, but she's home with the flu. I thought that since you're wearing such a beautiful spring skirt, you might want to show it off. Would you do us the honor of introducing the first song?"

Stunned, I leaned toward her and whispered, "Are you sure? I mean, with my boots and all?"

At that moment, I felt the chill by my ear again and heard the whisper. *"Believe the love you feel inside, not the fear that makes you hide."*

Immediately, I snatched the note card. "Yes, I'll do it!"

Once the music teacher had welcomed everyone to the concert, she nodded in my direction. I stepped forward to center stage and took in the colorful bouquet of moms, dads, grandmas, grandpas, sisters, and brothers. Then my eyes searched for Mom. Once I spotted the sparkles in her eyes, I waved my hand broadly and then tugged on my skirt so she could see the purple butterfly we made together.

Giggles filled the auditorium. The kids on the risers behind me started to whisper. Grabbing hold of my bracelet, I saw an image of the robin and the glittering skirt. Then, loud and clear, I read the title of our first song. When I was done, I blew a kiss to my mom before I turned for the riser.

The audience hushed their giggles and applause as the music began to play. I stood tall now, as I had in the bathroom, and snapped my fingers to the beat. I sang my heart out and looked down occasionally to see my skirt shimmer under the concert lights. I felt like a real live rock star.

༄

On the way home, I told Mom about the barn boots, Silvy's "you-know-what" on the floor, and my decision to wear the skirt anyway. I didn't mention how sad I felt that Dad hadn't shown up. Neither did I mention I'd heard mysterious whispers. Both of those things felt too personal to share.

When we pulled into the driveway, I headed straight for the barn. I opened Silvy's stall door and stood in front of him so he could get a good look at my skirt. "So, what do you think? Do you like it?"

Silvy greeted me with his endearing snort of approval, and I twirled around until the barn started to spin. To calm the dizzies, I grabbed hold of Silvy's mane and blabbed about my crazy special day. Silvy stood still and listened, nudging me with his head when I got so caught up in my story that I stopped petting him.

"And, of course, Dad missed it all," I sighed at last.

As I made ready to leave, I felt a cold breeze rush up behind me. When I stepped outside the stall, a thin strip of orange taffeta fabric lay fluttering on the ground at my feet.

How'd this get here? I wondered. I reached down to grab the fabric and heard the whisper: *"This symbol will remind you of your gift for creating beautiful works of art."*

Goose bumps erupted all over my body. "Is that you, Sienna?" I asked hopefully. "Don't worry! Dad doesn't live here anymore. We won't scare anyone else away . . ."

I gulped. *Is that what I believe? That I scared Dad away?*

I sat silent for a moment as I wondered about that. Then, I tied the strip of fabric onto my bracelet in a spot next to the feather. I tugged on it a bit to make sure it was firmly attached, and then I thought a little bit more. Sure, I had some doubts about myself and a lot of other things—but I did have some special gifts to be grateful for. I decided I would try to focus on them instead.

"Indigo!" Mom called from the back door of the house. "Caroline's on the phone!"

Who knew I'd be pushing the limits of my newfound confidence so soon?

CHAPTER 5
HERE COMES THE SUN

"Great job at the concert today," Caroline said all in one breath over the phone, then added excitedly, "I just found out that one of the teams backed out of the karaoke contest next weekend at the city park stage. Please, please sing a duet with me! I thought about entering alone, but I'd really like your support up there onstage."

Now that I had a taste of how it felt to be a "rock star," I didn't even have to think about it for a second. "Absolutely! Sign us up!"

She hesitated for a second, then added, "You know, Simone and her friends are going to be in it, too. Uh, is it still okay with you?"

Simone and her cronies had been making fun of me for so long that I was practically used to it, but lately, they'd been picking on Caroline. Although she didn't say it directly, I knew she was afraid they'd make fun of us, and she wanted some assurance from me, so I gave it to her. "We'll blow them away! There's no stopping us!"

That week, Caroline and I practiced every chance we got. We chose the old Beatle's song "Here Comes the Sun." And, not only would we be *singing* it, we would also be *signing* it to make it an extra-special performance for Caroline's five-year-old sister, Noel.

Eight months earlier, Noel had gotten meningitis and had been hospitalized for more than a week. Her hearing had been severely damaged, and the doctors didn't know if it would ever return to normal. She'd picked up sign language like a marvel and even taught me new signs whenever I went to Caroline's house.

༽ༀༀ

That day's plan was for my dad to take me to the contest, since this was a weekend I was *supposed* to spend with him. He was *supposed* to arrive in three hours, and today I needed him to be on time, since Mom's car was in the repair shop with a bad case of the flu. Caroline's parents wouldn't be able to drive me if Dad was a no-show because they'd be arriving at the park directly from one of Nicole's doctor's appointments in the city.

With fluffy orange slippers on my feet and my green fleece robe snugly wrapped around me, I stood in front of the bathroom mirror and practiced.

It was 8:30 when the phone rang.

Instantly, I knew it was Dad on the other end. My stomach somersaulted. I heard Mom's voice climb to an all-out yell, followed by the sound of the phone slamming down. *Yep, that was Dad.*

I banged my first and second fingers onto my thumb pad, signing a defiant "no" into the mirror. Then, all dizzy and weak, I reached for the countertop. As I leaned into the mirror, I gulped at the sight of me. My face was awfully pale, and I could feel dark storm clouds of anger rolling in to hover over my head, just like they had the day of the spring concert.

"Indigo, where are you?" Mom called from the upstairs hallway.

I rolled my eyes, bent my knees down to the tile, and cradled my head in my arms. "I'm in the bathroom."

Mom walked in, put the toilet lid down, and, with a sigh, took a seat. "Your dad is running late. He says he hopes to be here by twelve-thirty."

"Yeah, well, that's just great," I mumbled, feeling my hot breath blowing the hairs on my arm. "The contest starts at noon sharp and we're the third act, so that won't work."

"I know. I told him. But he's set on coming anyway."

My insides smoldered like hot coals. To vent the "What a jerk!" that heated up inside, I lifted my head and spewed, "I'm so angry I could scream past Jupiter and still have more scream left!"

Mom reached out a hand to comfort me. "I know your dad does this a lot, but he doesn't mean to hurt you, Indigo. He loves you very much."

I pulled my arm away. I usually just listened to her "he loves you" speeches and even tried to believe them, but this time around, I just couldn't. "Yeah, right, Mom. If he loved me so much, he'd be here. I told him how important this was to me. You told him." I fluffed my hair with my hand to make a point: "Look at these curls. It's just the icing on my Crazy Cake. No wonder nobody wants anything to do with me—not even my own father."

There was a silent, awkward pause before Mom asked, "Your bracelet, where is it?"

I jumped, startled. I had taken it off that morning to examine the fastening on the feather, and I'd forgotten to put it back on. "It's on my nightstand, why?"

"How about you go put it on and get dressed? You'll feel better."

"Yeah, I guess," I said, lifting myself off the bathroom floor. "Then I'm going to go hang out with Silvy. He doesn't mind my crazy ways."

Mom ruffled my hair, sending even more curls flying in all directions. "Be home by eleven o'clock. I'll make some calls. Maybe I can find us a ride."

∽

Silvy started out at a slow trot near the fence. My head was down, and I stared at his mane as it lifted off his neck with his every step. *Why couldn't Dad be here for me, just this once?* I wondered sadly.

As my body drooped and I sat heavy in the saddle, Silvy picked up the pace to a canter. Raising my head, I steered us through our pasture gate toward the Tree Canopy Trail. As we flew through the green-tree tunnel, the sound of wind rushed past my ears and silenced the depressing things my mind was saying.

Once Silvy caught sight of the open field and the pond at the end of the trail, he sped up to a gallop, snorting with excitement. "Whoa, boy," I said close to his ear. "The Looking Pond isn't going anywhere."

Silvy's legs snapped the tall grass as he raced through the wildflower field. As we drew closer, I caught sight of Jake and Luke by the weeping willow tree. They stood by their bikes and adjusted the fishing rods and gear that were stacked high on their handlebars.

Silvy and I trotted to the tree. "Catch anything?" I asked a bit cautiously, not sure if I'd be ignored or not.

"Yeah, look!" Jake replied. "We each caught our limit and we're headed back to my house for a fish fry."

"You're going to cook them *yourself?*" I exclaimed. Then I grimaced at the sight of all the bloody, dead fish that hung on a string from his handlebars.

"No, my dad has the day off," Jake answered. "He said if we caught anything, he'd gut 'em and fry 'em up."

"You mean you're not going to the karaoke contest?"

"Are you kidding?" laughed Luke. "We don't sing unless we have to. Right, Jake? Besides, we'd rather be here than anywhere."

My eyes lighted on root beer cans scattered on the grass beside the Sitting Log. I let out a loud cough: "Pigs!"

Jake and Luke frowned.

"Do you know how many times I take your empties home to recycle?" I shot out.

Jake and Luke looked at each other and shrugged.

"Can't you see? We're packed to the gills. There's no room for trash," Luke replied, pointing to their bikes.

Jake looked back at the cans, then back at me. Something told me he would've picked them up if Luke weren't there. In a flash, the boys hopped onto their seats. As they rode away, they called back, laughing, "Break a leg at the contest, Indigo!"

If I ever get there, I thought.

I jumped off Silvy's back and led him to the pond. After he'd quenched his thirst, I led him to the Sitting Log under the weeping willow tree. Just like me, Silvy liked the shade of the draping willow branches. I let go of the reins, gathered the four root beer cans, and stomped them flat with my boot. I carried them over to Silvy and put them in the saddlebag, then sat down on the velvety moss-covered log and stared out over the pond.

The water was perfectly still, and my gaze locked on the reflection of the violet, yellow, and orange flowers that surrounded us. While Silvy snacked on grass, I fiddled with the feather and the orange taffeta on my bracelet. It was then that I had an idea. If I couldn't make it to the contest, I could perform here in nature—where nobody ever loses.

That now-familiar chill traveled up my arm and came to rest above my left shoulder. Images of Pearl, my orange taffeta skirt, and my concert performance in barn boots appeared in my head. Then I heard the whisper: *"Nature speaks, and you listen."*

I stood up and looked around. Finding no one there, as I'd suspected, I walked to the pond's sandy shoreline, took off my boots and socks, and shoved my toes into the warm, wet sand. Something told me magic was afoot.

In a flash, I saw myself as a famous singer performing at the Looking Pond Theater. To fulfill my path to stardom, I retrieved a squished pop can from the saddlebag. I snapped the aluminum ring off the can and fit it around my right ring finger. Then I pulled the top and bottom of the can apart, brining it back to life. Next I found a stick near the Sitting Log and stuck it in the drinking hole. I gently plucked three yellow balsamroot flowers from the grass and tied them together by their long stems to make a necklace.

"Every singer needs a microphone and some bling," I said, as soft giggles bubbled from inside and followed me back to the water's edge.

I used my pop-can microphone to introduce myself to the water, trees, flowers, and wildlife hiding in the brush and then belted out our karaoke song. After a few verses, I set the microphone down and signed the lyrics as I sang.

I loved making the sign for "sun." Every time I did, I felt like I was five years old again and sprinkling fairy dust over Sienna Glass and me. My fingers would burst open just above my head and poof! There I was, as I imagined, a fairy as bright as the sun. And the sign for "darling," was pretty easy, too. I raised my hand, palm facing me, and waved with all my fingers bending down and up again, like a backward finger wave.

"Never seen anything like this, right?" I asked the pretend audience. " 'Here Comes the Sun' sung and signed by an eleven-year-old star from Fox Island, Washington —the isle where magic comes to life."

That's when it hit me: If we couldn't perform for Noel on a real stage at the contest, Caroline and I could give her a surprise performance here, at the famous Looking Pond Theater. We could bring popcorn and root beer, and even invite some of her friends.

Despite knowing there was little chance I'd get to the contest, I was happy again, and I didn't want that good feeling to end. I twirled my bracelet around to see the feather and orange fabric. As I did so, I felt that chill again, and then as if by some mysterious force, the ring from the can slid past my knuckle and balanced on my fingertip. It didn't just *slip* down—it felt like it had been pulled.

"What the heck?!" I cried, as the ring tumbled from my shaking hand into the shallow water. "Oh, no you don't," I said, stooping to reach in after it. "Come back here!"

The moment I grabbed the ring off the sandy bottom, I heard the whisper: *"You bloom in nature."*

I fought the urge to look around again. Instead, I took off my bracelet and strung the can ring around the braided leather. *No question—I do love being in nature,* I thought. I recalled all the times I'd made "magic" in nature while the wildlife watched on. I'd spend hours making mud pies, mushed weed doughnuts, flower potions, pinecone dolls, tree branch wands, and shell spoons. And I had definitely made magic today. "I guess I do *bloom* out here."

With the bracelet now clasped back around my wrist, I checked the time on my watch. *Eleven o'clock? Oh no, I'm late!*

I scooped up the pop can microphone and squashed it again, then ran to Silvy and put the flattened can back inside the saddlebag. Plunking myself down on the Sitting Log, I struggled to pull my socks up over my wet feet. Once I'd conquered the task, I slipped into my riding boots and climbed aboard Silvy.

"You can go as fast as you want now," I told him.

CHAPTER 6

RUNNING OUT OF TIME

I left Silvy to roam the pasture so he could cool off while I darted to the back door. Mom and her friend, Amy, watched me from the kitchen table as I stumbled inside. Right away, Amy's orange, vintage-type dress with bell sleeves caught my eye. She and Mom had similar taste and a lot of other things in common, which made sense since they'd been best friends since first grade. Amy was like Mom's version of my Caroline.

"Indigo, you're late!"

"Yes, I know," I replied. "I'm sorry. I got caught up at the Looking Pond. I feel better now, though," I reassured her. I turned to our visitor. "Hi! I didn't know you were coming over today."

"I hear you have a big karaoke contest at noon," Amy said with a smile. "I had to come by and wish you good luck."

"Sorry you drove all this way," I said, "but I'm not going to make it there in time."

Amy grinned. "Seeing as I'm your ride, you'd better get a move on!"

"What? Really?!" I exclaimed.

"Run upstairs and get ready," Mom urged. "We'll be waiting in the car."

I dashed to the staircase, jumped every other step on the way up, and burst through my beaded door. I put on a pair of green jeans and yellow T-shirt (I was going for the look of the sun over the mountains), and I grabbed the orange bandana from my dresser drawer to finish off my costume. Then I rushed to the bathroom, looked in the mirror, and saw the flower necklace from the pond around my neck. Gently pulling it loose, I set it on the counter and replaced it with the bandana. My hair was all poufy, with curls sticking out every which way. I had planned to braid it today. *No time,* I thought, so I grabbed two hair ties. *I'll braid it in the car.*

As I hurried back into my room, I passed Scarlett's cage and heard her coo *four* times. I whipped around, and our eyes met. "Scarlett, *four* coos? That's a record. Great job, girl! At this rate, it won't be long before you're flying again!"

When I reached the car, Mom and Amy were bent over inspecting the back right tire of Amy's yellow Volkswagen bug. "Are you kidding me?" I exclaimed, throwing my hands up in the air. "What's wrong now?!"

Amy delivered the bad news. "Looks like we have a flat tire."

I was speechless so Mom jumped in, "I'm assuming you don't know how to change one, right?"

"That's right," I admitted with a huff. "And the fact that we're all standing around tells me you guys don't, either?"

"I'm sure the three of us could figure it out, but by the time we've mastered the problem, I'm afraid it'd be too late."

Mom was right. I considered our options. In deep thought, I split my hair into two parts and started to braid one side. Seconds later I dropped the half-braid and announced, "I saw Jake at the Pond this morning. He mentioned his dad's home today. I'll run over and see if he'll come and change it for us."

I sprinted down our gravel driveway and hung a hard right across the neighbor's yard. Arriving at Jake's front door, I knocked twice. From inside, I heard Mr. Peterson call, "Just a minute! Jake, get the door. I'm covered in fish batter."

The door opened, and a surprised Jake greeted me. "What's up?" His head tilted, his bang-covered eyes fixated on my hair.

Mr. Peterson came up behind Jake, wiping his hands on a dishtowel. "Hi, Indigo. Everything all right?" Then *his* head tilted to the side, too.

Oh, crap! My hair! I proceeded to undo my half-braid and then smooth out the poof that was my hair. "Mr. Peterson, we need your help," I explained. "My mom's friend's tire is flat, and she's the one taking us to the karaoke contest. We're already running late. I was hoping you could—"

"I'll be right up. Just let me turn off the stove."

"You're a lifesaver!" I cheered with relief.

I hurried back to the car. No sooner had I announced the good news than Mr. Peterson, Jake, and Luke arrived. Jake stood by his dad's side and handed him the tools he needed. Luke stood back with his arms crossed, just like Amy, Mom, and me. The tire change took only five minutes. It reminded me of one of those speedy tire changes at a professional racetrack.

"Go on, ladies, get out of here," Mr. Peterson urged as soon as the job was done.

As I passed Jake, I whispered, "I owe you one."

"Oh, no you don't," he said. Then he actually kind of smiled at me.

༄

Amy drove like a police officer in hot pursuit: fast yet cautious. I rode in the backseat, while Mom sat up front with her fingers gripping the leather upholstery. It was a few minutes to twelve, and we were now just blocks from the city park.

Amy's car tires squealed as she rounded the circular driveway near the outdoor concert stage. A second after she slammed on the brakes and the car came screeching to a stop, she yelled, "Run, Indigo, run!"

As I ran toward the crowd, I realized that everyone was already seated. Principal Davis took the microphone and thanked the fund-raiser supporters for "coming on such a *glorious* Saturday afternoon." As he annunciated the word "glorious," my brain conjured up a million *other* words that would've described the day so far.

From that point on, I didn't hear a word the principal said because I was focused on a single thought: *Where is Caroline?*

I spotted her mom and Noel in the third row and let out a relieved *Phew!*

As Principal Davis introduced the first act, I ducked low and scooted down the center aisle to Caroline's mom and sister. "Psst! Where's Caroline?"

"Isn't she over there?" her mom asked, turning and pointing to the back row of the theater.

"No," I replied. "I'm sorry I'm late. I have to find her; we don't have much time."

I scurried up the aisle until I passed the last row, then stood and searched the crowd. When I determined that Caroline was nowhere in sight, I ran backstage. Still no Caroline.

I darted back to the park grounds, where I spotted Mom and Amy as they headed toward the seats. Behind me, I heard the audience clap, hoot, and holler. Whistles flew like streamers as the next act came onstage. I waved my hands wildly above my head to signal for help. Once Mom and Amy saw my distress, they hurried to join me in a huddle at the top of the center aisle.

"I can't find Caroline," I whispered in a worried rush.

"Check the bathrooms," Amy suggested.

I pivoted and sprinted to the restrooms. As the heavy, dented metal door squeaked open, I yelled, "Caroline?"

"Indigo, is that you?" Caroline's voice quivered.

"Yes, come on out!"

When there was no answer, I pushed each door open until I found Caroline seated, fully dressed in matching green jeans and yellow T-shirt, on a toilet, her head in her hands and her elbows on her knees. "This isn't your purple beanbag!" I exclaimed. "You can't just take a seat and hang out. Come on, let's get out of here. I'm sorry I'm late, but we're on in five minutes."

"You were supposed to be here twenty minutes ago!" Caroline cried. "When you didn't show, I thought you'd never get here, and when I imagined performing without you, I panicked. Now look at me; I'm a nervous wreck."

"I'm here now," I said placing my hand on her shoulder. "We got this! Listen to the crowd. Let's show them what a winning act looks like."

"You're going to have to do it without me. Remember how brave you were at the spring concert?"

Starting to lose hope, I reached for my bracelet. Time paused while I felt the feather, the taffeta, and the can ring. *Live the love you feel inside, not the fear that makes you hide.*

"I won't go up there without you. We created this act together, and we're doing it for Noel. You and I both know how happy she'll be when she sees us onstage. Come on, now. Get off that pot and let's go for it!"

I pushed the dingy gray door wide-open, grabbed her hand, and pulled her in the direction of the stage. We didn't hear music as we zoomed by, but we did hear sporadic laughter from the crowd. When we arrived backstage, we found Principal Davis peeking around the curtain.

"We're here!" I exclaimed, swiping my hand across my forehead in relief. Principal Davis smiled at the sight of us, then pressed his finger across his lips. But I continued to pester him—in a hushed tone, of course. "Whatcha waiting for, DJ Davis? You can start the music now."

"Wait just a minute," he whispered, nudging me ahead of him so I, too, could peer around the curtain. "See? Your mom just started a set of her favorite jokes to stall for time. Let's at least let her finish."

"What?" I gasped, my mouth falling open.

Caroline stepped forward to stand beside Principal Davis.

"Here's a good one," Mom announced. She leaned in toward the crowd. "What do you call a cute volcano?"

The audience turned to each other with facial expressions that read, "This woman's nuts!" As for me, I couldn't tear my adoring eyes off Mom.

"Lava-able," Mom answered after a pause, and, to my surprise, I blurted out a rolling snort-laugh.

Caroline whacked me on the shoulder. "You're the only one laughing."

I pulled myself together so I could save us both from further embarrassment. "Psst, Mom. We're ready," I whispered.

When she saw me smiling out at her from stage left, Mom bowed to the crowd and walked offstage to polite—*very polite*—applause.

"Light 'em up, girls," she cheered as she whizzed by.

I grabbed Caroline's sweaty hand. Time for us to shine!

CHAPTER 7
EXPIRED JUJU

I focused on the leafy trees that bordered the city park beyond the audience to keep calm. The music started, and I began to sing and sign. I glanced over at Caroline, who stood like a flagpole without the flag: straight, slim . . . and silent. When I realized we were short one in our duet, I became Caroline's "missing flag" and began to sing louder and performed the signs with even more pizzazz.

Noel danced in the aisle. She signed every word with me as she moved to the rhythm of her own beat. Still stiff and silent, Caroline kept glancing backstage. Simone and her groupies were standing there, whispering and pointing. I realized Caroline had fallen under their dark spell; she was blind to her sister's light beaming at us from the aisle.

I kept my focus on Noel. As awkward as she looked and probably sounded, hers was one of the most beautiful performances I'd ever seen. With two verses down and still not a peep or gesture from Caroline, I stomped on her foot. I had nothing to lose. And, miraculously, just as the third verse was about to begin, she finally started to sign and sing.

When the last verse ended, I grabbed Caroline's hand and pulled her into a bow with me. As the audience applauded, we watched Noel, who alternated between clapping her hands above her head to flashing them around like fireworks in the night's sky.

"She's thrilled," I whispered into Caroline's ear.

Caroline half-grinned, but then whipped her head around to see backstage. I grabbed her hand—and her attention—again and waved to Noel. Noel blew us kisses, so we sent a bunch back her way until Principal Davis motioned for us to clear the stage. Caroline, clearly spooked by the gaggle of girls who lingered behind the curtain, unhooked from my hand and sprinted ahead past Simone and her laughing posse.

"Caroline, wait up!" I yelled. But when I started to run after her, Simone blocked my path.

"Best get out of my way," I snapped, "unless you like a good bulldozing." Simone looked stunned, so I continued. "You just don't scare me anymore, Simone. You're like . . ." I tapped my finger on my temple, thinking. "Old news. A blank shot. Expired juju. Call it what you want; I'm immune to you."

Simone didn't move; I think she was still trying to comprehend the word "juju," which is just one of those words that, if you have to stop and think about it, you'll never fully get. So I charged ahead and, as I did, I heard Simone stumble. When I looked back, she was on all fours, calling to one of her friends for help. Funny thing was, I hadn't even knocked into her.

I scanned the park and theater seats. At last, I caught sight of Caroline standing in the doorway of the bathroom. She had the metal door propped open with her hip while she took one last look for danger. Certain she hadn't been followed, she dashed into her stinky hideout.

No one saw me running along the perimeter of the audience; their attention had shifted to the boy onstage, who was strumming away at an invisible guitar.

The metallic door squeaked to a close behind me as I entered the bathroom. "Caroline?" I called. "Come on, we did good, don't you think? Noel was beaming the whole time."

Caroline unlatched the stall door and peeked through the crack. "I was so nervous I could barely move! There's no way we're going to win."

With gentle pressure, I pushed the door open. Caroline got out of the way and sat down on the toilet. "Do we have to talk here?" I asked, wrinkling my nose.

Caroline nodded.

I leaned up against the frame of the bathroom stall. "Well, we may not win. But who cares? Noel was as big and bright as the sun the whole time!"

"But, Indigo," Caroline protested, "didn't you see Simone and her friends making fun of us? Every time the word 'sun' came up, they replaced it with 'losers.' It's true, I heard them!"

That was all I could take. Reaching for my bracelet, I felt the feather, the fabric, and the can ring between my fingers. Though I certainly understood her, I didn't feel the way Caroline did—not anymore.

I clasped my bracelet. "Look," I said softly, "I don't care what all the other kids think. All I know is how big Noel's smile got. If you want, we can take Noel to the Looking Pond, bring snacks and root beer, and you can perform for her there without worrying about your nerves or what other people think. What do you say?"

Caroline smiled. It was a weak smile, but I felt hopeful. Then she glanced at my bracelet. "Why do keep fiddling with that bracelet?" she asked.

I glanced down at the heirloom. "Well, this isn't just your average bracelet. I mean, it's really worn out, and with all the odds and ends dangling from it, well, I know it looks peculiar, but it helps me remember important things. My mom gave it to me."

Caroline touched the bracelet and began to examine the symbols. "Some things you do are pretty strange," she declared. Her head bobbed as she inspected my heirloom, her fingers stopping at the ring from the soda can. I think she was hung up somewhere between my quirks and her normal.

Then she snapped and tuned back in. Her hand detached from the bracelet now, and her finger pointed at my face. With a strong, upbeat voice, she said, "But you know what? I think you're . . . amazing and very brave. You saved me up there onstage." She wagged her finger. "And without you, Noel wouldn't have seen her sister perform in front of a crowd. I hope she knows how much I love her."

I smiled. "Oh, she knows; just you wait and see. And by the way, we were a team up there. Now come on, let's go sit with Noel and size up our competition. Who knows? Maybe we'll get an honorable mention—or better yet, a high-five from our greatest fan!"

When all the contestants had performed, Principal Davis walked back on stage holding the first-, second-, and third-prize envelopes in his hands. While he gave a speech about how proud he was of all the participants in the contest, Noel sat on Caroline's lap and played with her hair. I smiled over at them, and Caroline leaned over to whisper, "I don't know why she bothers. My hair is hopeless and not nearly as fun as playing with yours."

My eyes widened, and I would have replied, but then Principal Davis began calling out the winners. I reached for Caroline's hand.

"The first place winner is act seven, the beautiful duet from the Carson twins," he said. "Congratulations! You guys won the grand prize!"

Caroline signed, "We didn't win" to Noel, whereupon Noel took her big sister's face between her hands and kissed her all over, as if to say, "*You* are my first prize."

The second prize went to act two, and the crowd cheered as Jamie and Mike went onstage to receive their free-ice-cream-for-a-month passes for Henry's Sweet Shop downtown. *Those lucky dogs,* I thought, feeling mildly envious but happy for them.

"Last, but not least," Principal Davis continued, "the third prize goes to act three. You two were the first in school history to both sing and sign a karaoke song. Congratulations, Indigo and Caroline, you've won four free passes to the movies. Enjoy."

In shock, Caroline signed, "We won, we won!" to her sister. Then she grabbed Noel's hand, and together the three of us ascended to the stage to accept our prize.

⌒〜⌒

While the crowd dispersed, Caroline's mom reached for the movie pass in Noel's hand. All aglow, she pulled us into a group hug. As she gushed over our—how did she say it?—"super cheerful original performance," I winked and laughed with her.

Just as I was about to follow behind Mom and Amy, Noel grabbed my hand from behind and spun me around. As my eyes met hers, she presented me with a long-stemmed yellow rose. "This is for you," she signed. "I love you."

I took the brilliant flower and lifted Noel off the ground in a hug. When I set her down, I signed "thank you" and blew her a kiss. Tears began to well, so I twirled around and headed for Amy's car. I didn't want Noel to think I was sad, and I didn't know how to sign, "These are sweet tears, not salty ones."

I giddy-upped toward the car. Gumdrop tears dumped onto my cheeks, and I let them drip. I overflowed with an amazing feeling of goodness. Halfway to the parking lot, I heard the whisper in my left ear. *"You adore other people's beauty. It inspires you. What symbol will remind you of this gift?"*

I lifted up the rose to eye level, then swiftly looked down at my feather, fabric, and can ring. The chill swept across my hand. Instantly, something tugged at the rose stem, and the flower slipped from my fingers and landed at my feet. "Okay, okay, the rose it is," I answered as I scooped it up and walked on. "But there's one problem . . . how will I attach it to my bracelet?"

I found Mom and Amy leaning on the side of the car in the circular driveway, waiting for me. As I approached, they again clapped and yahooed as they had at the end of our performance. I wiped my face and gave them each a one-arm hug, careful to hold the flower at a distance so it wouldn't get crushed.

"Indigo, why the tears?" Mom asked. "You were marvelous up there!"

Just as I was about to explain my tears and the rose, Dad's red sports car pulled up. My heart thumped one loud beat, and then took off racing. My stomach suddenly turned rotten.

"He has some nerve," I growled, glaring at him as he exited his shiny new car. Once he reached me, he pulled me in for a hug—the last thing I felt like doing. So I didn't hug him back. I just clasped the stem of my flower and waited for it to be over.

When his arms released me, I looked down and saw my yellow rose bent over, the stem broken. When Mom and Amy caught sight of it, their jaws dropped.

"How'd it go?" Dad asked. "Did you win first prize?"

"Um," I stammered, shocked that the rose had been damaged. "No, we didn't win first prize."

Then, as I held the stem with one hand and supported the dangled bud with the other, I suddenly didn't want to keep my feelings to myself anymore. I blurted out, "What are you doing here? Didn't Mom tell you I had a ride?"

"I'm really sorry I couldn't make it, but we still have the rest of the weekend. We're going to my work party tomorrow. Remember? I told you about it last week. You're my date. It's been a long time since you've seen my partners, and they're bringing their kids, too. Did you pack an overnight bag?"

Stunned, I just stood there. Dad shuffled from one leg to the other in suspense. After several awkward moments, I huffed, "You know what? I don't want to go to the party, and I certainly don't want to hang with your partners or their kids. Honestly, I barely see *you.*"

Dad stammered, but nothing intelligible came out.

I took a deep breath and continued, "You think that whenever you show up, I should just jump at the *rare* chance to be with you? I'm just not normal or good enough for you, am I, Dad? You never want to hang out with me. Well, I don't want to hang out with you either! I'm going home with Mom, so don't try to stop me. I bet you didn't even notice you broke my . . ."

I looked down. I couldn't finish.

"Rose . . ." he said in the weakest voice ever. He hesitated, then stepped closer and leaned down. "Indigo, how about I take you home so you can pick up your clothes?

When I finish the leftover work at the office, we can see a movie or ride bikes. After we spend some quality time together, maybe you'll change your mind and we can go to the party after all."

Mom walked over then and placed her hands on my shoulders. When I didn't look up at her, she bent down and looked into my eyes. "Well, honey, do you want to go?"

"Ab-so-lut-e-ly not," I said forcefully. "Let's go home. Now!"

I guess Mom got the point because she took my hand, turned away from Dad, and called back to him that he'd have to make other arrangements for me to see his partners "next year . . . or next century."

As we drove away, I didn't even look back to see Dad's reaction. I decided that his juju had just about expired, too.

CHAPTER 8

WHOOP WHOOP

I opened my eyes to a dark room and glanced over at my clock. My eyes widened: It was five-thirty in the morning. I had slept a total of fourteen and a half hours.

I turned on my bedside lamp and spied a plate of food on my nightstand—a bunch of grapes and a dried-out turkey sandwich covered with a paper tent. The "tent" was a note from Mom that read, "Can we talk now?"

Mom must have left this for me last night, I concluded before noticing that, next to the plate, my bracelet was laid out in a perfect line. On top of it was another note. I opened it and read, "You are dynamite, Indigo. Never forget it."

Ah, Mom, I thought as I stretched my arms over my head. Then I recalled that five minutes into our drive home from the karaoke contest, I realized the yellow rose had broken off and was missing. When there was no sign of it in the car, Amy drove us back to the park to retrace our steps, but it was nowhere to be found. I'd sat cold and still all the way home, but deep down, my insides were firing up. The pain and disappointment of losing my fourth symbol at the hands of my dad had turned me terrible. The part of me that saw beauty in others was lost, and I felt possessed by hatred for my very own father. All those years of being treated like a second thought by my dad, even before the divorce, had caught up with me. I felt like I didn't exist in his world, just like Sienna Glass.

Once Amy had pulled into our driveway, I'd rushed out of the car and ran straight to my room. Ripping off my bracelet, I'd thrown it in the trash, crawled into bed, and pulled the covers over my head. In that dark moment, I honestly felt like I didn't matter. And, if nothing about me mattered, then the bracelet in the trash didn't matter either.

Seeing the bracelet so nicely laid out on the nightstand in the morning surprised me. I remembered that it had hit the top of the trash can and dangled over the edge. Mom must have seen it there when she'd brought me dinner. I imagined her peeking through the beads every five minutes, checking to see if I was awake and eating dinner. Mom tried hard to give me space when I was upset. I felt sorry for her long night.

I got out of bed, grabbed the plate of food, and walked to the door. Scarlett watched me leave and cooed at the top of her lungs *seven* times. "Shhh, that's *too* loud," I said with a grimace.

Tiptoeing my way to Mom's room, I peeked in to see if she was awake. I stood for a few moments and listened to the ceiling fan clinking every two seconds as the blades spun above her bed. She was fast asleep, so I went downstairs for breakfast.

In the kitchen, I discarded the stale sandwich and put the plate in the sink, then poured myself a bowl of Frosted Mini-Wheats. Once I took a seat at the kitchen counter, I dove my spoon into my cereal, unable to wait for the biscuits to get perfectly soggy. Marigold came up to me, barked once, and put her paw on my lap, but I was too hungry to care.

When my belly was full, I didn't feel any better. There was still a whole lot of sadness inside me, like it had seeped deep in and broken all my bones. I even heard my back crack, pop, and snap when I bent over and placed my spoon and bowl in the dishwasher. I was surprised when the dreadful noise didn't startle Mom awake.

No sooner had I closed the dishwasher than I heard Silvy whinny from the barn. *That's what I need. Silvy. The Looking Pond.*

I hobbled up the stairs. Perched on the edge of my bed, I slid on my favorite purple riding jeans and reached my arms through the sleeves of my orange sweatshirt. My white tube socks had gathered around my ankles, so I pulled them up over my jeans to their straight and tall position.

Fully dressed, I still felt like something was missing. Scanning my closet, I reached for my homemade tie-dyed skirt. In need of inspiration and confident it would just be me and Silvy at the Looking Pond, I slipped it on over my jeans. I didn't care if I looked like a clown.

When I stood up, I noticed my bracelet on the nightstand again. If fourteen and a half hours of sleep and

Frosted Mini-Wheats hadn't cured my blues, then I knew my bracelet wouldn't either. So, once again, I picked it up and tossed it in the trash can.

Scarlett was in a delightful mood; as I walked past, she again cooed seven times—and this time she actually flapped her wings.

"Scarlett," I called out, feeling a whole new ickiness come over me. It took me a second to detect the cause, but when I did, I found envy. Ewww! She was happy and I wasn't. Yep. Something was wrong with me, *really* wrong with me.

I shook my body from head to toe, replacing envy with a plan of action. "When I come back, I'll take you out," I promised. Suddenly, another answer rose in my mind. "I wonder . . . is it that time, Scarlett? You know, time to go home?"

She cooed eight times. Her answer was yes.

I walked to the barn, saddled up Silvy, and hurled my broken body up onto his back. Seizing the reins, I turned toward the gate. Immediately Silvy began to trot, evidently having a mind of his own that morning. Despite the darkness and gloom that hung over my head, I trusted he'd take us to our usual spot, the place where broken and sad were healed and made good again.

With each step Silvy took, the sun rose just a little higher over the horizon. I sat stiff in the saddle, squinting as I tried to picture Pearl, my spring concert skirt, my aluminum bling, and the yellow rose. But no matter how hard I tried, the happy, love-filled pictures never showed up. Perhaps it was a bad omen.

Silvy's trotting pace quickly brought us to the field, but he stopped suddenly just before we turned toward the weeping willow and Sitting Log. "What's wrong, Silvy?" I inquired. "What do you see?"

A familiar voice came out of the morning fog. "Hey, Indigo, what are *you* doing here so early?"

"Is that you, Jake?" I asked, peering into the dense haze.

"Yeah," Jake's voice replied, "but *shhh*. We're trying to catch Whoop, the biggest bass ever. Dad thinks he's the only one who can pull it off, but I'll show him."

"Come on, Silvy, it's okay," I whispered, not admitting I felt a bit embarrassed by my outfit. "It's Jake and Mr. Peterson."

We walked forward through the fog until we could see Jake and his dad seated on the upper bank of the pond. "Good morning, Indigo," Mr. Peterson said as he aimed another cast into the water.

"Hi, Mr. Peterson," I replied. I let go of Silvy's reins and jumped down so he could graze the dew-dusted grass. As I walked over to Jake and his dad, I pulled a teasing comment out of my bleakness: "So Jake thinks he's going to catch Whoop before you do, huh, Mr. Peterson?"

"Yeah, but he talks a bunch of hot air," Mr. Peterson replied. "I'm sure you've thought that before. Right, Indigo? Besides, Jake and I got in an argument last night, and when that happens, I drag him here and make him fish next to me in hopes we can work things out."

"Oh, thanks, Dad," Jake grumbled. "Real cool."

"I'll leave you guys to fight over Whoop, then," I

said, thinking that maybe my dad and I needed some fishing time to work things out between us, too.

"It's okay, Indigo," Mr. Peterson insisted. "Please, take a seat. Jake hasn't said a word all morning and you just got him to *thank* me. I think we've made progress since you showed up. By the way, how'd you do in the contest yesterday?"

"We got there in time, thanks to you guys, and we won third prize."

"That's great," congratulated Mr. Peterson. "It takes courage to stand up in front of a crowd. Come on, take a seat. We won't bite . . . though hopefully the fish will."

"All right, then," I said, gathering my skirt up from behind me and taking a seat on the ground. "I've never sat next to a father and son during a fishing contest before."

The three of us sat quietly, the silence broken only by the whizzing sound of sporadic casts. Sitting cross-legged, I watched my reflection in the water. My long red curls swirled in all directions with the wind, and my face was puffy and splotchy. I looked pitiful, actually.

I wanted to feel happy and proud, like I'd felt when I released Pearl from my hands. I wanted to feel brave like I'd felt during the spring concert. I wanted to feel excited and creative like I'd felt when I'd sung "Here Comes the Sun" here at the pond. And, more than anything, I wanted to feel love pour out of me like I'd felt when I'd watched Noel dancing and signing at the karaoke contest. But the problem was, I just couldn't feel anything but terrible.

Then, out of nowhere, that familiar chill crept up my

arm, catching me off guard. Freaked out, I jumped, startling Jake.

"Did a bug bite you?"

"Nope," I answered immediately, feeling embarrassed. "Just a chill on me, that's all."

I pretended to study the two red and white bobbers that floated on top of the water, but really I was just listening ever so carefully for the whisper's wise advice. To my surprise, it came super quick: *"You have two choices. Let fear trick you into thinking you're not good enough or live the love you feel inside, not the fear that makes you hide."*

I let that sink in for a moment. Then I made my choice: "I choose two!" I exclaimed aloud.

"Two *what?*" Jake asked.

"Oh, nothing," I replied, readjusting my skirt around my legs and acting like the bobbers were the most interesting things in the world.

I scooted closer to the edge of the bank and leaned in. To my surprise, I saw something floating in the water—a yellow rose . . . *my* yellow rose. "Oh my gosh!" I shouted, "I can't believe it!" And then I instantly tallied up the mysterious things that had happened since I'd been given the heirloom.

"What's the matter?" asked Mr. Peterson.

"Don't you see that yellow rose floating in the water?" I said, snapping out of wonder and pointing out at the pond.

He squinted and nodded.

"Lots of things get blown into the water," Jake said. "It's no big thing."

With my right hand shielding my eyes from the sun, I looked out over the water. My heart raced, and my cheeks ached from the huge grin that had spread across my face. "Do you mind if I borrow your fishing rod?" I asked Jake's dad. "Maybe if I cast a line out to it, I can hook the flower and drag it to shore."

Jake scooted behind me as we switched spots so I could sit by his dad. Mr. Peterson handed me his rod and showed me how to use it. I gripped it firmly, made my first cast, and missed the rose by at least six feet. Determined to hook my symbol, I tried again, this time missing by what seemed like a mile.

Each time I cast, Jake ducked. I didn't think I was *that* bad of a fisherwoman. As proof of that, my sixth cast landed about two inches from the rose.

Now what? I let the hook sink while the bobber rested on the water. All worried, I asked, "Ahhh, Mr. Peterson, what do I do?"

"Let's see," he said as he reached for the rod.

Just as I was about to hand Mr. Peterson the pole, Jake yelled, "Your bobber's down. You've got a fish! You've got a fish!"

I held the rod tightly with both hands. The tug on the other end was fierce, so I stood up and moved to the edge of the bank, thinking it would give me better control. All the while, the reel spun faster and the fishing line vanished deeper and deeper into the water.

I decided to jerk the rod back to give myself a better hold on the fish. But as I did so, I lost my balance.

"Jake, take the rod!" I yelled.

He caught the pole just as I slid into the pond.

"Are you all right?!" Mr. Peterson shouted. He leapt to the edge of the bank ready to dive to my rescue, but the wide grin on my face gave him the answer he needed to stay put.

"Dad, look, it's Whoop!" Jake shouted, fist-pumping the air. "Whoop, Whoop, Whoop!"

As he reeled the large fish up to the bank, I slid sticky, soaked curls off my face, using my other hand to brace myself in the shallow water. I felt surprisingly refreshed.

"Congratulations, Jake, you won the bet," I said. "It's your lucky day."

Mr. Peterson took out his measuring tape, while Jake unhooked the cold, slimy fish and held it for his dad to measure. "This bass is twenty-three inches long. Can you believe it?" Mr. Peterson announced. "That's pretty awesome for the Looking Pond!"

"So *that's* what a bass looks like," I said. I stood up in the waist-high water. "He's kind of cool and prehistoric-like."

"Indigo, come on, get out of there before I throw prehistoric Whoop back in. I'm pretty sure he could eat you for breakfast," Jake kidded.

"Wait, you're going to throw him back?" I questioned. "I thought you ate everything you caught."

"Oh, not Whoop," Jake replied solemnly. "He's special."

"All right," I replied, "but just hold on to him for a second longer. I need that flower."

Pushing down the skirt fabric that had floated up all around me, I looked across the pond to the rose. It bobbed up and down on the surface from the waves I'd created as I moved. Determined to rescue it, I ducked down into the water, submerged, bent my legs, and pushed off from the bank, my feet now free from the slimy thick clay on the bottom of the pond. I glided, not taking a breath or opening my eyes until I came close to where I thought the flower floated. When I popped my head up, I was within arm's reach of the symbol, so I reached out and snatched it with my hand. I swam the breaststroke to reach the shore, my rose locked in my paddling right hand.

Within moments, I climbed onto the shore. The second Jake saw my feet hit the sand, he stood up on the bank and held the crazy bass over the water. It jerked and flapped between his hands until he lost control and finally let go. I don't think any of us took a breath until we saw Whoop make his grand splash into the water.

"Whoop, Whoop, Whoop!" we all cheered as Jake and his dad high-fived. I raised my right arm and drew circles in the air with the yellow rose in my hand. And, to my surprise, the excitement went straight to my head. All dizzy and wet, I knew it was time to go home.

"Silvy and I had best be on our way," I announced, tugging my skirt and soaked jeans away from my skin. Once my legs were free to move, I walked toward Silvy by the weeping willow tree. "Congratulations, Jake. Whoop is quite the catch."

"I didn't hook him, Indigo—you did," Jake countered with a chuckle.

"If it weren't for your dad's fishing rod, we wouldn't have caught Whoop at all," I said.

I sloshed my way to Silvy. My boots squished water up my leg with each step, and my heavy skirt, jeans, and sweatshirt dripped a trail of water behind me. But even though I was cold and drenched, I felt something so good inside. I was overwhelmed with gratitude that, yes indeed, I was happy again, and that, even when I thought life would never get better, if I took the plunge for what I loved, things do have a way of working out.

And just when I thought I couldn't take any more goodness, I noticed two empty root beer cans in a bag that hung from the handlebars of Jake's bike. *Wow, he's actually taking them home*, I noted happily.

Careful not to injure the petals, I slid the rose down into my saddlebag, buckled the flap, and hopped onto Silvy's saddle. This time my body felt strong. All my sad and broken parts had been healed by the glue of goodness. My fourth symbol was back, and I knew exactly what I needed to do the minute I got home.

CHAPTER 9

ELBOW DEEP

s Silvy trotted to the barn, I saw Mom by the side of the house, stuffing our two trash cans with white garbage bags. After I'd put Silvy in his stall and given him fresh water and hay, it occurred to me that Mom usually embarked on a cleaning frenzy whenever she was upset.

Oh boy, I hope I'm not in trouble, I thought as I retrieved the rose from the saddlebag and walked from the barn toward the house.

"Indigo, what on earth?" Mom called out. "You're soaking wet. Are you okay?"

"I'm great. Just freezing is all."

"I'll bet! Well you better change this instant, and then come right back so we can talk."

"I'll be back in a flash."

I walked to the back door, yanked off my boots, turned them upside down to let the brown pond water pour out, and set them on the first step so they'd dry out in the sun. Then I attempted to run upstairs to my room, but my wet skirt and jeans hugged my legs tight again, holding them back with each stride. When I finally reached my room, Scarlett flapped her wings in greeting.

As I admired her, she again cooed seven loud coos. "Yes, I get it," I replied cheerfully. "Sorry about this morning. I see you're ready to fly."

She tilted her head and flapped her wings again.

"Just give me a sec," I said. "I need my bracelet."

I set the rose on my nightstand and peeled off my clothes. Then I replaced them with a dry gray sweatshirt and pants and a pair of red wool socks. I felt cozy and warm.

"Now, bracelet," I called out. "I've come to rescue you from the trash. We have our fourth symbol! It was in the Looking Pond."

I looked down in wide-eyed panic. The trash can was empty. I rushed out of my room and down the stairs, opening the door with a violent shove. "Mom, wait!" I yelled. "My bracelet, it's in that trash!"

Mom came from the side of the house with three plastic bottles in her hand and gave me a comforting smile. "I put it on your nightstand last night."

"Oh no, Mom! When I woke up this morning, I threw it back into the trash. I felt like nothing mattered . . . like *I* didn't matter. But I know better now. We've *got* to find it."

Mom put the plastic bottles on the ground and took my hand. "Indigo Monroe, *everything* about you matters. Let's search for it together."

As we walked toward the garbage cans, Marigold barked *twice* from the back door, so I turned around to let her out. "Come on, girl," I invited, opening the door. "Help us find the missing heirloom."

Instead, Marigold ran to the kitchen counter, then back to the door, barking twice again. "Come on." I tugged on her collar and led her onto the porch.

Mom opened one trash bag. I untied the yellow fastener of another full bag of garbage and twisted the tie around my left index finger so I could reuse it once we found the bracelet. I dove my hand ferociously into the bag like I was unwrapping a Christmas gift. Aside from the crashing sound of trash hitting the driveway and Marigold's occasional bark as she watched the frenzy, there was only silence. Mom didn't even ask why I'd come home sopping wet.

"This reminds me of Jake and Mr. Peterson fishing this morning," I said after a while.

"Oh, why's that?" Mom asked.

"Mr. Peterson and Jake fished in silence this morning," I explained. "Mr. Peterson told me he takes Jake fishing whenever they aren't getting along. He thinks it helps them work things out. Though, come to think of it, I didn't see them work anything out."

"But we're not in a fight," Mom countered. "Though I guess a lot has happened since we last saw each other. Do you feel like talking now, over used cotton balls and rotten garbage?"

I laughed. "Yeah, that sounds okay."

I proceeded to tell Mom *everything*. I began with when Pearl delivered my lost bracelet, and then added the appearance of the fabric in the barn, then the magic movement of the can ring as it fell off my finger, and finally the whispers. From the trash bags to the recycle bins to the compost pile, Mom used her best-ever listening skills.

As we picked through the last few potato peels in the decomposing heap behind the barn, she asked, "Do you know why you found the rose this morning?"

I thought for a moment as I recalled how the whisper explained the two choices. "When I chose love over fear, my symbol just showed up."

"Wow, Indigo . . ." Mom's hands stopped digging, ending the search.

She looked deep into my eyes, like she could see right through me. It didn't feel creepy. It felt comforting, like she saw me—all of me. *I'm real . . . just as real as Sienna Glass.* "Pretty cool, huh?" I said.

"Beyond cool," she added. "You know, your dad cancels a lot of plans with you, but you've never had that sort of reaction. What made you feel so sad and angry this time?"

"I guess I'm just starting to realize how terrible I feel when Dad makes himself scarce. I always tried to brush it off. But really, it feels like nothing about me matters to him . . . just like the way Sienna Glass never mattered to him."

Mom blinked a few times and then swallowed. "That makes sense, honey," she said. After a few awkward moments of silence, she continued, "It took me a long time to realize that your dad just doesn't experience the world like we do. He couldn't relate to our relationship with Sienna Glass. He needed to find his own way in the world. But that doesn't mean he doesn't love you."

That was an epic moment. It was the first time Mom had shared *her* thoughts about Dad and Sienna Glass with me. I stopped picking through the slimy potato peelings and looked at Mom. Tears welled up. Aside from feeling really sad about all of it, the divorce, Sienna Glass, my missing bracelet, Dad, I began to wonder what else Mom had stored inside her.

"It's okay," Mom reassured me. "It's normal to feel lost in the dark sometimes. I've felt that way countless times, like when I lost your sister and when your dad and I got divorced. But you aren't your feelings, any more than you are your thoughts, Indigo. You're a beautiful . . ."

Mom was getting all "Mom" on me, so I said, "I got it, you can stop now."

"No, let me finish," she insisted. "You are Indigo Monroe, a girl who loves animals, who sews and wears dazzling skirts no matter what other people think, who loves nature, and who's a good friend, a terrific daughter, and so much more."

Feeling embarrassed, I rolled my eyes, but she squeezed in one more gush anyway. "Trust me, your dad sees you and your gifts and loves you more than anything."

I wiped the tears from my face. I wasn't sure whether I was crying over my lost bracelet or the words Mom had just strung together. Slamming my garbage-slimed hand onto my forehead, I reviewed the facts: We'd looked through every ounce of garbage, recycling, and compost, but we hadn't found the heirloom.

Mom could feel me beginning to stress, so she took my face in her smelly, dirty hands, and gave me a big kiss on the cheek. "We've fished in every trash pile I know of and we're out of luck."

"Thanks, Mom," I said looking in her eyes. Then I heard the whisper: "*Whoop is around here somewhere.*"

Mom draped her arm over my shoulder, and we walked to the back porch steps and took a seat. Marigold ran to my feet and barked twice yet again. "What is it, girl?" I asked. When she scratched at the screen door, I let her in. Running right to the kitchen counter, she barked two *more* times, so I walked into the house and bent down to her level. "Show me what you can't say," I encouraged.

Marigold stretched her paw out in front of her. I looked, and there between the base of the counter and the kitchen floor was my bracelet. "Oh, Marigold, you found it! Mom, Marigold found the bracelet!"

Mom rushed through the back door, her smile entering first. "Good dog! Way to go!" she cheered.

I knelt and wrapped my arms around Marigold's neck. "Thank you! You're the bestest furry friend I've ever had, and a great fisher-dog, too!" Marigold nudged her head into my shoulder and I knew we had an understanding. I let her go and turned to Mom. "I'll be right back, Mom; something's missing."

༄

After washing the goo off my hands, I carefully plucked the rosebud off the nightstand. Picking off two wilted yellow petals, I unfastened the twist tie from my finger, wrapped it around the petals, and then wrapped the ends around my bracelet. Next, I grabbed the orange bandana I'd worn for the karaoke contest from my dresser. When I neatly wrapped the rest of the yellow flower inside, I placed it on my nightstand. "Don't worry, Rose, I'll find you a special place," I explained, "but first, I need to do something extremely important."

Once I'd fastened the bracelet securely around my wrist, I walked to the hospital cage. Scarlett cooed and flapped with anticipation. "I know, I know," I said, "it's time. I hear you loud and clear."

I reached into the cage and nudged my right hand under her skinny feet. As I took her out of the cage, she sat perfectly still. Confident she wouldn't budge, I spread out her left wing and watched for signs of pain, but she neither flinched nor struggled. In fact, she looked great.

With both my hands wrapped around her body, I kissed her soft, fluffy back, then walked downstairs and out the back door. Marigold heard the door slam and ran toward us. Mom had already cleaned the trash off the driveway and was weeding the flowerbed next to the porch. She looked up as I approached.

"Very creative, Indigo," she said, running her fingers across the yellow petals on my bracelet, and then gently patted Scarlett.

"I'm not sure how much longer I can wear the brace-let with all these symbols. The petals will shrivel up and break away in a few days."

"I see what you mean," she said. Then a few seconds later she followed up with one of her favorite sayings, "Things always have a way of working out, Indigo."

"You hear that, Scarlett?" I said, holding her up to my face. "Things *do* have a way of working out. I know you're wiser now and won't be fooled by silly windows, right?"

I walked to the center of the backyard with Scarlett secure in my hands. Standing motionless, I took a deep breath and held her high above my head.

As I looked up at my bracelet and its peculiar sym-bols, I saw an image of Pearl flying out from my bedroom window.

"I'll miss *you*, pretty bird," I said to Scarlett with a smile. "Remember, when you're flying toward a win-dow, you have two choices: You can turn or you can fly straight ahead. I hope you'll always turn."

When I opened my hands, Scarlett took off instantly, her wings (and my heart) beating stronger than ever.

CHAPTER 10

UNRAVELING

Scarlett grew smaller and smaller until I lost sight of her completely. I couldn't help but wonder where she was headed and whether she would ever come back to visit, the way I'd always wondered if Sienna Glass would ever come back to visit.

A second later, I felt a chill swish across my left ear. *"The love you feel for others will always come back . . . even if you never see them again,"* said the whisper. *"Sienna Glass—like Scarlett—visited for a while, but the love you shared will be with you forever."*

With those words, tingly warmth spread throughout my body, like a cheerful alarm going off inside me. In that moment, I understood something I'd sort of known all along: The mysterious whisper I'd been hearing all this time was . . . My. Very. Own. Voice.

"We are the whisper and the wisdom."

I scratched my head and wiped my hands over my eyes. I felt dizzy, like a mystery had just blown up inside me. Observing each clue as it floated by, I guessed it did make sense:

It was a female voice—a girl's voice, *my* voice.

It had always encouraged me at just the right times.

It knew things about me, things that only I could have known about myself. It even knew things a part of me had refused to see.

The whisper was like a knight—or, in my case, a warrior priestess—who stood guard atop a castle. Whenever it spoke, it protected me with the wisdom gained from its high point of view.

But I had more questions. Like, for instance, *Am I really that wise?*

I ran to the garage where Mom was making a racket. When I peeked inside, she had just tossed a metal watering can out onto the concrete floor and stepped closer to the two fishing rods propped up against the garage wall. Once she'd kicked my red wagon and the stack of planting pots out of the way, she made it to her destination. When she grabbed one fishing pole, the other came, too; their fishing lines were all intertwined.

After catching my breath, I blurted, "Mom, you know the whisper I told you about, the one I've been hearing?"

She looked up. A smile played on her lips, and she nodded.

"It's me!" I shouted. "*I* am the whisperer."

"Isn't that wonderful?" she replied, almost too casually. She leaned up against the wall and began picking apart the tangled line.

I inched closer to her. I tiptoed through the maze of junk until I reached my dust-covered wagon, and I plopped down inside. My legs hung over the metal rim, like a towel over the rim of a bathtub. I felt oddly humongous. I guess it had been years since we'd played together, my wagon and me.

Mom's focused gaze on the twisted lines reminded me of a tiger stalking its prey, and I couldn't help but study her untangling technique. She took her thumb and index finger and dipped inside the twisted mess for a particular knot. As she moved her hand, she was careful not to snag the two dangling hooks into her skin. Once she'd freed half the line, she stopped and grinned at me.

"Do you know *where* those messages you've been whispering to yourself are coming from?" she asked with an air of mystery.

"Yes . . . I mean, no," I replied, confused.

Mom continued to untangle the line while she talked. "That's your inner voice, your *intuition*. Among other things, it helps you see yourself and honor and love your unique gifts. When you do that, fear has less of a hold on you. When you're not afraid to be who you are, the wisdom you hear becomes the truest expression of you."

I shifted in the wagon. "*Hmmm*. I guess that makes a little sense," I said with a gulp, knowing full well "makes a little sense" might have been a bit of an exaggeration.

Mom took a deep breath and continued, "Your intuition can sense things that are hard to see in the *real* world. Take Sienna Glass, for example."

"Yeah?" I urged her on, my ears set to full volume.

"When you told me about her, I knew that you were deeply intuitive—like me and many others in our family." She returned to untangling the line, tossing out more and

more things for me to chew on. "As you grow in awareness, your intuition will grow, too. The heirloom helps
you hear your inner voice. *Everyone* has a wise inner
voice, with or without a special bracelet."

I gazed down at the heirloom, as her words just kept
coming . . . "The bracelet is a tool, a reminder really, and
it's just the first step in your journey. I know you won't
lose it ever again."

I sighed. At least that last part made perfect sense: I
would *never* lose the bracelet again.

"Ouch!" yelped Mom. She sucked a drop of blood off
the side of her arm where the fishing hook had snagged
her. "It takes practice to be aware of two things at once."

When the bleeding stopped, which it did quickly,
Mom dove back into the fishing line, working even more
carefully to avoid getting hooked again.

Curious about why she was going through all the
trouble in the first place, I asked, "Who's going fishing?"

Mom gave me a look I couldn't read. "Your dad
called this morning," she answered cautiously. "He canceled his plans to go to the work party. He said that when
you stood up to him yesterday, he saw you, *really* saw
you for the first time in a long time. He wants to make
things right between you two."

I took a deep breath and felt for my bracelet. *Live the
love you feel inside . . .*

I reached for the free line that led to the tangled mess
in Mom's hands. As I did so, I heard a car door shut
behind me. We turned to see Dad walking up the driveway.

Before I had a chance to freak out, Dad walked past

the old red wagon, stepped over the tire pump and shovels on the garage floor, and leaned up against the wall next to Mom. He looked at me with puppy dog eyes and said, "Looks like we have some unraveling to do."

PART TWO

WATCH

CHAPTER 11

THEY'RE BITING

The rust-encrusted shovel sliced into our flowerbed, and I yanked back on the handle, accidentally sending a shower of dirt flying into the air. Dropping to one knee, I thrust my bare fingers into the moist, root-scented earth and instantly felt something cold and squishy.

"I'm sorry, little guy, but I need you," I said softly, plucking the worm up from his cozy hideout. "Dad and I can't catch Whoop without you."

As the helpless creature dangled wiggling between my thumb and index finger, I raised it to eye level, being careful to keep it a safe distance from my mouth. "I hope you can hear me, Mr. Worm," I said apologetically. "You'll be one of our offerings to the fish today. In return, I'll fill this hole with homemade soil for your worm friends to enjoy."

Using my free hand, I reached into the steel pail by my side with my shovel and scooped out a mound of rich compost. I'd extracted it that morning from the pile of decomposed fruit and vegetables Mom and I tended behind the barn. "Mom says worms love this stuff," I explained, emptying the fresh soil into the hole. Then, I patted the compost to firmly pack it in place. "Despite my having to sacrifice you," I told the worm, "I really do love all creatures. Even though you can't be one of my pets, you can help me be a better fisherwoman."

I dropped the wriggling creature into the empty yogurt tub I'd lined with a layer of soft earth, swallowing uncomfortably as I snapped the lid tight. Wandering over to the steps outside the back door, I clambered up onto the porch, opened the tackle box, and set the plastic tub inside. Then I sat down on the top step to pick gooey soil from under my nails, using my purple jeans as a napkin.

Once my hands were mostly clean, my attention turned to my bracelet. For the first time, I noticed that the leather seemed to shimmer with a brand-new reddish hue from within the braid, like it was coming back to life. *Interesting,* I thought.

At that moment, the rocks in the driveway made a lively crackling sound. Dad's red sports car pulled up. Glancing down at my watch, I saw it was right on eight o'clock. *Wow,* I thought. *This is the fifth week Dad has been on time for our weekly trip to the Looking Pond.*

I thought back to that day in the barn when we spent most of our time unraveling the fishing lines and gathering the tackle. Then Dad had had to retrieve Mom's old-fashioned green bike from the clutter in the garage, pump up the flat tires, and wipe cobwebs from the white wicker basket that decorated the front handlebars. I rode Silvy out to the Looking Pond, while Dad followed astride the super-cushiony old ladies' seat.

It was fortunate our time by the pond had been short that Sunday. The first half hour had passed in awkward silence as we'd watched our bobbers float undisturbed on the glassy surface, neither of us knowing what to say to the other. Dad had finally broken the silence by proposing, "How about I come by every Sunday and you and I go fishing until school is out for the summer?"

Thirty minutes without a word being said. It felt like hours. Did I really want to agree to Sunday mornings spent in stony silence? I'd felt positively uneasy. Nevertheless I'd given in, only to be shocked a moment later by what came out of my own mouth. "Our fishing trips will be enough time together, Dad," I'd announced. "If we do this, I don't want to come over to your city apartment for a while." Aware that his frequent no-shows and late arrivals had put thousands of miles between us, Dad had nodded.

Five weeks later, our fishing trips had become one of the highlights of my week—so much so that today I was on a mission.

Dad stepped out of his car, green Thermos under his arm and white paper bag in hand, and slammed the car door behind him. I loved seeing Dad in his new camouflage baseball hat. Dressed in jeans, a gray zip-up sweatshirt, and tennis shoes, he seemed very down to earth —way different than the suit-and-tie costume he wore to work.

Holding up what I guessed was hot chocolate and my favorite Bavarian-cream-filled doughnuts, he yelled, "I've got the goods if you've got the gear!"

Grabbing our tackle box, I raced down the steps,

snatched up the two fishing rods from the side of the house, and headed for the driveway, handing Dad the tackle in exchange for our scrumptious sugar-packed breakfast. We headed to the garage, where Dad plopped the rusty metal box into the wicker basket on Mom's bike and fastened our rods to the handlebars.

With Dad pedaling alongside me, we made our way to the pasture. Silvy stood in the middle of the grassy field, tacked up and ready to go. Hearing my familiar kissing sound, he turned and trotted up to me, but he showed more interest in nosing the sweet-smelling bag of doughnuts than in my attention. Jerking the bag to a safe distance, I dropped it into the saddlebag with the Thermos, clasped the reins, thrust my brown leather barn boot through the stirrup, and swung aboard.

"We're off like a herd of turtles!" I hollered, leaning forward in the saddle.

Silvy broke into a trot. As we sped across the field, my red curls bouncing against my back, it occurred to me that I was wearing my favorite purple jeans and orange fleece sweatshirt, the same outfit (minus the skirt) I wore when I hooked Whoop and the yellow rose—whose petals had now fallen off my bracelet. Luck was on our side; I could feel it.

We rode out of the pasture, following the Tree Canopy trail until we arrived at the Sitting Log, where I let Silvy graze under the willow tree while Dad and I set up camp on the high bank of the Looking Pond.

"Wait!" I exclaimed as we both reached for a gritty worm. I pulled out mine first. "Let's split this one."

Holding up my offering to the fish, I blew it a kiss, then used my thumbnail to cut it into segments, a technique Dad had shown me weeks ago that allowed us to sacrifice fewer worms. Since then, I had learned to be a bait-saving pro.

With our hooks buried in worm, Dad swung to the right and I to the left. "Thank you, Mr. Worm," I whispered across the pond as our bait and bobbers plunked into the water. "I know you'll bring us good luck."

Instinctively drawing deep breaths, Dad and I sighed in unison. Then Dad announced, "Let the games begin!"

After five weeks together, Dad and I had become comfortable sitting side by side, watching our bobbers on the pond. Of course the first few weeks he bombarded me with a million questions. For example:

"Do you understand why Mom and I divorced?"

"Do you know that I love your sister, Vienna?"

"Do you know that I can't see, hear, or sense things like you and your mom?"

"Do you understand that just because I don't experience the world like you guys that I love you all very much?"

"Do you know that I left the house because I had to, not because of anything you did, or Mom did, or Sienna Glass did?"

"Do you think there will come a time when you will feel comfortable staying with me in the city again?"

Some of my answers came easily. No, I wasn't comfortable in the city. For starters, it made me nervous when he drove and talked on the phone at the same time. I also got bored and homesick when I spent ages waiting for him to finish working. To my amazement, I even found the nerve to explain to him that I didn't like the white leather couch he'd bought for his living room. "It's just that every time I sit on it with a glass in my hand, you warn me not to spill. Then I get so nervous I might ruin the couch that I can't even enjoy my drink. Besides, the leather's so cold and clammy, not snuggly like the couch Mom and I have at home."

With the other more personal questions about the divorce, Mom, and Sienna Glass, well, I just listened. It was like the answers were in his questions already. It was funny, but all of that sitting with Dad by the Looking Pond was super helpful for me; it seemed to straighten things up in my head.

It was on our third fishing expedition that he had asked the really embarrassing question, "Indigo, do you know how much I love you?" Without waiting for my answer, he had gone on to tell me all the reasons he loved me. He'd even included how I talked with Sienna Glass as a reason. Now *that* was a shocker, considering I had spent years thinking that was one of the reasons he'd avoided me so much.

Dad had even written a list of all the reasons he loved me, a copy of which he handed me just in case I started to feel like I had earlier in the school year when I'd really questioned whether he cared at all. In complete shock, I silently folded the list and stuffed it into my back pocket.

The last blast of awkwardness had come as Dad had left that day. "I love you, Indigo," he'd said, suddenly clasping me in a bear hug and picking me up off my feet.

"Oh, I know," I muttered, staring down at the dirt driveway, tears filling my eyes as he got into his car and reversed it slowly into the street.

Five weeks into this adventure, our attention had shifted from our discomfort with one another to our mutual enjoyment of catching scaly water creatures. We now sat quietly, comfortable with the silence. We listened to the wind, admired the bright white, pink, and yellow seasonal colors the flowers wore, and turned our focus to the pond whenever a ripple broke the stillness of the surface.

Partway through the morning Dad brought up the question of summer plans. "School is going to end in five days," he began.

"Me and Caroline are signed up for a performing arts day camp," I quickly interrupted. "We'll be rehearsing a play all summer. But save August fifteenth on your calendar because that's the day of the performance."

"I wouldn't miss it for the world," he assured me.

With the good faith he'd banked the past five Sundays, I thought that maybe he meant it.

The conversation turned to how Mom would once again change her work schedule to "weekends only" so she could be home with me on weekdays, as she had done the past few summers since the divorce. I was to spend the weekends with Dad. In the past, I'd dreaded summer for this reason, but maybe things would be different now.

"I'll pick you up from camp every Friday afternoon," Dad said, reeling in his line. "And I'll drop you off at camp on Monday mornings."

I nodded. Dad prepared to cast again. Suddenly, my bobber dove below the surface of the pond.

"I've got a fish!" I yelled. Setting the hook, I felt a strong resistance on the line. "It feels like a big one," I said excitedly. "Get the net!"

"Net? We don't have a net!"

"Well, what do I do?"

"Hold on firmly—don't let go, whatever you do."

As I reeled in the line, the fish suddenly swam away from the bank. *Pop!* My rod was now light as a feather.

"He broke your line," Dad said.

"Darn! I bet that was Whoop," I said. "Jake and his dad are always trying to catch him."

"*Grrrrr,*" Dad growled with a wink. "Don't you worry, Indigo. We'll look that monster in the eyes someday. Next Sunday I'll bring a net in case you hook him again. I can't believe we've come all these weeks without one."

"Well, we've only caught four tiny fish, so we've hardly needed one," I said glumly.

We set our rods down. While Dad poured a cup of hot chocolate for us to share, I opened the white paper bag and retrieved two soft doughnuts stuck together with cream. Biting into them, we rolled our eyes in delight.

At that moment, I heard Jake's voice calling my name. Parking his bike next to Silvy, he ran in our direction. "I saw Silvy and knew you were here, Indigo. Oh, hi, Mr. Monroe. Nice to see you."

"Hi, Jake," Dad replied. "Come to fish? Is your dad here, too?"

"It's just me this morning. In fact, this will be my last

fishing trip for a while. The day after school gets out, I'm headed to Montana to stay with my grandparents for the summer."

Now that Jake was being nice to me after all these years, I wasn't so eager for him to go away for the whole summer, but I would never share that out loud. So I just said, "That's cool."

"Oh, by the way," Jake added. "Be careful on your way back today. I saw a stray dog on the trail. As I rode by, he growled. He had slobber all over his mouth. There must be something wrong with him."

Dropping my half-eaten doughnut into the paper bag, I brought the cup of hot chocolate to my lips for a quick last sip. Leaping to my feet, I felt for the worn, scraggly robin feather that dangled from my bracelet. "We're outta here, Dad," I announced. "We've got to find him."

"Wait just a minute," Dad protested. "Didn't you hear what Jake said? The dog might be dangerous. You are good with animals, but this one sounds like it needs a trained professional. This is something you can't do alone."

Instantly, the whisper took center stage and urged, "Look!" So I instinctively turned my attention inward, as if in daydream. There in my mind's eye I saw a vision of all of my symbols lying together on my orange bandana. "Keep looking." As I focused on the vision, a glowing line began taking shape around my symbols in a triangular pattern. As I concentrated, the center of the triangle pulsed, then a bright light flashed within. When the light dimmed, four small pale-blue crystal stones had taken the place of my symbols.

"Indigo, did you hear me?" Dad demanded. "This dog sounds dangerous."

I snapped out of my head and heard Jake and Dad talking about the sick dog. "Dad, I'm not alone," I replied. "You're coming with me."

I gathered up the Thermos and doughnut bag, as I charged toward Silvy.

"Thanks for the heads up," Dad said to Jake, pulling himself up. "The fish are biting, so get ready for a fight. Indigo, wait up! Someone's gotta pack up our gear!"

"Giddy-up, Dad!" I urged, stuffing the doughnut sack and Thermos into the saddlebag. Dad ran for Mom's bike, securing the rods and tackle box. As he mounted the seat, I urged Silvy into a trot.

When we reached the Tree Canopy Trail a few minutes later, I sat heavily in Silvy's saddle to slow him to a walk.

Huffing and puffing, Dad pedaled up beside me. "Pull over right now," he ordered.

"What do you mean 'pull over'?" I protested. "We've got to find the dog before it runs away!"

Dad got off his bike and demanded I dismount. I did, and both of us stood in the middle of the dirt trail, each with one hand resting on our hip.

"I know you've got a gift with animals," Dad began, "but having a sixth sense with animals sometimes means knowing when to let an animal go."

While Dad lectured me about the danger of approaching a sick dog, my foot traced a wandering tree root that bulged up from the trail. The image of a single icy-blue crystal, just like the ones I'd seen in my vision, popped into my head. My attention was so riveted by the angles of the stone that my foot slipped off the root, and I took a tumble.

Grasping my wrist, Dad pulled me up. I brushed my hands clean on my jeans. And, in that moment, a deep, raspy growl from the trail behind us caused us both to jump. We turned. A collie, his fur all caramel and white, stood behind us on the trail.

Walking forward, I said calmly, "It's okay, we're here to help you." As I drew closer, I saw froth foaming at the collie's mouth and burrs clinging to the fur on his belly and hind legs. Other collies I'd met had seemed like the sweetest dogs. It didn't seem right that this one would be acting so gnarly.

"Don't you dare!" Dad called. "Let's go home and contact Animal Control!"

"I just want to see if he has a collar."

By now, I was barely two arms' length from the collie, and I put out my right hand faster than Dad could stop me. In an instant, the dog lunged for my arm, sinking his teeth into my sweatshirt sleeve. I jerked away, stumbling backward.

Sprinting forward, Dad positioned himself in front of me, yelling in a commanding voice and pointing vigorously toward the woods. The collie lowered his tail, then turned and slunk into the underbrush.

Still kneeling, I cradled my arm and stared after the dog in shock.

CHAPTER 12

A METAL MONSTROSITY

"The bite didn't even break the skin!" I shouted in frustration.

My attempts to stop Dad's frantic download to Mom about what had occurred on the trail weren't going well. While they stood bantering back and forth, I sat at the kitchen table with my arm propped up on a pillow. Whenever the ice pack slid off—which it did a million times—I sighed loudly, then used big movements to reposition it back over my arm.

Marigold was confused by Dad's wild gesturing and Mom's curious facial expressions. Sitting at my feet, she turned her big brown eyes toward me to see if I was all right. When I smiled reassuringly, she returned her focus to the riveting drama taking place.

"We've got to call Animal Control right now!" Dad insisted.

Mom went scurrying for her phone to look up the

number. With cell phone in hand, she sat down across the table from me. "What were you thinking?" she implored, her brow furrowed. She handed Dad her phone, and he made the call.

My gaze went to the robin's feather on my bracelet. "I wanted to see if the dog had a collar," I replied. "I couldn't just leave him alone on the trail."

At that moment, the icy-blue crystal again appeared in my mind's eye. Mom leaned back in her seat, sighing heavily. Dad was relating what had happened to Animal Control. Distracted, I lost sight of the crystal and the calm that had come over me.

"Well, you're one lucky girl," Dad said as he hung up. "Your sweatshirt protected you from the dog's teeth. Since the bite didn't break the skin, we don't need to worry about rabies, but keep the ice pack on your arm for now; there might be some swelling. Animal Control will be here as soon as possible to search the trail and catch the dog."

"But if they catch him, they'll put him to sleep!" I protested.

"The dog is sick," Dad said firmly. "If he has rabies and the virus has reached his brain, he'll die within ten days anyway. Animal Control needs to capture and quarantine him to confirm whether he has rabies and to keep him from harming anyone else. With all that frothing at the mouth, he could very well have it! You need to keep Marigold indoors, by the way. Since this house is the closest to the trail, there's a chance the dog will make his way here at dusk looking for food."

"Did you hear that, Marigold?" I said, reaching down to pat her with my uninjured arm. "You can't roam the pasture with our pal, Silvy, until they catch this dog."

When Dad excused himself to use the bathroom, Mom seized the opportunity to question me. "Did anything else strange happen today, besides the dog bite? You seem preoccupied by more than what's going on here."

"*Umm*, yeah, well, kind of," I replied hesitantly. "My intuition, that thing you mentioned that lives inside me that senses things, well, it was really active today, and I saw a picture in my head of a beautiful light-blue crystal. It was the size of . . . I don't know, a penny, maybe. It had sharp angles and uneven edges, like a busted-up piece of ice. Inside, I could see layers and lines, like you see in frozen water. I wish I had a picture to show you."

"I have a book on crystals you can flip through," Mom said with a wink. "Maybe you'll find a picture of it in there. I used to collect crystals when I was a kid, so I've had the book a very long time. Remember that day in my room when we said a blessing for Sienna Glass and I'd arranged the crystals on my quilt?" Mom paused and stared out the window into our backyard.

How could I forget that day we said goodbye to Sienna Glass? It was a bittersweet memory. Trying to focus on the sweet part of it, I asked, "What makes crystals so special?"

Mom reached across the table and pushed the plastic bag of ice back up onto my forearm. "I know you love animals, but safety comes first. Remember to choose wisely. I mean, what if you had been by yourself? If your dad hadn't been with you, the dog might have gone on the attack."

"I know, Mom. But we were talking about crystals."

"Yes, I know. We *are* talking about the crystal," Mom confirmed as Dad returned to the kitchen.

Just then, the doorbell rang. Dad grabbed my good arm and the three of us rushed to the foyer. When Mom opened the front door, two men stood on the porch.

"Are you the Monroe family?" asked a tall, black-bearded man with a nametag that read "Joel."

"Hi, Joel," Mom said, reaching out her hand and introducing herself. "My daughter and I live here," she clarified. "Thanks for coming so quickly."

Ever since the divorce, Mom had been in total charge of the house. Dad was more like a guest in our home now, which felt awkward. He leaned in and gave both men a firm handshake.

"My coworker is checking out the trail now," Joel said, "but when he last radioed in, he hadn't found the dog. We're wondering whether you'd all be comfortable having a dog trap near your barn. No doubt that dog's hungry and just might sniff out your place for food and shelter."

"You're not going to kill it if you catch it, are you?" I blurted, my suspicious, squinting eyes piercing into Joel.

"Easy, Indigo," Dad warned.

"We'll just take it back to headquarters for observation," answered the second visitor, a gray-haired man with the name "Otis" embroidered on the pocket of his blue work shirt.

I couldn't back down. "Do we *have* to use the trap? It seems kinda cruel if you ask me. Why don't I put fresh food and water by the barn, and if I see him, I'll call you right away?"

"Miss Monroe," Joel stepped in to explain, "that only works if you're home and watching from a safe distance."

"And if we happen to be free to get here quickly enough," Otis added.

"Safety is the most important part of this process," Joel continued. "That's where the trap comes in. We put food and water inside the trap, and when the dog goes in, he'll be safely contained until we arrive."

"I don't know," I contested, feeling protective of the collie. Something just didn't feel right about trapping it. "This sounds way too serious. We've got Animal Control men in blue uniforms, dog traps, and talk of quarantine and rabies. It's like we're on a hunt for an alien or something. It's just a dog!"

"Indigo," Mom commanded, placing her hand on my shoulder. "Remember the conversation we just had? Let's make a wise choice here. Take a deep breath, slow down, and listen to what they're saying. They want to capture and observe this animal so he doesn't hurt anyone else. They want to protect us *and* the dog."

With those words, the vision of the icy-blue crystal reappeared in my mind. As I studied the crystal, I calmed down and focused on what Mom was saying. After all, she did know a lot more than me about the powers of crystals. "Safety first," Mom was insisting. "Then, if possible, care and love for the animal."

The vision vanished, and I nodded in agreement.

"So can we leave this trap with you?" Otis questioned, looking at Dad.

"Of course," Mom replied, shifting the men's attention to the woman in charge.

Otis glanced in my direction and raised his eyebrows.

"All right," I reluctantly agreed, sensing that my approval *was* important to them before they dumped the metal monstrosity on our property. I thought that was pretty cool of him.

"We already have a trap set up on the trail," Joel said. "We set it next to the big oak tree with those thick roots that cross the trail like a highway." He looked at me. "Do you know the place I'm talking about?"

"That's right where we saw the dog this morning."

"Otis and I will check the trap on the trail daily," Joel reassured us. "But if you notice the dog inside, please call and we'll come right away. Here's our business card. It has our office number and my cell number. You can call us day or night."

Dad thanked them, taking the card and handing it off to Mom. "And don't you worry," he told them. "Indigo will watch both traps like a hawk." Turning to me, Dad lifted his baseball cap off his head and ran his fingers through his scraggly brown hair. "Indigo," he said authoritatively, "if you see the dog inside the trap or anywhere near it, leave it alone. Come right home and call Animal Control. You hear me? Mom will put the card right by the phone on the kitchen counter."

I rolled my eyes. "Okay, Dad."

Otis retrieved the metal cage from the van, and we all followed him and Joel down the driveway. Mom directed the men to a place beside the barn where it could be seen from the kitchen window. Once the cage was in place, Otis set the trapdoor.

∽

"I'll get a water dish and some food," I called out to Mom and Dad as they watched the yellow van pull out of the driveway and disappear down the street.

"Wait up a second," Dad interrupted. He closed the distance between us and pulled me close. "I'm heading back to the city now. Please promise me you won't go near that dog."

"But what if it's trapped in that awful cage?" I protested. "Can I be near it then?"

Dad let out a big sigh. "Well, I guess," he said, "but *only* if the cage door is secure. . . . And, Indigo, you wouldn't even think of sticking your hands through the bars to pet the dog, right?"

With raised eyebrows, I half-asked, "Um, I imagine that wouldn't be very safe?"

"Correct," chorused Mom and Dad.

"Do you promise?" Dad asked, searching my eyes.

"I promise," I huffed with a hint of a smile, secretly grateful that Dad cared so much.

CHAPTER 13

THE KARAOKE DISASTER

"**W**e're leaving for Caroline's in ten minutes," Mom announced, heading back inside the house.

With all the commotion, I'd almost forgotten about my get-together with Caroline. I made a beeline for the storage room inside the barn and called over my shoulder, "I'll be right in!"

When I pushed the barn door open, a sharp pain erupted from my forearm. "Ouch!" I cried. Pushing up the sleeve of my sweatshirt, I ran my finger over the purple marks. *I thought I was doing the right thing,* I reflected.

Then I heard my whispering inner voice: *"Sure, I have a gift for caring for animals, but I better pay attention to what's going on around me."*

"I got this," I told myself aloud. Then, for good luck and fast healing, I kissed my sore spot and quickly switched my focus to the storage room, which was stacked with horse tack, cleaning supplies, and feed.

Two empty plastic butter containers rested on the wooden shelf next to my saddle. The last time I had used them was the day I found Marigold. Grabbing a can opener off the hook on a wooden post, I reached for the gourmet dog food on the feed shelf and scooped the entire can into one of the plastic tubs. I filled the other with water. Rounding the side of the barn, I managed to place the containers in the cage without trapping myself.

"Indigo, come on!" Mom called from the car window. "We've got to go."

I ran to the house to grab my jacket. Marigold looked at me expectantly.

"I'm sorry," I told her, "but you've got to stay inside today." Kissing her on the nose and getting my lips all wet in the process, I nudged her head away from the door. "I'll let you out when I get home."

I climbed into the car and secured my seatbelt, and Mom asked if I was excited to meet Caroline's new neighbor, Tess. She went on before I could answer, "From what Caroline's mom said, the girls are spending lots of time together. Tess is finishing out the year at her old school, but she'll be going to middle school next year with you guys. She's also attending the performing arts camp this summer. Won't it be nice to have a new friend?"

I thought for a moment about my response. Before I'd gotten the bracelet and started paying attention to my gifts, I might have worried that Caroline's new friend would think I was a crazy lion-haired girl, but I wasn't so worried about that now.

As we turned the corner onto Bridgeport Street, I

replied, "I guess if Caroline likes her, I will, too. Caroline said she likes karaoke, so that's pretty cool. We're going to use Caroline's new karaoke machine today. She told me that Noel hasn't let her hearing loss stop her from using it. She's been belting out the songs and even signs some of the lyrics."

"Well, then, you'll definitely have a good time," Mom said with good cheer.

"Well, Noel is out with her dad today," I replied. "And anyway, all I can think about is that poor dog. I know he didn't want to hurt me. He's just scared and hungry. What if he's caught in that trap on the trail, right now? He'll be there all day until someone checks on him. Can you pick me up at one o'clock?"

"That doesn't leave you much time," Mom said as she pulled into Caroline's driveway. "The dog will be okay, so just go on and have fun. We've got a good plan. Remember, things always have a way of working out."

"How about one-thirty?"

Mom gave me her "let's compromise" look and said with finality, "One forty-five."

I reluctantly agreed and hopped out of the car.

Caroline met me at the front door. "Come on! I can't wait for you to meet Tess."

We climbed the stairs to Caroline's room and opened the door. There was Tess, her short brown hair cut bob-style and her pink shirt sparkling with sequins. She was standing next to Caroline's dresser, looking through her jewelry box. With its heart-shaped glass window on the lid, the box was one of Caroline's treasures.

When Tess saw us, she slammed the lid shut and ran her fingers along the sides of her hair, tucking the strands behind her ears. Then she quickly dumped her hands into her jeans pockets. Stepping toward me, she said, "You must be Indigo. I'm Tess. Nice to meet you."

"Nice to meet you, too," I replied, pulling up the sleeve of my sweatshirt to reach for a handshake, flinching a little as I did so. But Tess, with her hands buried deep in her pockets, left me hanging.

My instincts told me that wasn't a good sign. I suddenly found myself wondering why she had been rifling through Caroline's jewelry box.

"What happened to your arm?" Caroline asked, looking concerned. Taking hold of my right hand and stretching out my arm, she said, "Look, it's all purple and swollen."

"Yes, I know," I replied, pulling my sleeve back down. "I tried to help a stray dog on the Tree Canopy Trail early this morning. He got scared and accidentally nipped me."

"That's ridiculous," Tess said scornfully. "Why would *anyone* go near a stray dog? Dogs don't *accidentally* bite people. Right, Caroline?"

"I guess not," Caroline said.

Clearly, saving dogs wasn't a good subject to discuss with Tess. I pointed to the karaoke machine on the purple carpet by Caroline's bed. "Wow, look at that!" I said excitedly. "Let's get this show started."

I lay down next to the machine and flipped through the songbook. Tess and Caroline lay next to me as we picked out our songs. Tess insisted on performing first "to show us how it's done." She picked out a fancy dress from Caroline's closet, borrowed several items from Caroline's jewelry box, and then stood on Caroline's bed as if it were a stage.

Tess didn't sing just one song—she sang six in a row. Between each song, she changed her outfit like a prima donna, handing Caroline her discards for rehanging. Caroline didn't say a word and just did whatever Tess instructed. I wondered why Caroline was letting Tess steal the show. I also wondered whether or not she even remembered I was in the room.

I just sat back and watched, too preoccupied by my thoughts of the collie to make any kind of fuss. When it was clear I wasn't entirely entranced by her performance, Tess finally surrendered the microphone.

"Indigo, you're next," she said.

The clock in Caroline's room read 1:29, so I bowed out. "I'm leaving soon. You go, Caroline."

"Wear this!" Tess commanded, pulling a black dress off its hanger. Caroline hesitated, then stepped into the dress. When she motioned for me to start the music, Tess pushed my hand aside. "I'll take it from here," she said, pressing the play button.

As Caroline sang, Tess analyzed her every move. By this time, a pit the size of a watermelon had settled in my stomach. Something about their friendship didn't feel right to me. I decided I'd talk to Caroline about it at school the next day—when Tess wasn't breathing down her neck.

A huge wave of relief washed over me when Caroline's mom called up the stairs for me to come down. "Gotta run, guys," I said. "Caroline, you're doing great! Thanks for having me over. See you tomorrow."

I raced downstairs, said a quick thanks to Caroline's mom, and got in the car.

"How'd it go?" Mom asked.

"Tess took over the karaoke show," I told her, "and I think she's taking over Caroline. She orders her around like Cinderella's evil stepmother. Something's not right. I can feel it."

Mom pursed her lips, then said carefully, "Trust your instincts, but also keep in mind that Caroline and Tess have spent lots of time together lately. This is your first time hanging out with them as a pair. Maybe next time it won't be so uncomfortable."

That was such a Mom thing to say; she was always trying to cast the situation in a better light. I wasn't too hopeful, but I let out a quick "Yeah, maybe." Anyway, I had other things on my mind. "Have you seen the dog?"

"He wasn't in the trap by the barn," Mom replied.

∽

When we pulled up to the house, Mom told me she'd walk Marigold, so I hurried to the barn and saddled Silvy. Silvy and I set out to inspect the cage on the trail straightaway. Upon finding it empty, I headed back home with a heavy heart.

Mom must have known I'd need something to take

my mind off the poor dog because, when I got back, she had a surprise waiting for me on the kitchen table: her book on crystals.

While a pot of water and spaghetti bubbled on the stove top for an early dinner, Mom and I silently leafed through the delicate pages, many of which were dog-eared.

It was a thick book, like a dictionary. Down the lavender spine, it read, CRYSTALS. The cover was a deep yellow, and all around the title—*The Secret Lives of Crystals and Gemstones*—were pictures of different crystals and symbols. The outside edges of every page shimmered gold, but the pages were worn out, so a lot of the gold coloring had rubbed off, and tiny tears had begun breaking through the thin edges. It had this sweet old-person smell that reminded me of my grandmother's rose-scented talcum powder. Everything about the book felt antique, like its value had increased with age.

The book contained information on hundreds of crystals, including their history, healing properties, and other uses. Mom explained that each crystal held a specific kind of energy, and it was this energy that could be used, like medicine, to heal. After several minutes of eagerly flipping through the book, I asked, "Do you have a favorite crystal?"

"Oh, my goodness, there are so many!" Mom closed the book. "Each has its own special qualities. I pretty much love them all."

Mom had always had an affinity for all things mystical. She had totally embraced the idea that Sienna was with us, even though she couldn't see her. She loved to tell me about angels and other "spirits from the stars." When I was little, she used to make up bedtime stories in which *I* was a winged one who solved problems and healed the sick. If Sienna was around to hear the story, Mom would add in a part about her, too. Some days I wondered if Mom was a real-live angel herself, but then I'd come back to earth and remember that she was solid, a nurse, and my very own real-life mom.

"The crystal I keep seeing is icy-blue," I reminded her.

Mom got up to check on the spaghetti. I knew it was close to ready when she poured half a jar of sauce into another pot. Opening the book again, I flipped through more of its pages, finally coming to a page that show-cased a crystal—blue calcite—that matched the color in my head. Pointing to the page, I exclaimed, "It looks just like this!"

After Mom strained the spaghetti, she came back to the table for a second to glance at the picture. "What does it say about blue calcites?" she asked, returning to the stove to stir the sauce.

"The summary says, 'This is a grounding and cen-tering stone. It has a calming effect and helps people see things more clearly.' Oh, and on the side here, there's a word written in cursive. *Umm*, I think it's pronounced *dis-cern-ment?* Right next to it someone wrote 'to choose wisely.' Those words aren't in cursive and the handwrit-ing looks different. Did you write them?"

Mom returned to the table with two bowls of piping hot spaghetti smothered in red sauce and placed one of the bowls in front of me. "Let me see that," she said with a chuckle. Picking up the book, she set it down across the table where she had set a place for herself. Twirling her fork in the spaghetti, she peered at the words written in the margin of the book. After a few moments, she confessed, "Yes, I wrote *to choose wisely.* But grandma wrote *discernment.*"

"Is choosing wisely what *discernment* means?"

"That's how I used to think of it," Mom answered, then switched the subject. "Calcites come in different colors, too; they can be green, orange, yellow, and even pink."

I angled the book so I could see it better. "Oh, look here. It says, 'Blue calcite promotes speedy healing, especially of wounds.' Maybe that's why I keep seeing it, so it can heal my dog bite. . . . *Hmmm*, except I saw it *before* the collie bit me." I glanced out the window at the trap, which still sat empty. "I know we need to find the dog, but I can't stand the thought of tricking it into that cold metal contraption. There's got to be a better way."

"Maybe there is, so keep listening, and"—Mom pointed at the blue calcite page—"choose wisely." She winked at me, and then asked, "How is your arm?"

"It hurts." I pulled up my sleeve to peek at the purple bruises. "A lot, actually."

Mom leaned over to inspect the marks. "You are lucky those teeth only bruised your skin. I've heard that rabies shots are really painful."

"I guess, but I don't feel lucky."

I finished my spaghetti and gathered the empty bowls. Once the kitchen was clean, Mom went to the family room to read on the comfy couch. I sat at the kitchen table with one eye on the crystal book and the other on the cage by the barn. I read about lots of different crystals, including the hawk's eye, rainbow quartz, watermelon tourmaline, yellow jasper, and sunstone. Then I turned to the page on red carnelians. *Interesting.*

"Hey, Mom," I called, "it says here that red carnelians quiet an aggressive animal if worn on their collar or placed in their water dish. Of course I can't get a crystal around that dog's neck," I said, walking into the family room with the crystal book in hand, "but if I had a red carnelian, I could put it in the water dish in the trap. Do you know where I could get one?"

"*Hmmm,* let's see," Mom replied brightly. "I just might have one upstairs."

I followed Mom to her room. She knelt beside her bed and reached beneath it to pull out a golden platter. On the platter was a red velvet cloth, which she unwrapped to reveal all sorts of crystals. Big, small, dark, pale—you name it, she had it.

"Remember these?"

"Yeah," I sighed, again thinking back to the crystal grid she'd made on her bed the night we'd said goodbye to Sienna Glass. Examining the crystal collection, my eyes fell on one stone in particular. "A red carnelian!" I gasped, holding up the Ping-Pong-sized stone. "Right? Can I put it in the dog's water dish?"

Mom nodded, and I slipped the stone into my pocket. I looked again at the rest of the collection.

"Where did you get all of these crystals?"

"Well, some I found when I was young. Others I bought in different crystal shops. You can even buy them on the Internet now, but it's always most special when you feel drawn to a crystal in person."

My eyes then fell on a nickel-sized, jagged, icy-blue crystal. "Blue calcite," I said, lifting it up to inspect it more closely.

"That's the wise one," Mom said simply.

At that moment, Marigold's "I-want-to-go-outside-and-pee" whine sounded up the stairs. "I'll take her," I said, and I dropped the crystal into Mom's open palm.

She placed the calcite on the red cloth and wrapped the velvet over all the crystals. As I headed out the door, I looked back. There she was, with her eyes closed and her hands resting on the bundle. Instantly, I imagined her with beautiful glowing wings just like the ones I pictured on Sienna Glass the day she flew home. *Yep, that's my mom,* I thought with a wide smile.

⌒

"Come on, girl," I said. "Stay close, now."

Seeing us approach, Silvy trotted across the field toward us. Marigold crawled under the pasture fence and stood next to Silvy. "Good dog, Marigold," I said, sensing she realized she needed to steer clear of the trap.

Walking over to the barn, I held the red carnelian to my lips and kissed it, then dropped it through the top of the cage into the water dish. Then I hurried into the barn and grabbed Silvy's brand-new horse blanket and a rawhide bone from the storage shelf and returned to the cage. Careful not to trigger the trapdoor, I placed the bone and blanket on the floor of the cage.

"I feel much better now," I told myself, touching the robin feather on my bracelet. This way, if the dog were trapped inside, he would be comfortable. Along with gourmet food, he had a bone to chew on and crystal-infused water to help heal him.

Corralling a curly lock that had fallen across my right eye, I saw the robin feather symbol fall from my bracelet and float down toward my shirt. "Oh, no," I gasped, "you broke off!"

Not knowing what to do, I listened. Holding the feather between my left thumb and index finger, I waited. All was still, except for the butterflies that flapped in my stomach. When my inner voice didn't speak, I panicked. Peering at the feather's worn and frazzled shape, I heard myself silently ask, *What do I do with you now?*

It was then that I heard the whisper: *"Everything has a way of working out. Look."*

As if on cue, the blue calcite crystal appeared in my mind's eye, allowing my belly butterflies to settle peacefully. As I calmed down and my head cleared, the crystal image faded, and in its place was an image of my bandana sitting on my nightstand. Inside the bandana lay the yellow rose, placed there the morning I'd found my lost bracelet and released Scarlett back into the wild.

Great idea! I thought. *I'll wrap it in the bandana with the yellow rose and put it under my bed, just like Mom does with her crystals.*

Gently tucking the orange feather into the front pocket of my purple jeans, I secured Silvy in his stall for the night and strolled back to the house with Marigold following at my heels. From the back doorstep, I took a last, lingering look at the cage.

"Wherever you are, don't be scared!" I called toward the woods. "Good food, a soft blanket, and crystal water are waiting for you. I promise not to let anyone hurt you."

Blowing a kiss into the air, I opened the door and headed upstairs to my room. I changed into the new white satin nightgown Mom and I had sewn a couple of weeks back.

I removed the robin feather from my jeans pocket, picked up the bandana bundle from my nightstand, and then sat down on the floor. Gently unfolding the bandana, I placed the bedraggled orange feather next to my dried-up rose. Wrapping them up carefully, I slid the bundle under my bed.

CHAPTER 14

PLAYING IT SAFE

"**M**arigold, stop it!"

Being nuzzled awake by Marigold's wet nose was hardly the way I wanted to start my day. "What time is it?" Opening one eye, I glanced at the glowing green readout on my bedside clock—only 5:53. Pushing Marigold's nose away from my face, I insisted, "One more hour of sleep."

Not to be ignored, Marigold barked twice, then began sandpapering my face with her tongue.

"My goodness, Marigold!" I said, becoming annoyed. "It's not even six yet! What is it?"

She barked twice again, this time running out through the strings of beads. A moment later, she ran back in to my bedside, put her front paws up on the mattress, and barked again.

"Okay, I'm coming," I complained, resigned to giving up my cozy nest. Unwrapping myself from the warm blankets, I snatched up my robe from the back of my lounge chair. Thrusting my feet into my slippers, I followed Marigold downstairs, where she sat under the big kitchen window and let out another big *woof*.

"Sorry to wake you, Mr. Magoo, and finches, too," I apologized to the birds, all fluffed up and resting in their cages. Peering through the kitchen window, my eyes lighted on the trap. Inside was a caramel-colored, long-haired dog, asleep on Silvy's new horse blanket.

"Oh my gosh!" I breathed. "Oh my gosh, it's the collie . . . it's the collie."

Marigold ran two circles around my feet, went to the back door, and barked.

"Shush, Marigold! I know. But we can't wake up Mom. Be quiet while I think." I looked out the window again and noticed the cage door was still propped in its open position. "The trapdoor didn't work!"

Marigold looked at me, tilted her head, and barked again.

"Shush, I know! I want to meet him, too."

I felt an urge to run out the back door, sit at the entrance of the cage, and pet that soft, furry head. I wanted to tell him that I knew he was scared and hadn't meant to hurt me. I wanted to tell him all about Marigold, Mom, the birds, Silvy, and me, and invite him to stay and live with us forever.

As daydreams of befriending the collie flooded my mind, an image of the blue calcite appeared. The jagged edges commanded my attention. Totally captivated, I felt my mind fill with calmness. "Even though the dog is asleep," I whispered to myself, "don't go out there. Be safe. Call Animal Control."

I rushed over to the kitchen counter and grabbed the phone. Scanning for the number, my eyes fell on a blue calcite resting on the Animal Control business card on the countertop. I blinked. I staggered back, dropping the phone. This wasn't some vision I was seeing. The crystal was *really* there. It briefly occurred to me that my mom had placed it there the night before, but my intuition told me otherwise. This wasn't Mom's doing. Inside I heard, *"I chose wisely. This crystal can unlock many doors."*

I picked up the penny-sized, icy-blue crystal and twirled it between my fingers. Surveying all its sides and rough edges, I sighed. "It's beautiful . . . and it's my very own."

Sitting by my feet, Marigold looked up at me and whined.

I pulled my attention away from the crystal. "I know, but we can't go out there yet." I stashed the crystal in my robe pocket. "First things first. I'll call Animal Control."

I picked up the phone, relieved to see that it hadn't cracked in the fall. Marigold finally gave up and lay down on my slippers while I dialed the number and left a message on the after-hours voice mail.

Wide awake with anticipation, I poured myself a bowl of Frosted Mini-Wheats and planted myself at the kitchen table. While I ate, my eyes fixed on the sleeping dog in the cage. As I swallowed my second bite, I felt a weird chill rush up my spine—not at all like the whisper chill. It was something way more intense.

My head started to spin and my eyes grew blurry. For a moment, I felt like I was being spun around in circles.

When my eyes came back into focus, there before me on the kitchen table was a small pineapple-sized silver pyramid. Totally freaked, I jumped back in my chair and knocked the bowl of Mini-Wheats onto the floor. The plastic bowl bounced, and Marigold instantly pounced, devouring the spilt cereal and milk.

I pinched myself. I *had* to be dreaming.

I leaned forward and poked the pyramid with my index figure, as if touching it would make it go away. But it didn't budge. It reminded me of the time that I'd first seen Sienna Glass. She was real, and I decided that wherever the pyramid had come from, it was real, too.

Feeling braver now, I looked closer and noticed a small rectangular door outlined with the same silver etching that decorated my bracelet's clasp. An infinity sign was inscribed in the center of the door with a tiny keyhole where the two circles intersected.

Everything, everywhere, became still. Entranced by the mysterious treasure, I forgot about the dog outside, Animal Control, school, Tess and Caroline, my dog bruises, breakfast, Silvy, Marigold, Mom still asleep upstairs—even my new blue calcite.

What am I supposed to do with this?

I heard the answer speak inside me: *"Listen, and choose wisely. Everything always has a way of working out."*

That very next moment the earth began to spin again. Marigold barked, Mom's alarm blasted from upstairs, and the phone rang. I hopped up to answer. "Hello?"

"This is Otis from Animal Control," said the voice on

the other end of the line. "Sounds like you caught a live one over there."

"I guess you could say that," I replied. "He's sleeping so peacefully right now. Do you think you could wait a while before you take him away? I don't leave for the bus for another two hours, so I can watch him closely."

"No need to watch him. He's not going anywhere. When Joel gets here, we'll drive over and bring him back for observation."

"Yes, but the trapdoor didn't close," I explained. "He crawled into the cage, cuddled up on the blanket, and hasn't left. He's resting so peacefully, he's not a threat to anyone right now."

"In that case, don't go outside," Otis warned. "I'll call Joel and have him meet me at your house in ten minutes. Bye for now."

"But—"

Otis was already gone. I heard Mom's footsteps on the stairs.

Without thinking, I dropped the pyramid in my robe pocket. Fortunately, my pockets were pretty roomy, but the pyramid still made a big bulge in my robe. It just felt right to keep this mystery to myself until I knew more about it. I met Mom at the foot of the stairs.

"Who called?" she asked sleepily.

"Animal Control," I said, avoiding eye contact as I brushed past her. "They're on their way."

I hurried upstairs to my room. Lying belly down on the floor beside my bed, I slid the pyramid beneath it, next to my bandana. With my arms outstretched under the bed, I focused on my new treasure, running my fingertips over the metal. The infinity symbol captured my attention. The metal surrounding it sank in four slight indentations, two each in the center to the left and right sides of the symbol. *Hmmm, that's interesting.*

Unfolding the bandana, I reached for my new crystal in my robe pocket and placed it next to the feather and the rose. As I lay there, motionless, in awe of my new treasures, time fast-forwarded . . . and in the next instant, Mom was calling, "They're here for the dog!"

Placing a kiss on my right index and middle fingers, I touched them to the infinity sign on the pyramid door. Then I quickly rewrapped the contents of the bandana and snuggled it next to the pyramid.

"Coming!" I yelled, darting down the steps.

Joel and Otis stood in the entryway with Mom, and I explained the circumstances that morning, how I really wanted to go outside to check on the dog but had called them instead. "I think it's pretty neat that the door didn't shut," I said truthfully. "I couldn't stand the thought of the dog being trapped inside. Anyway, he just walked in and didn't leave, even though he could have. I really don't think the dog has rabies." Mom gave me a look, and I quickly added, "But you guys are the experts."

Joel and Otis made their way to the back, and Mom and I scurried to the kitchen window to watch. The dog appeared to still be asleep as they snuck up to the trap and dropped the door into its locked position. No sooner had they done this than Marigold and I burst out the back door. As Marigold sniffed the cage perimeter, the collie lifted his head, dazed but wary of all the commotion.

"He's not drooling—and look, he drank all the water!" Otis said. "That's a real good sign. An animal with rabies usually won't eat or drink. We still need to watch him closely for the next ten days though."

"Yep, I know," I agreed. "Can I call to check on him? I'll be thinking about him all the time."

"Of course," said Otis. "I have a feeling that all this dog needs is lots of food and rest. There's a good chance he could be up for adoption by the end of the summer."

"Did you hear that?" I said with a big smile as Mom approached. "Maybe I'll be able to pet and comb his beautiful coat after all."

Mom gave me a playful roll of her eyes and said, "Pretty soon our house will be a petting zoo." She draped an arm over my shoulder. "What matters right now is that the dog gets the care he needs. We don't know what will happen after that. Maybe his owners are searching for him. Let's take it one day at a time." She half-frowned, knowing I'd have a hard time waiting this out. "Speaking of days, you need to get ready for school. The bus will be here soon."

I knelt down by the cage and blew the tired dog a kiss. "Don't worry, you'll be just fine," I promised. Then, giving the two men a long, serious stare, I added, "These guys are trained professionals."

The collie cocked his head to one side and our eyes met. I felt a connection. "Trust me," I said.

CHAPTER 15

COURAGEOUS LIONESS

O n the bus ride to school, I reflected on the morning's wild events; I daydreamed about the crystal, the silver pyramid, and the possibility that someday I could adopt the collie. I'd dressed in a hurry, and I'd forgotten to brush my hair and feed the birds. Now it occurred to me that I hadn't checked to make sure my outfit matched, and somehow I had left the house wearing my red-and-blue bandana skirt and a pink-and-white striped shirt. Oh, well. At least I wasn't wearing barn boots.

"Sorry you didn't get a chance to sing yesterday," Caroline said as she emptied her backpack into the cubby next to mine.

"You and Tess spend lots of time with that karaoke machine. I'm sure one of these days I'll get a chance to check it out, too."

"What did you think of Tess?" Caroline asked.

I hesitated for a moment. "Um, well, she seemed kind of bossy."

"You think so?"

"Yeah," I replied gently. "She took over the show, stole my karaoke job, and then told you what to wear and when to sing—in your own room."

"I guess," Caroline said with a perplexed look. "She's fun though—and plus she knows *a lot* about performing, so she has really great ideas."

I shrugged.

Changing the subject, she asked, "How's your arm?"

"It's fine. With all the excitement this morning, I'd actually forgotten about it."

"Take your seats, girls," said Mrs. Harris.

"Excitement?" whispered Caroline. "I want to hear all about it."

I smiled at her. "I'll tell you later."

And that's exactly what I did over lunch. I thought about bringing up Tess again, but then I remembered what Mom had said about giving it another chance. Caroline listened intently as I filled her in on everything that had occurred, leaving out the part about the crystals and the pyramid and just focusing on the dog part. Honestly, I couldn't think of how to describe the magically appearing pyramid without sounding like I'd gone crazy. I could tell Caroline almost anything, but I'd never tried to tell her about Sienna Glass, and the pyramid thing felt like it wanted to stay quiet inside me, too.

The rest of the school day flew by. Before I knew it, I was staring out the bus window, headed home, lost in the same thoughts I'd had that morning.

When we reached my stop, Simone glared at me as I walked down the aisle, then turned to whisper to the girl next to her. Ever since I'd told her off at the karaoke contest, she hadn't said anything directly to me, which was fine by me. I could easily ignore her whispers.

Stepping off the bus behind me, Jake asked, "Did you ever see that dog again?"

"Uh-huh," I answered, "but it's a long story."

"Tell me," he said as we walked toward our houses.

"Okay, the short version. I looked for him. I found him. He bit me. We called Animal Control. We caught him in a metal trap. He'll be in quarantine for ten days. Hopefully he'll be up for adoption at the animal shelter by August."

"Wow," Jake said, clearly impressed. "You don't mess around, Indigo Monroe."

"Yeah," I replied. "I'm a crazy lion-haired girl, remember?"

"Oh, yeah," Jake said, looking a bit embarrassed. "Sorry about that." Then, laughing, he added, "Now I'd call you a courageous lioness."

I liked that. It had been weeks since I'd batted away an insult or annoying comment from him—ever since I rescued Eddy from the tree. I was just being me, but it was nice to know it had made a good impression on him.

Jake walked on, and I turned right up our gravel driveway.

Inside, I grabbed a stick of string cheese from the refrigerator, and I went into Mom's office and sat down on the gray, velvety loveseat.

"How was school?" she asked, looking up from her laptop.

"Excellent."

"Now that's what I like to hear," she said encouragingly, but then her tone changed. "Listen, Otis called to let you know that the dog is eating and drinking. He hasn't shown any aggressive behavior. Based on his experience, Otis is pretty sure the collie doesn't have rabies. He's already contacted the animal shelter, and they're expecting the dog in nine days. They're real surprised he lunged at you. Maybe he was so hungry and thirsty that his mind was playing tricks on him, making him think you were a threat. Anyway, don't get your hopes up on adopting him. We can't afford another set of vet bills, not to mention dog food. Okay?"

"But, Mom!" I sprang forward until half my bottom was hanging off the edge of the couch. "I can't bear to think of him in a cage at the pound! We have a pasture he can run in and another dog to play with. He needs a home, and we have a *great* one."

At that moment, an image of the blue calcite crystal popped into my head. I stopped talking to pay attention. As I turned my focus to the image in my mind, the crystal slowly expanded into nothingness. Taking a deep breath, I let out a heavy huff and fell back into the couch.

We sat in silence for several moments as Mom began another email. When it seemed she had finished writing, I asked, "Did you put a crystal on the kitchen counter, um, or anything else in the kitchen recently?"

"No, why?" she asked.

"Well, this morning, there was a blue calcite on the kitchen counter. It's beautiful. I wrapped it in my bandana and put it under my bed." I decided not to mention the pyramid just yet.

Mom turned away from the computer and flashed me a smile.

"I keep seeing images of the crystal in my head. Did this ever happen to you?"

Mom gave me a sort of *uh-huh* and then said, "Just trust what you see and find—the way you did with the symbols you found for your bracelet."

The blue calcite crystal popped back into my mind, and instantly, I had an idea. "If we can't bring the collie here, maybe I could help care for him at the animal shelter over the summer. Can kids volunteer at the shelter?"

Mom opened up the browser on her laptop and typed in the words "Pierce County Animal Shelter." Getting up, she offered me her seat. "See what they say about volunteering."

I clicked on "Volunteer Opportunities" and scrolled down to the part that read "Kids Care."

"Kids under twelve years old have to be accompanied by an adult to volunteer." Scratching my head, I read on. "Down here it says younger kids can donate art to decorate the center. They can also donate homemade cat toys and cardboard cat forts, or run a fundraiser in the community like a carwash or bake sale. And look at this! We can donate bandanas for dogs and cats to wear. That's it! I can make homemade bandanas for the dogs. I could even embroider their names on the material."

"We would need to visit the center to meet the dogs

and get their names," Mom said with a twinkle in her eye. She knew I'd eat that up.

"Will you take me?" I asked eagerly.

"If you're sure you want to commit to the idea, yes. But remember, you're signed up for performing arts camp. Whatever you decide to do, it's important that you give it your all."

"Yep, I know. . . . Look here. There's a Volunteer Welcome meeting this Friday at four-thirty. I won't have any homework because it's the last day of school. And you don't work this Friday, so can we go?"

"Absolutely," Mom replied.

I could hardly wait for Friday to come—a new adventure awaited.

ᘒ

Otis called with an update on the collie's condition each day. He told me that when an aggressive stray dog is found without a collar and is suspected of having rabies, it is usually euthanized. But since the collie had been a "perfect gentleman" with everyone at their office and Otis knew how much I cared for him, he made sure the dog was given every chance to live. I flooded him with a gazillion thank-yous.

For the last day of school, I decided to wear my spring concert skirt. Mrs. Harris complimented me again on the hand-sewn felt flowers, and my classmates seemed to sigh with relief that I wasn't wearing my crusty barn boots. Simone turned her nose up at me, but I just waved her off.

We had a last-day of school party and played games —it wasn't like a school day at all. At lunchtime, Caroline and I talked about how we'd both miss our elementary school . . . and Mrs. Harris. Middle school was going to be a whole new story, both terrifying and exciting at the same time.

Once I stepped off the bus into summer, fifth grade was officially over.

"Have a good summer, Indigo," Jake said.

"You, too," I replied, no longer surprised by his niceness. "Have fun at your grandparents."

"Don't catch all the fish, okay?" he shouted when I turned down my driveway. "Save some for me when I get back!"

"You have nothing to worry about!" I called back with a quiet laugh.

༄

Mom met me in the kitchen and handed me a banana for the road. "We need to run," she said. "The meeting starts in a half hour."

I dropped my school bag and snatched the snack.

Twenty minutes later, we entered the meeting room at the Pierce County Animal Shelter, where I counted eight adults and six kids, including me. We sat in a large circle and listened closely as Miss Thompson, the exuberant volunteer leader, told us about the center's policies and proper animal-handling techniques. Then we each shared how we wanted to contribute to the center.

A thirteen-year-old boy announced he would be coming with his dad to walk dogs once a week. Another girl and her mom would build cardboard cat and rodent forts, just like the ones I'd read about online. An older man with a black-and-gray speckled beard said he would come twice a week to clean and maintain the dog kennels. He also said he was a good handyman and could help fix things like leaky faucets and plugged drains. And then there was a girl named Lucy, who said she and her mom would sew fleece blankets for dogs.

I was the last one to share. "I plan to make each dog a special bandana with its name embroidered on the material." An image of the blue calcite popped into my head. Then I thought of the red carnelian I'd put in the collie's water dish. "And, depending on the dog's health and behavior," I added, "I'll make a little pocket on the bandanas where I'll insert a special healing crystal. The crystals can comfort the dogs and hopefully help them find new families."

Mom smiled, reaching over to place her hand on top of the purple felt flower on my skirt.

"We're so lucky to have all your support!" Miss Thompson said to the group. "We hold weekly meetings in this room on Wednesdays from four to six p.m. I'll talk about animal care, pet safety, and the shelter events that are happening in the community. We'll also spend time helping you with your crafts for the center. You'll have an opportunity to share your ideas, help one another complete your donations, and build new friendships. If anyone is interested in attending these meetings, please put your name on the sign-up sheet before you leave."

"Mom, can you drive me here every Wednesday?" I asked as everyone stood up.

"You'll be at camp—remember?" Mom replied. "You get back from camp at four-thirty. You wouldn't be able to make it here before five. It won't work, honey. I'm sorry."

My shoulders slumped.

"Remember how excited you and Caroline were about camp and the big end-of-the-summer musical?"

"I suppose so," I replied half-heartedly. "But for some reason, I'm not excited about it like I was. I'm having second thoughts. Tess signed up, too, and I just know she's going to steal all of Caroline's attention—and maybe even the show. Camp might be a total disaster."

"Maybe it will, but maybe it won't," Mom concluded, reaching deep into her purse for the car keys. "Give Tess another chance. Try camp for at least a week. I already paid the fifty-dollar registration fee and the first week's tuition. If it still doesn't feel right by the end of the first week, we can talk about it again."

"Fine," I said, but it didn't really feel fine.

CHAPTER 16
HEALING CRYSTALS

To celebrate the last day of school, Mom took me to an early dinner at Duke's, our favorite restaurant. Over the best fish tacos ever, we exchanged bandana-making ideas sprinkled with lots of giggles. We continued to buzz with excitement as we drove across the Tacoma Narrows Bridge toward home. We fell silent as the sun began its fiery descent below the snow-capped peaks of the Olympic Mountains.

Once we reached home, I went to visit Silvy in the barn.

"Hey, boy, guess what?" I gushed as I approached his stall, reaching down into a rough burlap bag full of apples. "School's out for the summer!"

I watched as Silvy practically inhaled the two apples I handed him. Then Marigold ran into the barn, wagging her tail so jubilantly that it made a rhythmic thud each time it whacked Silvy's stall. "Happy to see you, too," I told her, rubbing her ears.

I told my animal friends about the meeting and how I planned to make bandanas for the dogs. I also told them about Tess and my concerns about camp.

"She kind of reminds me of Simone," I explained.

Even though I felt confident that Simone couldn't hurt me anymore (I simply wouldn't let her), my stomach felt sick at the thought of hanging around with Tess at camp all summer. Noting the feeling, I quickly pushed thoughts of Tess out of my mind and changed the topic back to bandanas.

Design ideas flowed through my mind as I twisted the worn-out orange taffeta on my bracelet. Suddenly, I felt the material come off the bracelet and into my hand.

Instead of feeling alarmed, I thought, *I know just where I'll put you.*

"See ya later, Silvy!" I said and headed back to the house.

Marigold followed me to my room, where she watched me pull out the bandana from under my bed and place the taffeta beside the feather and calcite. Next, I pulled out the pyramid and ran my fingers over the indentations and the infinity sign on the door.

"I wonder what's inside," I said, addressing Marigold.

I pushed on the door, but it didn't open. Then I shook the pyramid. I heard something inside clinking around, which made me want to get it open even more.

"How am I going to get this open?"

Marigold tilted her head.

I hopped up and grabbed a bobby pin from the bathroom. Then, lying on the floor next to Marigold, I held the pyramid in my right hand and stuck the pin inside the keyhole and jiggled it around. I poked and prodded—but nothing. The door just wouldn't budge.

"Choose wisely," my inner voice whispered.

I wasn't sure how that whisper related to opening the pyramid, but it was clear I didn't have the tools to open it—yet. I slid the mystery box back under the bed and went downstairs to say goodnight to Mom.

I found her snuggled up on the couch with a cup of tea in one hand and a book in the other. Careful not to spill her tea, I squeezed in next to her, sniffing the fragrant steam of cinnamon that rose from her cup.

"May I have a sip?"

Mom handed me the cup. "Hey, how does your arm feel these days?" I held out my arm for her to inspect. "Wow, the bruises are just green specks now. What a relief. Does it still hurt?"

I slurped up a long, slow sip of the tea before responding, "Nope, I'm pain-free."

Mom took the cup back without looking; her eyes were fixed on me. "So what's up? Got something on your mind?"

I hesitated for a moment. "As a matter of fact, I do," I said. "You might think this is a little strange . . ."

Mom gave me a dubious look as if *she* would ever find anything strange.

"While I was eating breakfast the morning I found the collie in the trap, a pyramid, like this big"—I showed her how big with my hands—"appeared out of nowhere on the kitchen table."

Mom's mouth curled into a smile. "How mysterious," she said, then sipped her tea, keeping me in suspense for a few moments. At last she continued, "Your first tool, your bracelet, helped you discover your second tool."

"The crystals," I confirmed.

"And now you've earned another powerful tool."

"The pyramid."

Mom nodded. "Excellent work, Indigo. When you listen closely and choose wisely . . .

"Things always have a way of working out," I finished for her.

With a proud smile, she offered me her cup again. I scrunched up my nose and took another long, slurpy sip. I knew she had some insight into the pyramid's purpose, but I didn't push for more. I wanted to discover its mysteries for myself.

"So, are you reading the crystal book?" Mom asked, changing the subject. "There are only ten weeks of summer vacation, and you have lots of crystal bandanas to make. This is our last weekend together before my schedule changes. If we have all the materials you need, I could help you get started this weekend. Let's take inventory of our bandana-making supplies, and you can decide which crystals you want to buy. We can go to the crystal shop tomorrow."

"Great idea," I replied, my excitement growing. "Dad and I are going fishing Sunday morning, and Caroline invited me for pizza and karaoke Sunday afternoon."

"That should be fun," Mom commented. "Will Tess be there?"

"Probably. I didn't ask. Either way, I miss spending time with Caroline and Noel."

The thought of Tess turned my stomach sour, but then Mom finished the last sip of her tea and nudged me to stand up. "Bedtime can wait for a little while. Let's go take a look at what material we've got and make a list of what more you'll need."

I jumped up, feeling instant belly relief. I had better things to think about than the Karaoke Thief.

⌒⌒

Wind howled through the trees outside my bedroom window. Curious about the night song, I looked out through the glass. Branches danced in the moonlight, so I swayed along with them, my satin nightgown flowing with every move. Dizzy with delight, I fell back onto my bed, grinning.

I reached for the crystal book on my nightstand and retrieved a notepad and pencil from the drawer. I opened the book and began studying the properties of each crystal. I knew that the happier a dog was, the greater his or her chances of being adopted. I thought back to how Miss Thompson had described the temperaments of the shelter dogs. Some were playful and sweet, but others were afraid, skittish, or sluggish. Some were hyperactive, insecure, and defensive—borderline aggressive.

With all this in mind, I wrote down the names of the crystals that seemed like they might help the various dogs feel better. At the top of my list was a red carnelian. Next came citrine, rose quartz, garnet, moss agate, clear quartz, and, finally bringing up the rear, amethyst. With my list complete, I closed the book and fell asleep.

When my eyes opened in the morning, I leapt out of

bed ready to shop. As I wrestled my red curls into a pony-tail, images of bandanas with crystal pockets and custom decorations and embroidery appeared in my mind's eye.

"Indigo," Mom called from downstairs, "breakfast is ready!"

Throwing on my tie-dyed skirt and denim shirt, I raced downstairs.

Mom and I ate side by side at the kitchen table, syrup dripping from our French toast as we chatted about bandana decorations. Mom had laid out all the goodies we'd collected the night before on the table—buttons, yarn, metal charms, and sequins. As I surveyed the assortment, the blue calcite popped into my mind.

"I just realized something," I said, concerned. "Attaching small decorations to the bandanas isn't very wise. What if one of these large buttons falls off and a Chihuahua tries to eat it?" I coughed and pretended to struggle to breathe. Mom clearly understood the point I was making; I probably didn't even need to add all the dramatics. "I think I'll just stick to embroidering the dogs' names on the bandanna and make a secure pocket so the crystal can't escape."

Mom put her hand on my shoulder and winked. "Good thinking."

Sweeping the decorations off to the side, she picked up a pen and notepad, and together we drew a pocket bandana pattern that would safely enclose a crystal. Putting our heads together was something Mom and I were very good at.

∽

An hour later, the door chimed as we entered the crystal shop in Tacoma. The air smelled of sweet incense, and I took a deep breath. Hardly believing I'd never stepped foot inside the shop before this, my eyes eagerly scanned the bright, colorful room. The stones, categorized by color, were neatly organized and displayed on the shelves, some in glass bowls and others on stands or velvet pads. I felt like I'd entered a rainbow, the light of each stone drawing me farther in.

It made total sense that my eyes were immediately attracted to the blue calcites in the front left corner. I walked over and placed my hands above the stones. When I closed my eyes, I saw their icy-blue color fill my mind. With that vision came a knowing that I belonged there in that moment, among the stones.

Opening my eyes, I read the description on the shelf that stated those blue calcites came from Mexico. When I picked up the largest one in the pile, I imagined I was in Mexico, which was funny because I suddenly felt like I had a sense of the land where those rocks had once lived. Then I got to wondering if stones were imprinted, like they held the history of their homeland. With that thought in mind, I looked all around. Scanning the labels and origins of all the crystals nearest me, I suddenly felt connected to faraway lands.

Mom tapped my shoulder. "Pretty amazing, huh?"

I placed the blue calcite back in the pile and advanced down the wall to the collection of blue topaz. "Anyone can find awesome stones in their own backyard," I said, "but this is different. These stones are from all over the world. And you can tell by just touching them. Each one makes me feel a little different. I can only imagine how the dogs will feel about them."

Mom handed me a small handheld shopping basket, and we walked through the store collecting magical rocks. We placed them in labeled baggies: citrine to help newly rescued dogs settle into the shelter without fear, rose quartz for hyperactive or traumatized strays, garnet for insecure dogs, amethyst for the dogs who barked too much, red carnelian for aggressive dogs, moss agate for the real nervous dogs, and clear quartz for any dog who needed an energy boost to be even more healthy and playful.

I felt at home in the crystal shop, and Mom and I made a plan to go back someday to pick a couple of special stones for ourselves. For now, the dogs were our main focus.

Following that, we made a quick stop at our local fabric store—another place where I felt totally comfortable. But this time, the shopping experience felt pretty basic. For now, it couldn't compare to the exotic, crystalled journey around the world we'd just taken.

CHAPTER 17

THE KARAOKE THIEF

On Sunday morning, while Dad and I were fishing, I filled him in on the good news about the collie's health and told him that he'd be transferred to the animal shelter on Wednesday. I also added the fact that Mom wouldn't let me adopt him because we had too many mouths to feed.

He quickly agreed with her decision—to my dismay. Then, more cheerfully, I told him how we'd come up with another way to help not only the collie but also the other dogs at the shelter. I explained my plans for the crystal bandanas.

"Are you spreading yourself too thin?" he asked. "I know you, and when you put your mind to something, you give it all your heart and time. You've got camp and your end-of-summer performance to think about, too."

"Oh that," I said. Then, feeling really comfortable with him, I shared my feelings about Tess and my concerns about summer camp. "That's why this afternoon at Caroline's is so important to me. Maybe I'll get to know

Tess better and decide that camp with her and Caroline won't be so bad."

"I hope so," Dad replied. "And if that's the case, you'll be very busy this summer. You'll probably need to catch up on your sewing project at my house over the weekends."

I realized he was right and my shoulders slumped. I wouldn't have access to my sewing machine at his house. I told him as much.

"Well, isn't it fortunate then that you have a new sewing machine waiting for you at my apartment?"

My eyes popped. "Really?!" I exclaimed, throwing my arms around his neck.

"Mom phoned me and told me how you chose to call Animal Control the other morning instead of putting yourself in danger—even though I know every part of you wanted to run out and comfort that dog. I'm proud of you, Indigo, and I wanted to do something to show you how much."

I felt a change in Dad, like he was really *seeing* me, not looking past me the way he did with Sienna Glass. It wasn't just that he saw me, but he actually listened to me, too.

"Of course, as with everything, there's a price to pay," Dad teased, taking off his baseball cap and replacing it sideways on his head. He looked goofy. "Let's see," he said, tapping his index finger on his lips. "First I need a few new work shirts . . . and some slacks. . . . You'll be so busy making me a new wardrobe this summer that you'll have to stay up nights sewing the bandanas."

He looked totally serious, but then we just cracked up

over the absurdity of it all. We wound up sharing a fun morning at the Looking Pond, even though we caught only a few minnows and zero Whoops.

Later, once I'd said goodbye to Dad and cleaned out Silvy's stall, Mom drove me to Caroline's. Tess met me at the front door.

"Oh, hi," she said. "Come on in. Noel is upstairs. Caroline and I are just getting plates for the pizza. We'll be right up."

Noel was lying on her side on the floor when I entered the room, looking at a piece of paper and eating a slice of pizza. She leapt to her feet and ran to hug me. Her pizza, still in her hand, entangled itself in my sea of curls. As I backed away, Noel signed "sorry" and began pulling ringlets off the greasy pizza. When she held up a particularly gooey strand, we broke into laughter. Gathering my hair behind my shoulders, I realized my fingers were coated in cheesy red sauce. Noel frowned and pointed me in the direction of the bathroom.

When I returned a few minutes later—my strand of hair now squeaky clean from a quick sink shampoo—Tess and Caroline had joined Noel and were gobbling down their slices of pizza. Choosing a spot on the floor, I picked up Noel and plunked her on my lap.

Tess handed me a slice of pizza, then announced, "You're on after the intermission. I hope you like Britney Spears because I chose one of her songs for you to sing."

I stiffened. Noel looked at me, her expression confused, then went back to twirling my ringlets.

"I like a lot of singers," I told Tess, "and that's why I'd like to choose my own song to sing."

"The show's already made up," Caroline chimed in. "And look, Tess showed me how to write a professional-looking program. See? Noel's going to be my back up singer!"

I reached for the piece of paper Noel had been looking at when I'd entered. Reviewing the lineup, I said with surprise, "You guys are singing a Billy Ray Cyrus song? Caroline, you don't even like country music."

"That's okay; Tess thinks it's a good song for me," Caroline said. "You know, producers and all," she added with a chuckle. "Come on, let's just give it a try. We'll have fun." Seeming anxious to change the subject, she added, "Hey, how's your dog bite? And whatever happened to that dog?"

Grateful to talk about anything other than country music, I gave Caroline the full rundown. "The bruise is almost gone, and the dog is doing great. Mom won't let me adopt him, though, so he'll go to the animal shelter on Wednesday. Mom and I went to a volunteer meeting there on Friday afternoon. We found a way to help the collie and other dogs by making crystal bandanas and donating them to all the dogs in the shelter. It's an exciting project but will take me all summer."

Caroline's eyes lit up, but she looked away when Tess interrupted, "What *are* you talking about? Crystal bandanas? Sounds ridiculous!" She shot up to her feet and clapped her hands, going into full production mode.

"Come on, guys, we've got to get dressed—we have a performance to do."

Caroline gave me a quick "Sounds cool" before she shifted her focus to Tess, who was holding out a dress for her to wear. Then, after instructing Noel to change into her tights and tutu, she walked over to me with a brown cotton dress. I felt a nervous flutter in my stomach. At that moment, an image of the blue calcite formed in my mind.

As I was studying the stone in my mind's eye, I heard Tess say, "Here, wear this."

Glancing down, I looked at the dress she had dropped on my lap. "You know, Tess," I said, trying to sound polite but firm, "I'm happy with what I'm wearing. I think it will look great for the show."

"That tie-dye skirt will look ridiculous for your song," Tess snapped. "I can't let you wear that 'onstage.'"

I liked my skirt, and I had no intention of letting her opinion hurt my feelings. I was way past that. Then the blue calcite reappeared in my mind again, and turning to Caroline, I asked, "Do you mind if I wear this skirt?"

"I like your skirt just fine," Caroline replied. "But if you would wear the dress, we can get on with the show."

Noel got up off the floor and stood by my side. I pointed to my skirt, gave Noel two thumbs up, then put my hands out as if I was asking whether she liked the skirt. Her face creased in a big smile as she mirrored my two thumbs up.

"If you don't wear the dress," Tess announced, "you can't be in the show."

I saw the blue calcite again. It was showdown time. Taking a deep breath, I replied, "That's settled. I'll be the audience."

Tess looked startled and pulled Caroline into the bathroom. Noel and I sat together on the floor. I found myself shaking a little. Noel tapped my shoulder and motioned for me to braid her hair. Grateful for the diversion, I separated her hair into two parts. On the back of her neck, I noticed her Diamonelle pendant stuck to the necklace clasp. I released the pendant, sending it down the chain to the center of her neck.

Suddenly, Tess stormed out of the bathroom. "Fine," she exclaimed, "you're the audience! Caroline, you'll have to redo the program." Then she grabbed Noel's hand and pulled her up. With big mouth movements, she ordered, "Come on, Noel. Get ready."

Caroline came out of the bathroom and flashed me a half-smile, then joined me on the floor. I gave her a long, hard, searching stare. She seemed oblivious of Tess's lack of kindness. I tried to figure out why Caroline liked her so much. Maybe Tess was different when I wasn't around.

I sat quietly and watched them perform their songs. Tess directed the show, and Caroline and Noel did whatever she said. For the grand finale, Tess dressed in Caroline's favorite black velvet dress and borrowed Noel's necklace. I guess it must have caught her eye since it now dangled front and center.

After she'd performed Taylor Swift's "You Belong with Me," Tess jumped off the bed stage and hugged

Noel and Caroline, and they all took a bow. I didn't feel envious; rather, the whole scene made me feel a little queasy. I clapped politely.

When Tess vanished into the bathroom to change, I complimented Caroline's and Noel's performances. When I stood up to stretch, I realized that my bladder was about to burst. I knocked on the bathroom door, but Tess didn't answer, I *really* had to go, so I turned the doorknob and went in—just as Tess was tucking Noel's necklace into her jeans pocket.

"What are you doing?" I asked.

"Don't barge in like that!" Tess yelled.

"Why did you put Noel's necklace in your pocket?" I asked as my stomach flipped over.

"I didn't want it to get lost," she said. "I'm going to give it to her right now, see?" Brushing past me, Tess walked over to Noel, pulled the necklace out of her pocket, grabbed Noel's wrist, and dropped it into her hand. Then she turned and glared back at me. "Do you honestly think I would steal Noel's necklace?" she demanded, mustering up three quick gasps, two sniffles, and a tear.

"Indigo!" Caroline interjected. "I can't imagine Tess, or anyone for that matter, stealing anything!" She placed a consoling hand on Tess's shoulder and gaped at me. "You think maybe you're a little jealous that she knows more about performing than you do?"

I felt utterly shocked. Caroline and I had been best friends since first grade; there had never been a time when we hadn't been on each other's side. Was I wrong?

I knew what I saw, and it gave me a bad feeling. Sure, she'd said she intended to give it back, but something in me just knew she planned on keeping it and would have done so if I hadn't caught her. Should I apologize and act like it didn't happen?

The image of the blue calcite crystal flashed in my mind. In seconds, I was clear-headed.

"You know what, Tess?" I said firmly. "Maybe Caroline trusts you, but I don't. I'm sorry, but I really don't like the way you treat my friends. The thought of spending five days a week with you at summer camp makes me ill."

I could hardly believe the words had come out of my mouth, but after dealing with Simone's mean-spirited ways for the past five years and having conquered that particular challenge, I wasn't about to let someone else take her place.

"I have a suggestion for you then," Tess said, instantly perking up out of her fake cry. "Let Caroline and me have our own fun this summer. Find someone else to hang out with."

Caroline stood expressionless, as Noel frantically signed to her to listen to me.

"Indigo, your mom's here!" Caroline's mom called up the stairs.

"Perfect," said Tess. "It's about time you leave!"

I quickly said goodbye to Noel and flashed a confused look at Caroline. She looked away. I ran down the stairs, threw myself into the passenger seat, and let out a huge sigh before telling Mom everything. The thought of seeing Tess again made my skin crawl.

That night as I lay in bed, I realized I'd probably just lost my only true friend. The thought made me feel more awful than I'd felt in a long time. But I just couldn't let anyone treat me poorly—even if it meant losing Caroline's friendship.

Out of the darkness in my mind, a new image emerged: This time I saw two blue calcite crystals sitting side by side on my bandana. My inner voice whispered four short phrases of reassurance: *"You listened carefully, you were aware of your surroundings, you trusted your instincts, and you chose wisely."*

Curious about the image of two crystals, I reached under my bed for the bandana. Placing it on my belly, I unfolded it, and there, beside the rose, the feather, the orange fabric, and my blue calcite, was a *second* blue calcite, small and jagged. Part of me couldn't believe it had just miraculously appeared, but another part, the part that could see Sienna Glass, could.

Holding the crystals in my hand, I kissed each of them, and then set them back on the bandana. I wrapped up the bundle and slid it back under the bed. Then I retrieved the pyramid. No amount of pushing on the door would get it to open. As my eyelids began to droop, I cradled the pyramid in my arms and snuggled under my covers.

"How do I open you, pyramid?" I asked.

I listened to silence until sleep took over.

CHAPTER 18

CAMP: DAY ONE

After breakfast Monday morning, Mom drove me to camp for my first day. On the way, we talked about how Otis from Animal Control had called that morning with an update: The collie was definitely being transferred to the shelter on Wednesday.

I told Mom that I was sure the carnelian in the water dish had helped calm him down—which incidentally Otis was planning to return along with the blanket on their way to the shelter on Wednesday. Otis had referred to it as the "red rock," and when I explained its purpose, he told me that it had worked like a charm.

"Maybe I should put a carnelian in Tess's water dish," I joked to ease my nervousness.

Seeing how upset I was about the prospect of facing Tess and Caroline at camp, Mom promised to take me to the shelter after camp on Wednesday. "You can catch the end of the meeting, visit the collie, and get to know the other dogs in the shelter," she said cheerfully, looking at me from the corner of her eye to see if that idea raised my spirits.

It did. "I'll bring a notebook to record all the data," I replied. "That way, I'll have a list of each dog's name and temperament. Then I can start making the bandanas by the end of the week. And did you know, Mom, that Dad got me a sewing machine for the apartment?"

Mom smiled. "He called me late last week for advice on how to buy a good sewing machine. I thought that was pretty cool. He's excited about spending the weekends with you this summer."

"Me, too," I said truthfully.

The drive to camp was over too soon. When Mom stopped the car, I opened the door and stepped out.

"Make the best of it," Mom called after me, pumping her fist in the air. "Remember, things always have a way of working out."

"Okay, Mom, whatever you say," I said with a half-smile, shutting the car door. Strolling over to the entrance of the auditorium, I pressed the bracelet's pop can ring between my fingertips. "Make the best of it," I secretly whispered to myself.

Taking a seat in the back row, my thumb and index finger still pressed against the ring, I watched as at least forty kids found seats in front of me. Tess and Caroline walked in and sat in the very front row by the aisle. When Caroline turned to survey the room and our eyes met, I raised my hand and waved. Pretending to barely recognize me, she nodded her head once and then quickly looked away.

I felt deflated, as if all the life in me had drained out with my sigh. Slumping deep down into the chair, I realized nothing had felt so awful since Sienna Glass had gone home to the angels. Yes, Caroline had been my best friend, but in many ways, she had been like my sister, too. I felt I couldn't bear to lose someone so close to me again, so with all my might, I breathed the life back into me and sat up straight.

I shifted my gaze to the center aisle, where I saw Lucy, the girl from the animal shelter who'd planned to sew fleece blankets for the dogs, looking for an empty seat. Instinctively, I held my hand up to catch her attention. She pointed at herself as if to ask, "Me?" I nodded and waved her over.

As she walked toward me, I squeezed my bracelet's pop-can ring between my fingers. To my surprise, the metal snapped, and the ring parted into two pieces on my lap. I grabbed the freed symbol and quickly buried the pieces in the deep pocket of my skirt, knowing exactly where I'd put them.

Dressed in jean shorts and a light-blue shirt, Lucy sat down next to me. After some awkward silence, she spoke. "I like your bandana skirt; it's totally original."

"Thank you," I said, feeling the sincerity of her compliment. I wasn't used to compliments on my clothing from kids my age (aside from Caroline) so I knew she was a special sort of person.

We reintroduced ourselves and then talked about the shelter and our sewing projects for the dogs. That initial awkwardness had totally faded. A few minutes later, a young woman with brown curly hair walked to the microphone and introduced herself as Mrs. Rose. Her flowing yellow skirt and embroidered red floral shirt lit up the stage. I liked her immediately.

As she highlighted the camp events for the summer, Lucy and I were transfixed. Every camper was going to sing and dance in a play, and we could even learn costume design if we wanted. Lucy and I turned and looked at each other, grinning spontaneously.

When Mrs. Rose announced that we would be doing a production of *Annie,* lots of kids—including Lucy and me—yelled and clapped with excitement. I loved the story of *Annie,* an orphaned girl, and her dog, Sandy, and how they found a loving home after years of being alone. Then Mrs. Rose whistled and, from behind the side curtain, a medium-sized black dog appeared. "This is Gertie," Mrs. Rose said, introducing the furry newcomer, "and she'll be playing Annie's dog, Sandy."

The dog sat by her side and looked out over the auditorium, and I wondered how Tess, who was clearly not a dog lover, was receiving the news.

"We're going on a fabulous summer journey together, guys," Mrs. Rose declared. "Let the fun begin!"

Everyone applauded, and spirited cheers filled the room. I immediately felt better about the prospect of attending camp for the entire summer.

Mrs. Rose's assistant handed her a clipboard, and soon we were split into groups named after famous musicals and ballets. We would rotate among music, drama, dance, and set or costume design classes. Luckily, Lucy and I were placed in the same group—Cats. Then, like all the other campers, we spent the day exploring what the camp had to offer.

At lunch, Lucy and I talked again about our sewing projects. When she shared that blankets and nightgowns were her favorite things to sew, I chuckled. "That's funny. I just recently made my first nightgown. They are a lot harder than making skirts."

"The sleeves can be tricky," Lucy agreed. "You have to be really precise. Sometimes my mom helps me line up the fabric around the armhole. Oh, but then," Lucy giggled, "my dog Patch would lie down on the cut-out fabric as we tried to pin the pieces together on the floor."

"You have a dog?" I asked eagerly.

"I *had* a dog," Lucy said sadly, "but he died of old age two months ago. I hope we can get another, but right now, Mom isn't too excited about taking on the responsibility of training a puppy."

"I'm sorry to hear about Patch. I bet you guys were super close."

"He followed me around the house and slept by my bedside every night." Lucy cast her eyes down at her lunch, falling silent for a moment. Then, popping open a reusable metal container, she took out a chocolate chip cookie. "How about you, Indigo?" she asked before taking a bite. "Do you have any animals?"

My face broke out into a huge grin. "I have a horse, a parakeet, two finches . . ." I hesitated; it was clear she was still sad about Patch's death. "And a dog," I concluded, trying to slide by the fact that I had Marigold.

"Wow! A whole menagerie! That's so cool," she replied, not appearing to be too upset by the mention of a dog.

As the first day of camp drew to a close, Lucy and I waited outside for our moms to arrive. Tess and Caroline exited the building and stood at the curb some two car lengths away from us.

"Do you know those girls?" Lucy asked, nodding toward Tess and Caroline. "They keep looking this way."

I kept my gaze on Lucy and replied truthfully, "Caroline, the one in the pink shirt, is—or maybe *was*—my best friend, until she met Tess, the one standing next to her. It's a long story, but basically, I don't trust Tess, and now Caroline won't talk to me."

Lucy gave me a sympathetic look.

"It feels really weird," I confided. "It's not like Caroline to be so cold. I'm glad they're in Nutcracker Group, and not Cats."

"Hey, I was thinking," Lucy said with an upbeat change of subject, "maybe we can sew together after camp some days this summer."

"That's a great idea!" I agreed, as Mom pulled up to the curb.

I introduced Mom to Lucy, and Mom recognized her from the meeting at the animal shelter. She thought it was cool that we'd met up again—and even cooler that we both shared a love of sewing and animals. Then Mom waved to Caroline, who smiled shyly at her before looking away. Anyway, despite losing my best friend to the Karaoke Thief, I felt a glimmer of hope about the summer ahead.

That night, I placed the pop can ring pieces inside my bandana bundle with the crystals, the feather, and the taffeta. As I stared at the "freed" symbols and the gems resting on my bandana, I heard the whisper: *"When I value my gifts, I don't need the symbols to steer me back to them."*

I intuitively understood this, but then I asked myself aloud: "What's with the crystals and the pyramid?" I searched inside, but there was only silence. As my eyes became heavy with sleep, I heard my mom's often-repeated words: "Everything has a way of working out."

⌒⌒

Wednesday couldn't have come any faster. It was the day I'd get to visit the animal shelter. I couldn't wait to officially meet and pet the collie—as well as see all the other dogs. First, another day of camp was at hand.

After Mom dropped me off, I ran into Tess in the lobby.

"Caroline thought you were her BFF," she practically hissed, "but it looks like she was wrong. You've already replaced her with that girl Lucy. Caroline confided in me that she was only your friend because she felt bad for you."

I knew that couldn't possibly be true, but the horrible, sick feeling settled in my stomach again. Just then, Lucy walked into the lobby. Seeing her approach, Tess beat a hasty retreat, throwing me a nasty look as she turned away.

"Hi, Indigo," Lucy said. "I saved you a seat." I quickly followed Lucy into the auditorium and we took our pair of seats in the back row.

"Are you all right?" she asked.

"I guess," I replied. "Tess gives me a bad feeling."

Instantly, I saw the two blue calcites in my mind. I reached for my bracelet and felt for the last remaining symbol—the twist tie that had held the petals of the rosebud I had saved in my bandana bundle under my bed. Though the petals themselves had long since dried up and broken off, the yellow twist tie still hung securely to the bracelet. "Well, she can't," I said.

"Can't what?"

"Make me feel bad," I clarified. Changing the subject, I asked, "Tell me about your blankets. Have you made any since Monday?"

"Just one," she replied. "And before I forget, I asked my mom if you could come over on Saturday. She said yes. What do you say?"

"Oh, I can't," I replied with disappointment. "I'm staying at my dad's apartment in the city every weekend this summer."

"Your parents are divorced, too?"

"They split up two years ago. It's been pretty hard. How about you?"

"My parents divorced when I was one or something," Lucy answered. "I've never even met my dad."

I squeezed Lucy's hand sympathetically. I couldn't imagine not knowing my dad, although there had been times when I wished I hadn't. But that was all in the past.

I couldn't say more to Lucy because Mrs. Rose had taken the stage.

"Welcome to day three!" she said with bubbly excitement. The room filled with cheers. "The tryouts for *Annie* will be held tomorrow. By Friday, everyone will have their part. If you would like to work on set or costume design—or both—find me center stage during the break. In a musical, the behind-the-scenes participants are just as important as the lead actors."

Lucy and I looked at each other at the same time, and I asked, "Are you thinking what I'm thinking?"

"I've always wanted to learn to make costumes!" she confirmed.

At break time, Lucy and I sprinted down the side aisle to the stage. Nine campers wanted to work on sets and costumes, and Mrs. Rose explained that, if we wished, we could even sing in the chorus, which sounded great to me since I loved to sing.

At the end of the day, Lucy and I were standing together at the curb waiting for our moms when Tess and Caroline approached.

"So you guys are going to make our clothes just like peasants in the olden days," Tess sneered. "Well, I'm trying out for the part of Annie, and Caroline here is trying out to be one of my 'sisters,' right, Caroline?"

"That's right," Caroline agreed, though she wore a mildly startled expression. "I can't believe it, Indigo. You don't want to be center stage wearing one of your homemade costumes?"

"Nope, I just want to be a part of the production,"

I said confidently. "Singing and costume making sounds perfect to me." I paused for a moment, then asked hopefully, "Want to join us? It'll be fun."

"No, thanks," Caroline muttered, and then Tess gave her a little nudge, as if prompting her to say something. Caroline took a breath and said, "You know, Indigo, it was mean of you to accuse Tess of stealing Noel's necklace. You hurt her feelings—and mine. Honestly, who would ever take anything from Noel?"

"That's exactly what I thought when I saw Tess put the necklace in her pocket," I responded, glad we were finally airing the issue.

Caroline's face softened a bit. I could see that she was struggling. Tess must have noticed it, too, because she pulled on Caroline's arm and said, "We're outta here."

CHAPTER 19

ROOTS

Later that day, Mom and I entered the Pierce County Animal Shelter and found Dad sitting in the lobby. "What are you doing here?" I asked.

Standing up to hug me, Dad explained, "I'm interested to see how the dog turned out. We had quite an encounter with him on the trail that day. I'd like to know what he's like when he isn't viciously lunging at you."

"Thanks," I said, burying my head into his chest. I leaned into him, and he didn't budge. It felt so good, and it was at that moment when I realized how Dad's recent "show ups and be there's" had become a huge comfort to me.

A friendly lady entered the room and greeted us. "Welcome! I'm Gwen, and I'm a volunteer here. Are you Indigo?"

I told her that I was, shook her hand, and then introduced her to my parents.

"Wonderful to meet you, folks," she said. "I'll get the collie. Meet me in the petting room."

After a few minutes' wait in the petting room, in

pranced a beautiful longhaired dog, freshly bathed that morning and with all the mats and burrs brushed out of his fur.

"We named him Roots," Gwen said with a smile. "I hope you like the name. Otis from Animal Control told us where you first encountered the dog on the trail. Thinking about the animals here, it's our hope that they'll all grow roots inside the hearts and homes of loving families."

She left the room to give us some private time to get to know the collie.

Smiling, I called out to him. "Here, Roots!"

To my surprise, he walked straight to Dad first. "Hi, boy," Dad said, greeting him. "You're coming to say you're sorry for attacking my daughter? Is that right?" Dad laughed as the dog sniffed his hands.

Wagging his tail, the collie crossed over to me, sniffed my leg to catch the scent of Marigold, and then sat patiently while I petted his head for the first time. I felt happy and proud; I couldn't imagine him hurting anyone now.

"See, Mom?" I said. "He'd be a wonderful addition to our family, and he'd have such a great home in island country. Can't we take him with us?"

Though I persisted for ten minutes, citing all my reasons for wanting the collie, Mom wasn't buying my arguments. When I realized it was hopeless, I broke into a cold sweat and salty tears rolled down my cheeks.

"Honey, each dog here needs a home, not just Roots," Mom explained soothingly. "We can't rescue every dog who needs a family. I'd have to get another job to pay for all the food, and you'd have to be a full-time poop-scooper-upper."

I giggled a bit, then dried my eyes. I knew Mom was right—there were a lot of responsibilities at home, especially since it was just the two of us—but that didn't make me feel better.

When Gwen returned to take Roots back to the kennel, she offered to give us a tour of the facility. We agreed. Though I hated to see the collie go, I was excited to meet the other dogs.

As I strolled, notepad in hand, I recorded the dogs' names, breeds, and any behavioral or health problems they were experiencing. When we arrived at the kennel in which Roots was being kept, I blew him a kiss through the kennel door.

Roots's homemade bandana would be yellow with a blue border, I decided. Since he was as calm as a lamb now, he wouldn't need the red carnelian anymore. He'd need something to help him adjust to his new surroundings—especially since he'd been in many cages and places the past two weeks.

"Citrine's the one for you, Roots!" I announced.

"That's perfect," Mom said, placing her hand on my shoulder. "It will give him a sense of peace until someone can adopt him."

"I think citrine would be great for a lot of these dogs," I said. "I read in the crystal book that it helps pets settle into new places."

"Do you have all the info you need to get started on

your bandanas?" Dad inquired, leaning in for a peek at the data on my notepad.

"I'm all set," I answered, feeling really good about the task ahead of me. I just wished I could bring Roots home with me. I guess making his bandana would be the next best thing.

That night, I embarked on my adventure by sewing Roots's blue-bordered, yellow bandana. I embroidered his name on the edge with dark blue thread so it could be clearly seen, and then I placed a small citrine in the secure pocket affixed to the center of the bandana. It came out perfect.

As Mom inspected my creation, I told her that Lucy and I were making plans to spend Wednesdays after camp together. I'd work on the crystal bandanas while she sewed the dog blankets. It would be like our own Wednesday shelter meetings. Mom agreed it was a great idea.

∽

When Friday came around, Dad picked me up from camp. On our drive to his place, I filled him in on who had gotten which roles.

"That's great that you're part of the chorus, too," he confirmed. "You'll get to be onstage singing and backstage making costumes with Lucy. Sounds like a perfect fit for you. How about Caroline? What will she be doing?"

Dad knew only part of the story about Tess and Caroline, so I filled him in on the rest, ending with "Caroline and I aren't friends right now." Then I related how, when

Tess and Caroline won only supporting roles—those of the French maids, Annette and Cecille—Tess had cried hysterically. "And when Caroline tried to console Tess with a hug," I concluded, "Tess pushed her arm away and ran off."

"Doesn't Caroline see what's going on?" Dad asked.

"I don't know. She hasn't returned my calls. Truthfully, I only called twice: one after the fight, and then again the other day. It's hard to believe Caroline doesn't trust my instincts about Tess. We've been best friends forever. But, on the other hand, I don't trust her new friend, so she's probably feeling just as shocked as I am."

"Well, I really like Lucy," Dad replied. "Maybe some weekend Lucy could stay with us in the city."

"Really? That would be so much fun!"

As Dad opened the door to his apartment, he dropped his keys on the glass entrance table, and they slid across the surface, coming to rest up against a red dog leash. *That's funny*, I thought. *Dad doesn't have a dog.*

Then, I heard a familiar-sounding pitter-patter on the floor, and sure enough, Roots came bounding toward us.

"What? Dad! Are you kidding me?" I exclaimed, kneeling down to put my arms around Roots.

"It's not exactly what you think," Dad said, tempering my enthusiasm. "Take a seat on the couch and I'll explain."

As we sat down on the white leather, Roots came and plopped his butt right on my feet.

"When I was at the shelter on Wednesday," Dad began, "Gwen talked with me before you and your mom arrived. She wanted to know if I would consider fostering Roots. She explained that foster parents can be helpful to the shelter by taking dogs into a home environment to assess their social behavior—you know, to make sure they're not aggressive to visitors or dangerous to kids. Gwen said that after a dog has been in a foster home, they know more about its behavior and are able to match the dog with an ideal family. So I thought about you and Roots. I figured we could foster him for the summer. That way, you can spend more time with him, and we can help the animal shelter find him the right family."

I threw my arms around Dad in a gigantic hug, then I ran to my weekend bag and dug through the clothes and sewing materials until I located Roots's bandana. I had planned to make it my dog bandana prototype until I delivered it to him next week, but I'd just have to manage without it.

"Come here, boy!" I called. "I have something special for you. I hope you like it."

Roots came immediately. When he'd obeyed my command to sit, I wrapped the yellow bandana around his neck and tied it securely. As I stood back to see how it looked, he tilted his head and examined me.

"You're extremely handsome," I said, giggling with delight.

"Come here, boy," called Dad, and Roots jogged to the couch. "Indigo, this is really cool," he said, pulling the bandana around to see Roots's name and the enclosed crystal pocket. "You and your mom have taught me a lot about the power of things we can't always see."

"Like Sienna Glass?" I asked hesitantly.

Dad ran his fingers through his hair. Motioning for me to sit next to him on the couch, he confided, "Even though I don't see the world the same way you guys do, I trust you. I don't want you to think that who and how you are is wrong or to blame for anything. The same is true for me, too. Just because I didn't see Sienna Glass and couldn't relate to her the way Mom did, doesn't mean there is anything wrong with me."

I gulped as I looked up at him. I'd never thought about it that way.

"Okay, Dad," I said, and without warning, a few sweet tears trickled down my cheeks. In that moment, my heart expanded, and my body seemed to melt. I let go of the gripping pain that had lurked deep inside that told me I was wrong for seeing Sienna Glass or that I was to blame for Dad wanting to leave our family.

"There's a citrine inside the bandana," I said quickly, changing the subject and wiping tears off my face. "I hope it helps Roots feel at peace here."

Dad wrapped his arms around me. "I know he will, Indigo."

And there we sat for a good ten minutes, thinking up ideas and planning a fabulous weekend for Roots. On Saturday we would walk him, take him to the dog park to play with other dogs, and visit the pet store to buy him treats and toys. Then, on Sunday morning, Dad had work to do, which was all right because I had lots of bandanas to make for next week's drop-off.

The weekend flew by. Everything went pretty much

the way we had planned it. I missed Marigold and Silvy of course, but Roots turned out to be a great companion, too. Dad even let him sleep with me on my bed because he was acting like a perfect gentlemen in his fancy apartment. I wondered if maybe the following weekend he'd even let Roots keep me warm on his cold leather couch. *If that happens, then I'll know Dad has really turned into a softy.*

Sunday night before bed, I wanted to make sure Dad knew just how much I appreciated his efforts—the quality time together, the sewing machine . . . everything, but especially for taking Roots in to his home.

"I can tell he's happy, and I'm crazy happy, too," I said sincerely. "But I bet you knew I would be, huh?"

"I had a feeling," Dad said with a wink.

I gave him a peck goodnight on his scruffy cheek, and Roots and I headed off to my bedroom.

CHAPTER 20

THE BEGINNING OF AN IDEA

Dad and Roots, with his wet nose out the car window, dropped me off at camp Monday morning after our fun weekend together. When I walked into the building, Lucy was waiting for me in the hallway. Together we met with the other team members in the costume and set design room, where we spent most of the day learning about our duties for the production.

Meanwhile, in the theater, the actors sat on folding chairs in a circle and ran through the entire script. An hour before camp ended, all the campers came together to perform drama exercises and play-acting games.

I was grateful for the distance from Caroline and Tess, but as the camp days went on, the entire cast blended more and more. Our team outfitted the set and fitted the actors for the costumes we were designing. I loved my comings and goings from the design room to the stage, except when I accidentally caught glimpses of Tess powering over Caroline. On one occasion, I saw them huddled together stage left.

"I hate this stupid role so much that I keep missing my cues," Tess whimpered, swiping a "tear" from her left eye.

Caroline consoled her by placing her hand over her shoulder and whispering, "It's okay, everyone else misses their cues sometimes, too. Don't worry. You'll get this."

"It's hardly worth it," Tess whined, backing away so Caroline's hand fell off her shoulder.

Caroline looked at Tess with a confused expression, as if trying understand her cold distance. Looking annoyed, Tess grabbed Caroline's hand and tried to pull her back in, but Caroline hung back, arms crossed, her gaze bouncing back and forth between the unpredictable Tess and the hard wood floor.

On a different day, I overheard Caroline talking to Tess backstage. From the sound of it, Tess had borrowed Caroline's treasured Lucky Brand embroidered sweatshirt weeks ago and still hadn't given it back.

"Tess, it's been two weeks," Caroline was saying. "You told me you'd have it for me today."

"Seriously, Caroline? We live next door to each other. It's not as if I ran away with it."

When Caroline narrowed her eyes, Tess held up her index finger—a sharp signal to wait—then she drifted over to the wall where her bag rested. She rummaged in the bag for a moment, grabbed something, and returned to Caroline. "Here," she said.

Caroline, looking happy yet puzzled, accepted the candy bar Tess offered. "Thanks. Twix are my favorite."

"I know," Tess replied, turning all her attention to the actors onstage and away from Caroline.

Despite that, all in all, camp was turning out to be pretty awesome. But what was even more fun was the evening and weekend time I spent with Lucy. Every Wednesday after camp, Lucy and I sewed bandanas and blankets for the shelter dogs as planned at one of our homes, and sometimes she stayed with me at Dad's for the weekend, bringing her mom's sewing machine so we could sew together. Dad let us drape fabric over the couch and big screen TV, too, and he didn't even mind the tiny pieces of thread and fabric scattered on the floor.

Sewing together with Lucy created more than just blankets and bandanas; it stirred up mega amounts of laughter and required lots of snack breaks to refuel. "Puppy Chow"—a mixture of rice cereal, melted peanut butter, chocolate chips, butter, and powdered sugar— was our favorite sewing snack. Whenever we stayed at Dad's, we'd whip up a fresh batch. Dad pretty much left us alone while we sewed—that is, until he was taken over by the Puppy Chow craving, which happened pretty much every hour.

I had to give it to Dad: When we weren't sewing, he was always ready with a new activity we could do, like roller skating, painting pottery, and shopping for and creating our own ice cream sundae bar at home. And, of course, we all took walks with Roots and played Frisbee with him at the park.

During Lucy's second sleepover with me at Dad's in late July, we were hard at work in our sewing shop (aka

Dad's living room), and I noticed that Lucy was paying extra-special attention to one blanket in particular.

"Don't you just love purple and orange together?" she questioned as she cut two blanket-sized rectangles out of the brightly colored fleece that was laid out on the living room floor.

I was trying to rethread my sewing machine, my gaze focused on the tiny eye of the needle and the spindly fiber between my fingers. "Yeah, that's a cool color combo," I muttered, my head now tucked in real close to the machine.

When I finally looked up, Lucy was cutting out the makings of a fleece tree. She'd cut out a large green cloud-looking shape and was snipping the final edge of what looked like a tree trunk.

"That's so awesome," I cheered, eyeing the blanket she was piecing together on the floor.

She smiled. "You think so? I'm going to add yellow fleece fringe all around the perimeter, too."

I nodded a big yes, and for the rest of the weekend, Lucy took extra care with her creation. Then, Sunday night, before we went to bed, Lucy met Roots in the hallway. I put my toothbrush on the counter and turned off the bathroom light when I saw her standing just outside the bathroom door, concealing something behind her back.

Kneeling down to Roots's level, she petted him with one hand. "I hope you like this," she wished. "I made it extra-special just for you."

Then she flashed him the purple and orange, yellow-fringed blanket, lifting it up so he could see the humongous, hand-sewn tree in the center. "You're such a good dog," she said, putting her arm around his neck. "You are my Roots to this tree." She smiled, then buried her face in his neck.

"Wow," I cheered, walking over and kneeling next to them. "How'd I miss that this was a gift for Roots?"

"Surprise!" Lucy giggled.

I felt real close to Lucy after that, which, strangely enough, made me think of Caroline. Lucy and Caroline had so much in common; they were both smart, clever, kind, funny, and generous, and I knew that if Lucy got to know the old Caroline, they'd be friends in a heartbeat. So somewhere deep inside me, I felt pretty bummed that Caroline wasn't part of the fun. And, in that same dark place, I faced the truth that Lucy and I wouldn't get to see each other as much after the summer. Since I lived on Fox Island and she lived on the other end of town, we wouldn't be going to the same middle school.

But Lucy and I agreed we wouldn't talk about that until camp ended. Why is it that when fun is being had, sadness that it will end creeps in?

∽

In mid-August, after Lucy's last weekend with Dad and me, Roots sat between us in the backseat of our car as Dad drove us to camp. As we circled around and stopped in front of the auditorium, Lucy hugged Roots goodbye.

"You remind me so much of my dog, Patch," she said. Before shutting the backdoor, Lucy thanked Dad for having her over that weekend, then whispered to Roots, "Love you."

Dad turned around and planted his eyes on Roots, and then on Lucy. "You're welcome anytime, Lucy," he announced with a huge smile on his face. "Have a great week, girls." As he drove away, I knew something good had just flashed in his mind.

Walking toward the auditorium, I noticed a tear trickling down Lucy's cheek.

"Are you okay?" I asked.

"I just miss having a dog," she replied sadly. "Last week I asked my mom if we could get one, but she said she still wasn't ready for the added responsibility of a puppy and that I needed to be patient until the time was right."

Giving her a one-armed hug as we walked into camp, I said, "At least she didn't give you a flat-out 'no' like my mom did."

CHAPTER 21

A MAGIC TWIST

Like a hummingbird, summer was fluttering by at rapid speed. Not only had Lucy and I created and delivered thirty-three crystal bandanas and twenty-nine dog blankets to the Pierce County Animal Shelter, but also I'd made sure to focus on my bracelet, the pyramid, and the crystals I'd acquired.

I slept every weeknight that summer with the silver pyramid by my pillow. Before drifting off to sleep, I'd trace the infinity sign on the door and wonder what secret code I'd need to open it. But the wondering didn't solve the mystery; it just made me cuckoo-curious for the hidden clues.

Every morning, I placed the pyramid under my bed next to my bandana. Whenever I did so, I always unwrapped the bundle for a few moments, holding the two crystals in my hand and running my fingertips across their jagged blue edges. As I marveled at them, I thought of the words written in mom's crystal book: "Choose wisely."

I was also acutely aware of the heirloom around my

wrist and the twist tie still attached to it. From the day Marigold had recovered my bracelet in the kitchen, I hadn't taken it off, feeling sure it was the reason I had been so happy lately, despite losing my best friend. Mom even said she thought I was the most confident and peaceful she'd ever seen me.

The last week of August—and our last week of camp—came so quickly I could hardly believe it. *Annie* was slated for six o'clock Saturday night, which meant dress rehearsals ran all week long. On Friday, after our final costume fitting, Lucy and I were thrilled we'd finally be able to see our creations onstage.

Five minutes before our day ended, Lucy and I left the design room and went back into the theater to collect any costume accessories that had been left behind. All the other kids were in the dressing rooms changing into their street clothes—except for Caroline. There she sat, all by herself in the front row, her head down, forehead propped up on her fists. Lucy and I walked over and knelt in front of her. Tears streamed down her face.

"Caroline, what's wrong?" I asked. "Why are you crying?"

"I feel terrible, Indigo," Caroline replied bitterly. "You were right—Tess *isn't* trustworthy. In the dressing room, I saw her take Alycia's silk scarf off the floor and stuff it in her backpack. She doesn't know I saw her."

"Oh, no!" I said sincerely. "I'm so sorry. I know you really like her."

"Well, I guess. But now I'm not sure I *do* like her. I'm just really mad." Caroline sniffed, swiping her sleeve across her wet nose. "She probably *did* intend to steal Noel's necklace, just like you tried to warn me. Why did I trust someone I hardly knew over you?"

Lucy pulled a pink-tinged Kleenex out of her pocket. "It's kinda used," she said, handing it to Caroline. "But it just has a tiny bit of blush on it from Annie's cheeks."

Caroline looked up at Lucy. "Thanks," she said, accepting the tissue.

At that moment, we heard the theater door squeak open. Tess, dressed in rhinestone-bejeweled jeans and a shimmering silver T-shirt, ducked in and barreled down the middle aisle toward us, arms pumping.

"What's going on here?" she demanded. "I've been looking all over for you, Caroline!"

Caroline wiped the tears from her cheeks, then turned around and faced Tess. "I saw you steal Alycia's scarf," she said in a gloomy voice.

"Don't be ridiculous," Tess snapped, waving her index finger at me. "I think you're seeing things that aren't true, just like this here Indigo."

Lucy and I fixed a laser-like stare on Tess. As I fiddled with the twist tie on my bracelet, an image of the two blue calcite crystals swirled into my head. All mindful, I calmed right down.

"Well excuse me, Tess," I said, "but I know what I saw, and my instincts told me you tried to steal Noel's necklace." I was surprised by my bold tone and the evenness of my voice. "You lied to me, Noel, and Caroline back then—just like you're lying now."

Seeming emboldened by my words, Caroline stood up

and faced Tess. The composure I'd always admired about her had been magically restored. "Return the scarf now," she demanded, "or I'll tell Mrs. Rose what I saw."

Then Caroline turned away and walked up the center aisle with Lucy and me following at her heels. Tess remained behind, her arms crossed, tapping her left foot on the royal blue carpet.

"Come on, Caroline, don't be like that!" Tess finally called, realizing that the exiting Caroline was serious and determined.

"Do you have a ride home, Caroline?" I asked as Lucy opened the dressing room door for all of us.

Snatching up her backpack, Caroline replied, "My mom's picking me up. But thanks, guys. You didn't have to do that . . . I mean, you know, support me back there."

"You're welcome," Lucy and I chorused, holding the door open for her as she walked out of the dressing room and made her way to the front of the building. Gathering our things, we, too, hurried out to the circular driveway.

No sooner did Caroline's mom drive away than Lucy's mom arrived. "I'll call ya later," said Lucy, giving me a quick hug goodbye.

Lucy's mom called out to me from the passenger side window. "It's been great getting to know you and your family this summer, Indigo. We're sure going to miss seeing you guys throughout the year."

"Me, too," I said with a half-smile, waving to Lucy and her mom. They waved back with that same happy-sad look, then drove off.

An air of excitement rippled through the crowd on the

curb in anticipation of tomorrow night's performance. I stood motionless and quiet, sad to have seen Caroline's red, splotchy face and teary eyes when her mom's car had pulled away. I felt bad that her faith in Tess had been unwarranted, but at the same time, I felt angry that Caroline hadn't believed in me.

When Mom pulled up, I opened the passenger door and plopped into the seat with a heavy sigh. She glanced over at me with a concerned expression. "What's up?"

I explained how Caroline had seen Tess stealing a girl's scarf in the dressing room. "I think Caroline's feeling pretty bad that she trusted Tess, and I feel bad for her." I hesitated for a moment. "And to be honest, I'm feeling pretty bitter, too . . . but not at Tess—at Caroline."

As I spoke, an image of the blue calcites appeared in my mind's eye and I heard my whisper: *"Choose wisely."* The images faded as I quickly changed the subject, not giving Mom any time to comment on my confession. "What's for dinner?"

"How about bean burritos," she replied, "with your favorite mango salsa? That should cheer you up. Come on, let's celebrate. It's our only weekend together all summer."

Despite Mom's upbeat attitude and the fact that she had taken the weekend off from work to come to Saturday's performance, I didn't feel good. Mom knew it, too.

Once we reached home, I hurried in through the back door and dropped my stuff near the shoe pile on the kitchen floor. "I'll be in my room," I called out, heading upstairs. "Let me know when you need help."

Just as my hands parted my doorway beads, the door-bell rang.

"Got it, Mom!" I yelled as I hurried back downstairs. To my surprise, when I opened the door, Caroline stood stiff and tense on our welcome mat. "What are you doing here?"

"I wanted to tell you something."

"Come on in," I offered.

"That's okay," Caroline replied. "My mom's waiting in the car."

Leaning against the doorframe, I swung forward and waved to Caroline's mom in the driveway.

"Indigo," Caroline mumbled, her voice full of regret, "I'm sorry. I'm really, really sorry. I should have trusted you that day at my house. We've been friends for forever, but for some reason, I believed Tess instead of you. She's just so sure of herself, and I liked that about her. I really envied it. It was too hard for me to believe she would try to do such a terrible thing. I hope you'll still be my friend."

Everything around me froze, as if someone pushed the pause button on time. I stood there staring blankly at Caroline as *three* blue calcite crystals appeared in my mind's eye. *"Choose wisely,"* said the whisper.

"Did you hear me?" Caroline interrupted. "Can you forgive me for turning my back on you?"

I felt an understanding rising up in me. With a friend like Caroline, forgiveness wasn't a hard choice to make. "Of course, I do—I've really missed hanging out with you."

Caroline's face lit up. Hugging me tightly, she whispered, "Thank you."

Hugging her back, I said, "Best friends forever, right?"

"Right! Best friends forever!" Now Caroline looked into my eyes. "Well, I better get going. Mom's waiting." She turned and dashed to her mom's car.

"Thanks for coming!" I shouted after her.

Closing the front door, I jumped every other stair to my room, squatted down beside my bed, and reached for my bandana. Sure enough, a third blue calcite was inside. Gathering the crystals in my hand, I became acutely aware of their ice-like configuration and color.

Something magical had just happened. Not only had I been gifted another crystal from who knows where, but Caroline and I had our friendship back. Mesmerized by the crystals, I rolled them back and forth in my palms. As I did so, I noticed that the twist tie on my bracelet dangled precariously from the leather band. When I transferred the crystals to my right hand, the twist tie fell to the carpet.

At that moment, I heard the whisper: *"Forgiveness is a wise choice."* All of my symbols were free now, and I knew that meant something important.

I reflected on all that had transpired. First of all, I had been valuing my gifts and living without being afraid of what others think of me, so I didn't need the symbols to remind me anymore. As for the crystals, I knew they had something to do with making wise choices. If I listened carefully and stayed aware of myself and my surroundings, I ended up making wise choices—like when I called Animal Control when Roots was sleeping in the cage, when I stood up for myself in front of Tess at Caroline's house, and when I chose to forgive Caroline.

I tried to remember the word written in the crystal book next to *choose wisely.* All I could remember was that it started with a D, so I grabbed the book to check. *Discernment,"* I read aloud. "The ability to judge well— and that's what I've been doing." I repeated the word to be sure I'd commit it to memory—and to remember to keep using it. My next chance came when Dad called a few minutes later.

"The animal shelter called today," he said. "They received our six-week evaluation of Roots and believe he is ready for adoption."

"I see," I said. Then I fell silent.

Dad broke the silence. "I know how you feel. I'll miss Roots, too. He's an amazing dog, and the three of us will never forget each other. But he deserves a bigger home than my apartment, don't you think? We knew this moment would come. And so I was wondering . . ." He paused. "How about I ask Lucy's mom if Roots would be a good fit for their home?"

Instantly the three blue calcites appeared in my head. I clutched my hand to my chest to keep my heart from breaking. But at the exact same time, I remembered Lucy's teary eyes when she'd hugged Roots goodbye. "She loves Roots as much as I do!" I shouted.

"Whoa, Indigo, not so loud," he laughed. "But you know what? I think you're right. Even though it's hard for me to imagine anyone else loving him so much, when I've watched Lucy with him I—"

"I know. I saw the same thing. I bet Lucy's mom would go for it because Roots isn't a puppy; he's fully grown and potty-trained."

"As long as I have your go-ahead—"

"Yes, of course!" I cheered. "Call her mom right now, Dad!"

"Also, I was thinking—wouldn't it be cool to send Roots off with Lucy tomorrow night after the show? Lucy's mom and I will have to complete the adoption process before Roots can go home with her, but as long as her mom agrees, I think I can make it happen."

I fell silent. Dad's ability to amaze me was at an all-time high.

Dad broke the quiet. "I've got a dinner meeting tonight and a work proposal to write in the morning. If you don't hear from me before the curtains open at six, I'll give you all the details after the show."

Later, over burritos and mango salsa, I filled Mom in on our hopeful plans. When the phone rang again as I cleared the dinner plates from the table, I hoped it was Dad with good news. It was Lucy.

"Anything new?" I held my breath awaiting her answer. *Had her mom already agreed and told her about the adoption?*

"My mom wants to know if your mom can take me to the preshow rehearsals with you tomorrow. She has a last-minute errand and doesn't think she'll be home in time."

I checked with Mom, who quickly agreed. I could barely contain my excitement as Lucy and I made the arrangements for her to be dropped off at my house the following day. Once our plans were settled, Lucy brought up Caroline. "I can't stop thinking about her. I hope she's feeling better."

I filled Lucy in on Caroline's apology and how we were friends again. That made Lucy feel better. "When you get to know her . . . and you will . . . you will really like Caroline. She's a good friend . . . just like you."

Lucy made a little *aww* sound and then said, "You're a good friend, too, Indigo. I'm so glad we became close this summer. Lots of sleepovers this school year?"

"Definitely," I agreed.

I hung up the phone, feeling good inside—and not just because Roots would (hopefully) be Lucy's dog.

Whoop! Whoop! I cheered.

CHAPTER 22
CENTER STAGE

Following the smooth-flowing final run through, all the cast members gathered together in a big circle onstage. Lucy and I were dressed in "you-can't-see-me" stagehand attire: black leggings and black T-shirts. It was the most ordinary getup I'd ever worn.

"I was looking for you guys," Caroline said, approaching. "Can I sit with you?"

Lucy and I scooted over to make room. "Are you excited or nervous?" Lucy asked.

"Nervous," Caroline replied with a smile, "but not as nervous as I was for that karaoke contest."

"Oh, you worked it out just fine," I said, putting my arm around her shoulders. "You're going to be great out there. And, might I add," I said with a giggle, "you look totally marvelous in your costume."

Across the circle from us, Tess sat sandwiched between two boys and was swatting at their knees, trying to force greater distance between them and her.

Mrs. Rose walked to the center of the circle, wearing

a smashing red dress that flared at the knees. "Ladies and gentlemen," she began, "we come together now to share any final words of cheer or fear about tonight's performance. You've all worked so hard, and I know tonight's show will be spectacular. But sometimes it's good to check in as a group to air any last-minute concerns." Mrs. Rose smiled. "I'd like everyone to join hands, and quietly chat amongst yourselves, sharing any words of inspiration, concern, or encouragement you may have. In a few minutes, we'll end the circle with our camp cheer and cast mega-hug."

I happily reached for Lucy's hand on my right and Caroline's on my left. Right away, Caroline noticed my bracelet. "Indigo, your bracelet—it's naked!" she exclaimed. "Where are all your symbols?"

I giggled. "They fell off one by one. I still have them though, tucked away for safekeeping, just in case I need them again."

"What do you mean, *need them?*"

"Well, they reminded me of my gifts—you know, those things I'm good at and that come naturally to me? So when I felt sad or uncertain, I looked at them and remembered my strengths when I was feeling weak."

"Wow, I could sure use one of those bracelets," Caroline said wistfully. "I'm pretty sure I'm lost. Just the other day, Noel told me she missed me and wanted her sister back. She said I'd been acting like Tess."

Knowing how it felt to be lost inside myself, I suddenly had the urge to take off my bracelet and give it to Caroline. *Maybe it can help her like it helped me,* I thought. *After all, she's right—it's naked now. Maybe she's supposed to have it.*

But as I touched the bracelet, the whisper came: *"Choose wisely."*

I sensed that as much as I wanted to help Caroline "find herself," giving her my bracelet wasn't the answer. As I released the urge to take it off my wrist and hand it over to her, I saw *four* blue calcites in my mind's eye.

"Hello, Indigo?" Caroline said, playfully tapping on my forehead. "Are you in there?"

I tuned back in. "Oh, yeah. I'm here. You have lots of gifts, Caroline, and once you see and love 'em, you won't be lost anymore. Trust me."

Listening closely, Lucy bent forward and smiled at Caroline. That was one of the things I really liked about Lucy: She was always really encouraging, even when she didn't say anything.

"Are you guys ready for the show?" I asked.

"Can't wait!" Caroline said, and Lucy agreed.

Mrs. Rose began clapping out a steady beat, and we all stopped talking and joined in. Soon the auditorium rang with happy hoots and hollers, and we clutched one another in the cast mega-hug. Then, the stage lights flickered twice.

"Okay, everyone!" shouted Mrs. Rose. "You know what that means. The auditorium doors will open in five minutes. Everyone take your places. And silence, kids, silence!"

Lucy and I ran to the dressing room where the actors touched up their makeup and Lucy and I primped their exquisitely designed costumes. Once everyone had left the room, we rejoined Caroline backstage.

"I hope all three of you break a leg out there," said a threatening voice from behind.

We turned around to see Tess. I was about to respond when Caroline whispered, "Oh wow, really? How original, Tess. And just so you know"—she leaned in closer to Tess—"Mrs. Rose knows about the scarf. I wasn't the only one who saw you steal it yesterday. If you haven't already, it would be real brave of you to come clean."

Tess's jaw dropped. The house lights dimmed. Everyone, including the audience, fell silent. Instrumental music flowed from the speakers, and the red velvet curtains opened. Caroline, Lucy, and I clutched one another's hands with excitement.

The first act went smashingly well. I sang my heart out in the chorus, feeling great to be part of something so fantastic. When the curtains closed, the chorus filed offstage. "Come on, Indigo," Lucy said. "We've got to get back to the dressing room, pronto!"

"I'll be right there. I just wanna see if I can catch a glimpse of my mom and dad in the audience."

I peered around the side curtain. There was row 4, seat 26—and there was Dad. I sighed with relief. Beside him in seat 27 was Mom. Truthfully, I didn't have any hopes that my parents would get back together—they were just too different, almost from two different worlds, it seemed—but it was nice to see them interacting and sitting together. Then I noticed Lucy's mom in seat 28. I didn't know they had seats together, and I thought it was pretty cool.

I pulled my head back behind the curtain and sprinted to the dressing room. "Lucy," I said excitedly, "did you notice? Our moms are sitting next to each other."

"Really?" Lucy replied, looking surprised. "Mom said she was sitting in the back. She was really bummed she couldn't get any closer."

"Well, it looks like she got an upgrade," I said, smiling.

Time flew by as Lucy and I went back and forth between the dressing room and our chorus parts onstage. I was too busy organizing costumes and setting up and taking down props to get an idea of how the show looked from the audience's perspective, but by their applause after every song, I knew it was going well.

One thing I did notice though was the way Lucy's eyes focused on Gertie, Mrs. Rose's dog. Whether I looked over her shoulder or stood on tiptoe to catch a glimpse of her across the stage, it seemed that no matter whether we were backstage adjusting costumes or onstage shifting props, Lucy made sure Gertie was in view. Seeing her so drawn to Gertie only confirmed how much I knew she needed Roots—maybe just as much as Roots needed her.

Before I knew it, the finale was upon us. As the show came to a close, the audience rose to their feet applauding ecstatically. We all took our bows at predetermined intervals and, section by section, we left the stage. Then Mrs. Rose moved to center stage with a microphone in hand. "Thank you, everyone, for being such a wonderful audience tonight," she began.

A hush descended on the auditorium. "This summer's production has been such a blast and we're so lucky to have your enthusiastic support," Mrs. Rose continued. "But before you all get up to congratulate your children, I'd like to invite Mr. Monroe and his friend Roots to come onstage. We have a delightful surprise for one of our cast members. Would the cast and crew please come back onstage?"

"Come on, Indigo," yelled Lucy, seeing I had frozen. "Your Dad and Roots are onstage!"

"Indigoooo!" said Dad into the microphone. "Oh, Indigo! Will you please join me out here?"

Wide-eyed, I looked at Lucy. I took little, quick, nervous steps toward Dad, while Lucy found a place among the cast. Dad put out his arm as I met him. Then, drawing me close, he began telling Roots's story, sharing how the collie had come into our lives and how we had fostered him for the summer.

"As much as we would love to keep Roots," he explained, "we can't support another animal in our households. But I want to take this opportunity to draw your attention to a table in the lobby with information about fostering and other programs at the Pierce County Animal Shelter. A lot of animals could use good homes."

Dad cleared his throat. "Now that the summer has come to an end, so has our fostering time with Roots. We enjoyed getting to know and trust him, and both Indigo and I wanted to find him a loving home. And we did.

Indigo has made a new friend here at camp. Lucy, would you please join us out front? Someone real special is waiting to see you."

As Lucy made her way through the cast wearing a dumbfounded expression, Roots's tail began whipping back and forth with excitement, his tongue dangling from his mouth. "Lucy," Dad continued, "I called your mom last night and asked if she thought you might want to adopt Roots. Somehow, she knew you would. So she and I met at the animal shelter this afternoon. As a result, it's official. You are the proud owner of Roots!"

Lucy was speechless, holding back tears of joy, so I grabbed her hand, drawing her close to Dad and me.

As the applause died down, Mrs. Rose again stepped to center stage. "Annie's love for Sandy in tonight's performance reminds us of the powerful love that can grow between a human and a dog," she said, wiping away her own sweet tears. "It doesn't matter whether the dog is old or young, or whether it's from a breeder or the animal shelter. Once you find a dog you love, it's hard to let him go. I think Roots is ready for you to take him home, Lucy."

Dad handed Lucy the red leash. Bending down, Lucy snuggled Roots's neck, causing the audience to let out a loud collective *Awwwww.*

Love exploded inside me, and I couldn't help it. To steady myself, I knelt down beside them both. Leaning in, I said, "You two deserve the very best. And look! You've found it."

Lucy wrapped her arm around my neck to steady

herself. She looked up gratefully at Dad, then out to the crowd. We hovered there and took it all in.

While the audience and cast filed into the lobby, our families, Caroline, her mom, and Noel walked onstage and surrounded Lucy, Roots, Dad, and me.

"He's beautiful, Lucy," said Caroline. "You're so lucky!"

"Oh, thank you, Caroline!" Lucy said, then stood up to face Noel so the little girl could read her lips. "Indigo says you're really great." Lucy reached out her hand and Noel grabbed hold.

I took a seat on the floor. My heart beat so fast as I watched my friends and family come together. "Don't mind me down here," I said to Caroline's mom. "I'm just taking this all in." Then I signed to Noel, "I missed you!"

Noel grinned and jumped in my lap.

"Come on, girls, we better get going," Caroline's mom urged. "Your dad probably has the car pulled around by now. Indigo, we sure do miss you. We hope you'll come over soon."

I suddenly had a vision of myself standing at Caroline's front door with a rolled-up bandana in my hand. The last time I'd seen the bandana vision, it had had four blue calcites lying on top of it. Something was a-brew; I could feel it.

"I'd love to come over," I said, waving excitedly as Caroline and her family left the stage. Noel blew me a kiss, and then scampered off after Caroline and her mom.

I gazed out over the retreating audience and my eyes fell on Tess, her parents, and Mrs. Rose deep in conversation near one of the exits. Tess was squirming and looked very unhappy. So did her parents. I guessed they were talking about the scarf she'd stolen. I felt a little twinge of sympathy for Tess—not because she'd been caught, of course, but because it seemed she had a real problem and had lost a good friend in Caroline and the chance to be part of our growing crew.

I turned my attention back to Lucy, who was thanking my dad again and again.

Dad grabbed my hand and pulled me up so that we stood side by side. "It was our pleasure, Lucy," he replied.

I reached out to hug Lucy. "We have to introduce Roots to Marigold and go to the dog park with them both. We'll have lots of fun! Remember, this isn't goodbye!"

"You got it!" affirmed Lucy with a wave. She walked away with Roots glued right to her side, and my smile was so wide it nearly broke my face.

CHAPTER 23

ALL AGLOW

In the parking lot, I grabbed Dad in a tight hug. "We're on for fishing in the morning, right, Dad?"

He stood strong, squeezing me tight in response. "I wouldn't miss it, honey."

I buried my grin deep in the comfort of his arms. I'd tell him tomorrow how much what he had done for Lucy and Roots meant to me. It all felt too big for words at the moment.

"What a night, Indigo," Mom said, waving goodbye to Dad as we walked toward our car.

"Unbelievable," I said. "And guess what? I saw *four* crystals today." Remembering I hadn't told her about the third, I quickly filled her in on that part, then I went on, "I saw four in my mind when I decided *not* to give Caroline my bracelet." Mom let out a little gasp, but quickly smothered it as I went on, "The strange thing was, I knew the heirloom could really help her, but then again, it's *our* treasure; it's not something to give away in the rush of a moment."

Mom tapped her head with her index finger. "Good thinking," she said, as she started the car.

Once our tires came to a complete stop in our driveway, I jumped out, and moments later, with Marigold beside me in my room, I knelt down and reached for my bandana under my bed. But when I tried to grasp it, my fingertips connected instead with the pyramid. I peeked under the bed, located the bandana, and moved my hand toward it. As my hand moved, the pyramid followed.

"Okay, so you want to come out," I said, my voice quivering.

There was no explanation for the magical movement, so I didn't try to come up with one. Hands shaking, I pulled both the pyramid and bandana at once. Marigold sniffed the pyramid while I watched for more mysterious movement.

"Come on, girl," I instructed, "lie down next to me. Let's see if I have another crystal."

As I touched the bandana, rays of light began to emanate from the center of the bundle, growing brighter. Peeling back the folds, I found that—sure enough—there were four crystals, all aglow, clustered together.

Marigold growled.

"It's okay, girl," I assured her, petting her with my sweaty palms. "I'm certain there's a perfectly good explanation for this." I said the words before I really believed them. I just had to trust what I was seeing—the way I did with Sienna Glass.

I touched the feather, fabric, broken pop can ring, twist tie, and dried rose scattered among the crystals. As

I did, the light from the blue calcites enveloped my hand and my symbols. My heart fluttered like the wings of a hummingbird. "Wha—? Wh-what's going on?"

Marigold barked. As I turned to look at her, I noticed a similar light glowing around the seam of the pyramid door.

Marigold barked again.

I waved my glowing hand back and forth through the beams of light streaming from the pyramid. As my hands passed the door, the four indentations within the infinity sign started to glow. Instantly I had an idea, and I gathered the four blue calcites in my left hand and held it toward the pyramid. The light inside the pyramid grew even brighter.

"Four indentations on the pyramid door, four crystals, all sharing the same light."

I took a crystal and inserted it into the top indentation. The crystal fit perfectly into that spot. The glow intensified for a moment, and I heard a "clink!" When I pulled on the crystal, it wouldn't budge.

I quickly placed another crystal in front of the second indentation. Once again, there was a bright light. *Clink!* The second crystal was in place. Once I'd popped the third and fourth crystals in place, I heard a low creaking. The pyramid door was opening!

Marigold growled, stood, and sniffed the pyramid.

"Girl, we're safe," I assured her.

"There's nothing to fear," said the whisper.

The glow from my hand and from the pyramid

expanded into a balloon of light all around me. Marigold barked wildly and circled the light.

"Are you all right up there?" Mom called up the stairs.

At first, I couldn't respond. Then I called down, "*Umm*, yeah, it's all under control!"

As I sat up, the light followed and floated around me, like it was part of me, like it was *my* light. I felt peaceful, and I also felt ready to look inside the glowing pyramid.

There, inside it, an object rested on red velvet lining. Reaching into the pyramid, I pulled it out. I could hardly believe my eyes. It was an *exact* duplicate of my bracelet.

The image I'd seen on stage of myself with my bandana folded in my hand, standing on Caroline's porch, returned. "This is for Caroline," I said aloud, knowing deep down that giving it to her would be a very wise choice.

But where will I keep my symbols? I wondered.

The red velvet inside the pyramid glowed with a brilliant light. Without hesitation, I placed the feather, orange taffeta, ring pieces, twist tie, and dried rose on the illuminated floor of the pyramid. Then I wrapped Caroline's bracelet inside the bandana.

The pyramid began to vibrate, and my symbols danced about on the velvet cloth. The pyramid shook until its silver door slid closed. Then, the light surrounding me and the pyramid intensified. Marigold yelped, lay down, and buried her head under her paws. I had to shield my eyes, too.

In another instant, the blinding light faded, and there, on the floor before us, lay a golden platter lined with red velvet, just like Mom's platter. The pyramid and symbols were gone, apparently having transformed into this magnificent tray. I panicked for a moment and looked down. I breathed a huge sigh of relief when I saw that my bracelet was still safely around my wrist.

I took a deep breath and exhaled, enveloped in a new sense of wonder. Feeling like my mysterious adventures were far from over, I spoke my inner voice aloud: "Live the love I feel inside, not the fear that makes me hide. Be aware of myself and my surroundings. Being mindful leads to wise choices."

As long as I can do these things, I thought, *anything is possible.*

CHAPTER 24

AN IMPORTANT DELIVERY

I simply couldn't sleep. I felt like a neon sign that read "CAROLINE, I HAVE A SPECIAL GIFT FOR YOU!" Wide-eyed, I joyfully rehearsed telling Caroline about the brand-new heirloom created especially for her. Of course, I'd share how my bracelet had helped me, and at the same time, I would have to be careful not to give away any answers—the way Mom gave me only little clues. Caroline would have to find the answers for herself.

The following morning, I filled Mom in on my magical experience, never once thinking that she'd think I'd gone crazy. I mentioned the light, *my* light, and she called it an aura—a luminous field of energy that surrounds all living things. Then she let me in on a secret: She could even see it now. She ruffled my hair and told me how proud she was of me. Then finally she shared with me that she'd gotten her golden platter the same way I did when she was about my age.

"What did you find inside your pyramid?" I asked.

"Another bracelet, just like you did." She winked. "I gave it to Amy. She was going through a hard time, and it was one of the ways I could help her."

"Like mother, like daughter," I said with a laugh before hopping up from the breakfast table to tend to the animals.

Once everyone had been fed, I quickly got dressed, and Mom drove me to Caroline's house so I could make my important delivery.

"You got this, Indigo!" she cheered when we pulled into Caroline's driveway. "And you look fabulous, too."

I shut the car door and curtsied, my fingertips fanning out my spring concert skirt. There was no question that what I was about to do required style, so, along with my skirt, I wore high-top Converse tennis shoes and a white pocket tee. "Thanks, Mom!" I said, waving goodbye.

Caroline was expecting me. When I'd called that morning to see if I could make a delivery, she'd been super excited.

"What is it?" she'd pleaded.

"It's top secret, something I have to give to you in person," I'd said, pacing back and forth in the kitchen, too pumped to sit down.

And now, there I was, sitting beside Caroline in her dining room. She glowed with excitement in her yellow sundress and white cardigan, her brown straight hair pinned up with a silver barrette. It was just like her to be so clean and put together.

"Remember when we sat in a circle onstage before

our performance yesterday?" I asked. "You noticed the symbols were missing from my bracelet."

"Yes, I was surprised, knowing how special your bracelet is to you," Caroline nodded, pushing her long brown hair off her shoulders.

"It's a treasure," I explained, "not only to me, but to my family. Anyway, I really wanted to give it to you in that moment. I thought it might do for you what it's done for me, you being my best friend and all."

"Indigo, I could never—"

"Just wait. You see, even though I wanted to give it to you, inside I knew it wasn't a wise choice. Then, later last night, while working with my—" *Shhh,* I cautioned myself in my mind, and my voice trailed away.

"I'm listening," Caroline said expectantly, clearly wondering why I'd clammed up.

"*Um,* well, ever since I put this bracelet on," I recovered, "strange but good things have happened. It's like a key that opens the door to a place inside that has all the answers. It's really valuable and has helped me see things about myself and my surroundings."

Being such a devoted listener, Caroline nodded along with me, finally commenting with a "Wow, Indigo, you're lucky," though I could tell she didn't completely grasp what I was saying.

"Yes," I agreed, peeling back the folds of the bandana to reveal a second bracelet. "This one's for you. It was the treasure I found—"

Caroline gasped. "I don't know what to say."

"I didn't know what to say either when my mom gave me my bracelet." I patted my worn leather band, then pulled the silver etched clasp around to where it was visible. "See the clasp? It's an infinity sign."

"May I?" Caroline's hand hovered over her bracelet, which still lay snuggled in the folds of the soft bandana. Cautiously lifting the brown leather band out of the cloth, she turned it around to expose the silver clasp. "They're identical."

"That one's yours," I declared, pointing to the bracelet in Caroline's hand, "and it stays in your family forever. But there are a few things to remember: First, this bracelet is about love. Second, there's nothing to fear. Third, watch and listen. And fourth, remember that things always have a way of working out. So whenever you feel discouraged or upset, trust that you'll find your way."

"Okay," Caroline replied with a slight furrow of her brow. "I'll try to remember all that."

"If you forget," I reassured her. "I'm right here. I'll do my best to share what I've learned without getting in the way. May I help you put it on?"

Caroline blinked, holding back two tiny joyful tears, and handed me her bracelet. Unfastening the clasp, I wrapped the leather around her left wrist and hooked the sides of the silver infinity sign together to secure the treasure in place. Then Caroline and I held our wrists up to one another, our bracelets touching.

"Yours has that brand-new glow," I said, marveling at the stiff, red-brown leather and the shiny clasp. "And you know what? Now that I see your new one and my old one side by side, I think I've figured something out: When Mom gave me my bracelet a few months ago, it looked totally faded, light brown in color, and real thin to the touch. But look at it now. Can you see the red coming back into the braided leather? And see?" I held up my wrist. "It's thicker, too, and much stronger than the day I got it." I scratched my head with my free hand.

"Whoa!" Caroline gasped. "It's like it came to life or something."

"I think we both came to life," I said.

"I already feel better," Caroline announced, but when she got immediately quiet after that and her eyes drifted away from her bracelet, I could tell something else was bothering her.

"What's the matter, Caroline?"

"Don't take this the wrong way or that I'm not totally happy about this wonderful gift, Indigo," Caroline said, touching the bracelet on her wrist. "It's just that I was feeling kind of bad this morning about how I left it with Tess. We did spend a lot of time together, and well, she wasn't all that bad." Then she thought better of that statement. "Well, she *was* mean to you. I'm sorry I let that happen. I don't see us being *besties* or anything, but . . ."

"I know what you mean," I said, reassuring her. "She obviously has a problem."

"I was thinking I might walk over to her house this morning," Caroline said, gauging my reaction, "to see how she's doing."

"Well, I could go with you," I offered. "I mean, who knows? Maybe she's turned over a new leaf, and we can put all this summer madness behind us."

"That's what I'm hoping. You'd be willing to hear her out?" Caroline asked.

"Sure," I answered. Then I added wisely, "That is, if she has something kind and honest say."

⁕

A little while later, Caroline's sandal tapped rapidly on the doormat. She picked at her sweater and fluffed up her dress a gazillion times, so I could tell waiting for Tess to open the door was really nerve-wracking for her.

"It's times like these that your heirloom can really help," I suggested. "See?"

Caroline looked down at my hands, which I had folded over each other and rested just below my waist. Then she noticed the fingers of my right hand lightly grasping my bracelet. She grabbed hold of her bracelet and stopped fidgeting.

Tess's front door finally opened. "Oh, it's you," moaned Tess, staring only at Caroline. Realizing I was deliberately being ignored, I said nothing.

"Hi," Caroline muttered, "I just wanted to make sure you are okay."

"Why bother?" Tess exclaimed. "Because of you, I'm grounded for a month!" She crossed her arms over her chest, thankfully covering the green neon letters across her purple T-shirt that read "ROCK STAR."

Caroline gulped. "It had nothing to do with me, Tess," she said bravely. "You're the one who stole the scarf."

"Whatever," Tess said spitefully, "I can tell you right now, we're not going to friends anymore, especially if you're going to be friends with her. I don't even know why you're here."

Now she turned her glare on me, looking me up and down. It took everything in me to keep my mouth shut.

"Well, then that solves it," Caroline replied. "I had hoped getting caught had taught you a lesson. It was . . ." Caroline paused. "Tough knowing you. It looks like we'll be moving on. Indigo, it's time to leave."

She turned to me, her hands still folded together at her belly button, her fingers still grasping her bracelet.

"After you," I said, holding out my hand, inviting her to lead the way.

Before we could even turn around, Tess slammed the door in our faces.

As Caroline and I walked down the sidewalk to her house, I lightly bumped her shoulder. "You okay?"

"Oh, yeah," she said with a smile, bumping my shoulder back. "Everything has a way of working out."

PART THREE

UNFOLD

CHAPTER 25

A GOOD SCARE

A crescendo of quick footsteps sounded up the back porch, followed by silence and then a rapid tapping on the screen door.

"Indigo!" Jake called.

It was Sunday morning, following the last sleepover of the summer. Lucy had already left because she had an early appointment with her mom, so Caroline and I had breakfast without her. Standing side by side, rinsing syrup from our plates, we glanced over our shoulders at the screen door. I didn't even realize Jake had gotten back from his grandparents' house.

"What is it?" I called out. "Are you okay?"

"It's Ed," Jake replied, flipping his shaggy bangs away from his eyes. "I think she's sick."

Caroline realized I was about to let the plate I was holding crash into the sink and grabbed it out of my hands. As I spun around, I felt the hem of my green fleece robe lift from the rush of air.

"Come in," I urged.

As the back door creaked open, I pivoted, nudging Caroline in front of me. I pulled the collar of my robe across my chest to cover my nightgown and tightened the belt around my waist, tying it with a double knot.

"Have a seat," I said.

As I pulled out a chair, I caught sight of an escaped scrap of French toast on Jake's side of the kitchen table. I swiped it away, leaving a rainbow smear of maple syrup on the table. Shrugging my shoulders, I licked the sticky sugar off my pinky and took a seat opposite him.

"Ed's been in and out of that box a million times in the last hour," Jake explained. "She doesn't stay long enough to do anything, if you know what I mean. She's—"

"Meowing like crazy," I interrupted.

"Yeah," Jake answered with a frown. "How'd you know?"

"*Shh,*" I commanded.

Giving me a blank stare, Jake leaned back in his seat and fell silent.

In the stillness, I heard a repetitive *meow* in my head, and in my mind's eye, I saw Ed, her eyes wincing, her body hunched under Jake's kitchen table. A gray hue permeated the scene. Suddenly, I smelled smoke.

"Caroline," I gasped, "are we baking something?"

"No. Why?"

"I know this sounds crazy," I explained, turning to Jake, "but I see Ed meowing in pain under your kitchen table. And I smell—"

"Wait a minute!" Jake exclaimed, lurching forward in his seat and pointing at me. As his elbow met the table, the sleeve of his blue hooded sweatshirt landed in the smeared maple syrup. "What do you mean you *see* her?"

"There's no time to explain," I said urgently, not even sure I could explain it to myself. "Tell me, were you cooking something this morning?"

"Oh, my gosh!" Jake gasped, leaping to his feet. "My breakfast!"

He turned and raced out the back door. Caroline and I exchanged worried glances, then leapt up and headed after him in our robes.

We reached Jake's house and stood breathless on his porch in our bare feet, pacing back and forth to the blaring of the smoke alarm from the open front door. Peering into the entryway, I caught a glimpse of smoke.

"Jake, are you okay?" I shouted.

"We should go in, Indigo. Jake could be hurt!"

Without hesitation, I blurted, "Let's call for help first."

Caroline nodded, and together we darted back across the lawn. Suddenly, we heard Jake yelling after us. "All clear! Everything's okay." The alarm had stopped sounding.

We returned to the porch, where Jake stood waiting.

I was ready to rush inside to the cat, but Jake shook his head. "Hold up a sec. It's a bit too smoky in there. Get a load of these."

Our eyes dropped to the dirty white dishtowel in his palm. "Here are the culprits," he groaned, holding out the towel, upon which lay a large pile of burnt pieces of something totally unrecognizable.

Caroline and I gripped the collars of our robes and leaned forward. "What the heck is that?" Caroline asked, crinkling up her nose at the sight.

"They *were* Pop-Tarts," I answered before Jake could reply.

Jake let the blackened pastries fall onto the porch. "How did you—?" he asked, his voice trailing away.

Grabbing the white wicker rocking chair from beside the front door, I maneuvered it toward him, just as his eyes started searching for a place to sit down.

"Here you go."

As Jake took a seat, I nervously peeked into the house through the open front door.

"My family's—" Jake began.

"Not home," I finished for him.

"There wasn't a real—"

"Fire." Again, I'd finished for him. "What happened in there?"

"It seems you already know!" Jake replied, half-accusingly. "I mean, you know about the smoke and you knew that burnt mess was Pop-Tarts. And that's not all," Jake continued. "You said you could *see* Ed under my kitchen table, which is *exactly* where she was when I came to your house."

"No, I didn't," I said, feeling confused.

"*Um*, yeah, you did," Caroline confirmed.

"You're right," I said, warily backing away from them. Reaching behind me, I felt for a porch pillar and, leaning back against it, slid down until my butt hit the wooden floor. I closed my eyes and pressed my palms into them. *Now I'm having visions of other people's lives?* I felt a bit panicked over the idea until it sunk in that I was no stranger to things beyond the ordinary. Maybe part of being aware—well, at least for me—included knowing stuff about other people.

Jake slumped limply in the rocker. "I'm seriously spooked right now. How did you know those things?"

Caroline sat cross-legged beside me. Adjusting her robe to cover her legs, she put her arm around my shoulder. "It's a good question, don't you think?"

"Maybe so," I replied softly. "But I have no idea. I just knew. Anyway, you guys have never just known something?" I was reaching, but I hoped to make it seem like it was just an ordinary occurrence. I didn't want to freak them out.

"No way, Indigo," Jake firmly replied. "I've never seen, heard, or smelled anything that wasn't close to me."

"Me neither," Caroline added, in a gentle but puzzled voice.

"Are you spooked, too, Caroline?" I asked.

Caroline raised her arm from around my neck and reached for my left wrist. Then she brought her left arm across her body and placed it beside mine. Our two bare leather bracelets touched.

"No," she replied. "I'm not spooked. And, Jake, you know Indigo. She's harmless."

"Yeah, I know," Jake admitted. "You do have a way with animals, Indigo. I've seen you with Silvy at the Looking Pond. Then there was that bird on the soccer field. You risked *my life* to save it. And let's not forget when you rescued Ed from the tree and that sick dog on the trail. I figured you'd have an idea about how to help Ed."

"So, let's go see Ed," I suggested, trying to change the subject and conceal my delight that Jake and I had somehow become friends—despite everything.

Jake started into the house first, but Caroline held me back to make a request: "Just promise me this, Indigo, that when you know how you *just knew*, you'll tell me."

I nodded in agreement. "But can we keep this to ourselves? I seem quirky enough to others already . . . if you know what I mean."

Caroline offered me a fist-bump to seal her commitment to my request.

The sound of gravel cracking, popping, and scattering caused us to turn, just in time to see a red truck barrel up the driveway. Jake rushed back outside to meet his mom and dad on the sidewalk.

Caroline and I leaned against the wooden banister, observing the heated discussion that ensued. When Jake returned to the porch with his parents in tow, Mr. Peterson thanked us for our support. "Now if you'll excuse us,"—he sniffed as he entered the house—"we need to assess the damage."

Mrs. Peterson followed, pushing the front door wide-open, commenting with a wink and a smile, "We'll just need to air out the house a bit."

"Is now a good time to check on Eddy?" I asked.

"Wait, Indigo!" Caroline said. "Don't you think we ought to go home and change real quick?" When I didn't respond, she brought her head close to mine and mumbled, "I'm feeling a little *under*dressed."

"Good point," I said with a volume of ten to Caroline's one.

Suddenly bashful, Jake turned away, staring at a random bush near the side of the house.

I still felt compelled to check on Eddy first.

Caroline grinned, pulled her robe collar tight, held out her hand in the direction of the house, and looked at Jake.

Jake responded in a heartbeat. "Follow me."

Jake led us into the kitchen. All the windows stood open, and the butter-colored curtains danced in the breeze. The smoke had cleared, but the smell remained.

Jake and I crouched to look at Eddy under the table. She looked up at us with glassy eyes, and when she moved toward us, her body tensed up.

"Here, Eddy," I urged softly. "What's troubling you, pretty calico girl?"

As I spoke, I noticed a yellow light emanating from her head, neck, and chest, and a faint red glow encircling the lower half of her body. Remembering what Mom had told me about auras, I figured that I was seeing Ed's. Too worried about the cat, I didn't even wonder why I could suddenly see it. Instead, I noted that Ed's aura was dim compared to the light that had encircled me the night I opened the pyramid. I cautiously moved my left hand forward, hoping to pet and soothe her. But the minute my hand approached, she hissed, swiping the air with her dagger-sharp claws.

"*Hmmm*," I muttered. "Okay, safety first. Caroline,

let's make a quick run back to my house. Jake, I've got something that should help. We'll be back in a flash."

⌒

Mom was sitting at our kitchen table when we barged in. "Mom, can Eddy and I borrow your red carnelian?"

"Where have you been?" she asked, her expression worried. "Silvy's still in the barn, so I knew you hadn't gone to the Looking Pond."

"Good morning, Ms. Monroe," Caroline said. "We're sorry. We didn't mean to cause you concern."

That Caroline, I thought, *she has the best manners— and she actually feels just how she says she does.*

"Sorry, Mom," I said, taking a leaf out of Caroline's book and speaking more politely now. "Please excuse our absence this morning, but Eddy is sick and Jake came over looking for help. I've got a plan and wondered if I could borrow your red carnelian again?"

"Of course, honey," Mom replied. "I don't have to remind you—"

"Nope, you don't. Safety first!"

Mom led us upstairs. Sitting in a circle on her bedroom floor, the three of us admired her platter of crystals. I immediately spotted the red carnelian among the rainbow of stones and scooped it from its resting place.

"If you don't mind my asking, Mrs. Monroe," Caroline said, "what do you do with all these crystals?" Although she had zero knowledge of Mom's crystals or the experiences I'd had with the blue calcites, she seemed to have a genuine interest.

"That's a good question," Mom replied. "I use them to heal. I've collected them throughout the years, and I've found them to be some of the best remedies of all time."

"Wow," Caroline sighed, looking amazed. "That says a lot coming from you, I mean, with your nursing experience and all."

"They're not the *only* remedy, of course," Mom quickly clarified, "but they can be combined with other healing methods to promote optimal healing."

"That makes sense," Caroline said hesitantly, as if she only partly understood what Mom was saying.

"I'm going to put this in Eddy's water bowl," I interrupted, "just like I did for Roots. Once Eddy takes a few sips, the crystal's effect on the water will calm her down enough for us to take a closer look."

"Maybe Eddy needs to see the vet," Mom suggested, then thought again. "Well, today *is* Sunday. Jake's parents would have to take her to the emergency clinic in the city. I bet they'd be grateful for a remedy that would buy them some time until tomorrow when they can take her to the vet in town."

"We're on the job then, right, Caroline?" I confirmed.

Caroline gave me an excited nod. "Right-o, Indigo!"

"Run along, you two," Mom said with a laugh.

Caroline and I darted across the hall to my room, where we hurried to get changed. We were planning our next move when my butt slipped off the edge of my bed and hit the floor with a loud thud. There I was, one leg in and one leg out of my new homemade polka-dot skirt (one of two skirts I made over the summer between batches of crystal bandanas) while Caroline rushed over to me, half-laughing, half-concerned.

"No worries," I said, hopping up on one leg and swinging my other leg though the drawstring waistband of my skirt. "I'm indestructible," I proclaimed, addressing my remark to Marigold, who had come barreling through my door upon hearing the thump.

As Caroline and I stood side by side in the bathroom mirror fixing our hair, she said wistfully, "I wish I had curls like yours."

"What?" I exclaimed. There she was, with her dynamite straight brown hair. "Do you know how much I'd give to have straight hair? Just look at my curls. They have a life of their own."

Caroline watched as I tugged at the end of one of my red tendrils. I stretched the lock of hair until it was straight. Caroline watched with fascination as I released the ringlet and it flew up in the air and sprang back into place. "See? They only do what *they* want to do."

"At least your hair has a zest for life," Caroline countered. "Mine is lifeless, like I'm wearing two large cold pancakes down the sides of my head."

My eyes found Caroline's in the mirror. "I *love* pancakes. I thought you did, too."

Caroline giggled. "You got me there. Maybe if we love our own hair as much as we love each other's, our own hair would feel more beautiful to us."

"I think you're on to something," I declared, looking at her in the mirror.

Suddenly, Caroline closed her eyes and kept them shut. Her right hand reached over and grasped her bracelet on her left wrist. I fell silent. After a long moment, I inquired, "Are you with me?"

Caroline gave a sudden, rapid shake of her head and blurted out, "Sorry."

At that moment, our eyes met in the mirror again, four brilliant blues reflecting back with intense clarity. I sensed that Caroline had experienced a "bracelet break," a moment where loving truth whispered louder than fear.

I corralled my unruly hair and bunched it into a large ponytail.

Caroline turned her head toward me. "I'm ready if you are."

"Me, too," I agreed.

CHAPTER 26

SIRENS

Jake's front door was still wide-open when we returned to his house.

"Should we ring the bell?" Caroline wondered.

Just then, Jake appeared in the entry hall, startling us both. "I thought I heard someone out here!" he said. "Come on in. I just finished a *nonhazardous* bowl of Frosted Mini-Wheats."

I chuckled. Then, it occurred to me that we both liked the same cereal. A surge of admiration caused me to blush, and I suddenly felt bashful. A rush of butterfly flutter filled my stomach. I shifted my gaze away from Jake's eyes, and it landed on the swirling multicolored rug on which he was standing.

"Indigo, should we go see about Eddy?" Caroline suggested, nudging my shoulder with hers.

"Yes," I said, just as another vision of Eddy came into my mind. "She's still under the kitchen table, huh?"

"Gosh, Indigo," Jake said, sounding awed. "I have no idea *how* you know these things."

"Lead the way," Caroline directed.

We followed Jake to the kitchen, and I peeked under the table. "Don't worry, Eddy," I assured her, "I won't get too close. I'm just going to put this healing crystal in your water."

Holding the red carnelian in my open palm, I allowed Ed to inspect it from afar. As she did so, I noticed the dim light around the top half of her body again. Then a new vision appeared in my mind: a green tube, like a garden hose, with a stone-like object lodged inside.

"*Hmmm*," I murmured.

"What are you *hmmming* about?" asked Jake.

"Eddy, you have pain when you try to pee, right?" Though Eddy didn't respond in an obvious way, in my head I heard an affirmative *meow*. "Where's Ed's water dish?"

Jake led me to his utility room. Shoes were scattered about the floor, coats hung in layers upon hooks, and laundry piled high in three baskets waited its turn to enter the washer and dryer. "Over there," Jake said, pointing to a white dish resting on a placemat.

Opening my left hand to show Jake the crystal, I said, "I'm going to put this red carnelian in Ed's water dish, okay? This type of crystal calms aggressive animals. If Ed drinks the water, she'll calm down."

Resting one hand on his hip, Jake ran the other hand through his blond "I-just-woke-up" hair. "I suppose we've gone this far," he conceded. "Okay, go ahead."

I bent down and, positioning my hand a centimeter above the water, gently released the crystal, which ker-plunked its way to the bottom of the dish.

"So now what?" he inquired.

"We bring the dish to Eddy and hope she'll drink."

Jake and I returned to the kitchen to find Caroline cross-legged on the floor, keeping watch over the cat.

"Jake, *you'd* better place this next to her," I suggested.

Taking the dish from me, Jake carefully positioned it next to Eddy, who didn't flinch. Once Jake had moved his hand away from the dish, she bent over and drank daintily.

Quietly clapping my hands under my chin, I whispered with excitement, "Yes, Eddy, keep drinking. Keep drinking."

We froze in position, not wanting to disrupt her while she quenched her thirst. Once she was finished, Jake and I joined Caroline on the floor.

"You guys promise not to tell anyone?" I asked solemnly.

"Tell anyone about what, Indigo?" Jake asked, looking at me sideways.

"You know," I replied quietly, "about how I'm *seeing* things."

"Of course I promise," said Caroline.

"Yes, I swear, too," Jake agreed.

I took a deep breath, and then the words just flowed out of me: "All right, then. I saw something else in my mind, like a hose with a stone clogging it. You mentioned Eddy was in and out of her litter box this morning, right? I'm thinking maybe something is blocking her ability to go . . . uh, number one and causing her pain."

"That would make sense," Jake said, pulling up his blue sweatshirt sleeve, His fingers swiped over the sticky syrup left behind by our breakfast. He inspected his hand with a puzzled look.

Caroline chimed in, averting Jake's attention from the syrup. "How long before the crystal water has an effect on Ed?"

"That's a good question," I answered. "I used the red carnelian with Roots, but I don't know how long it took to have an effect because he was in an outdoor cage all night." Feeling for my bracelet, I pressed the leather between my fingers and tried to sense if Ed was safe to approach. Within seconds, I heard my inner voice whisper *"yes."* Trusting my instincts, I instructed Jake, "Stand by. I'm going to approach her."

Jake got into position, kneeling next to Caroline, while I scooted under the table toward the cat and sat with my legs crossed, listening. To my surprise, a faint purr emanated from Eddy. The light around her upper body appeared brighter now, although the light around her lower body was still dim and red. Hopeful she would allow me to advance, I slowly took my hand from my lap and placed it on the floor next to her. This time, she showed no aggression toward me.

"She seems better," said Jake.

"I think we've made progress," I whispered, repositioning my hand on the hardwood floor closer to Eddy. Remembering "safety first," I sensed my position was close enough, and that touching her, even though she seemed more relaxed, *wouldn't* be a wise move.

Now that I could observe Eddy closely, I again saw the vision of the hose with the stone blocking it. But this time, the stone lit up red and flashed. Blasted by the glare of the red strobes, I closed my eyes. I heard a faint siren swell out of the silence. As the moments passed, the noise swelled, louder and louder. My hands instinctively shot up to plug my ears and drown out the sound.

"What's going on, Indigo?" hollered Jake. "Are you okay?"

"*Shh!*" *Too much input,* I thought.

Jake backed off and anxiously awaited my response. As he did so, I had a growing sense that Eddy was in serious danger.

Suddenly, in my mind's eye, I saw three gigantic gray stones in a triangular formation. They weren't the ones causing Eddy's distress. They were magnificent and somehow calming. But, all the while, the red light flashed with increasing intensity, and the siren in my ears blared. Overwhelmed, I tried to focus on the giant stones in the background to relieve the pressure in my head. "One, two, three," I counted them in a whisper over and over again. "One, two, three."

Caroline had seen enough. Scooting past Jake, who was kneeling close to me and looking freaked out, she grabbed a wad of my polka-dot skirt and pulled hard, breaking my counting rhythm and calling my attention back into the room.

"What's going on?" she blurted. "You're beginning to scare us." Her eyes stared into mine, her arms now locked straight with her knuckles pushing down onto my knees.

I looked past Caroline to Jake. "This is an emergency!" I gasped. "Eddy needs to go to the clinic—now."

Shocked, Caroline sat back on her heels, leaving just enough room for me to crawl out from under the table. Hurrying out of the kitchen, I whispered loudly from the hallway, "Come out here, guys. We need a plan, quick."

"Why are you whispering?" Jake asked as he and Caroline joined me on the spiral entryway rug. "What's wrong?"

"I'm whispering because I don't want to alarm Eddy," I replied. "Crystals aren't enough to heal what's going on inside her body. She needs emergency care. Where are your parents?"

"My dad just went to the station," Jake answered. "There's been another case of arson in the recycling dumpster downtown." Caroline and I gasped at this news, as Jake continued, "Mom's here, though." He turned toward the stairs and called for his mom. Then he looked directly at me. "How am I going to convince her to drive Eddy to the city clinic if I can't explain to her how you know that he needs to go?"

"I dunno," I responded. "You're a quick thinker. Come up with something that will light a fire of concern." Remembering the Pop-Tart incident, I cringed at my choice of words.

Just then, Mrs. Peterson descended the stairs and met us in the entryway. "What's up?"

Jake scowled at me, then turned to his mom. "You know how I went to Indigo's this morning because I was worried about Ed?" She nodded. "Well, Indigo says Eddy's in danger. Right, Indigo?"

I froze up and blinked. How was I going to tell Mrs. Peterson how I had come to understand Ed's dire situation? I didn't want to spook her like I'd spooked Jake and Caroline.

"What Jake's trying to say," Caroline said with her usual finesse, "is that Indigo senses that Eddy is extremely sick and needs emergency veterinary care. We know it's Sunday, and it's inconvenient to get help for Ed right now, but there's no time to waste."

Mrs. Peterson gasped. "Jake, Indigo, is this true?"

Again, I blinked a couple of times, as Jake, sounding relieved, sighed a loud "yes."

"Indigo, you're awfully quiet," Jake's mom remarked. "I know Jake wouldn't have asked for your help if he didn't trust you. He told me about Eddy's symptoms earlier this morning. It's true; she's not her usual self."

I gulped. *That's for sure.*

Mrs. Peterson gazed into my eyes, awaiting a response. Though I could feel her trying to draw me out, I found myself at a loss for words, unable to tell the truth but unwilling to lie.

"Mrs. Peterson," Caroline interjected, "if you have time, it seems the best thing for Eddy is to have you and Jake drive her to the vet in the city."

"That's a good idea," Jake chimed in. "Mom, I'll get the pet carrier from the garage while you look up where to go."

Just then, I received a vision of a green stone lying on the red velvet lining the golden platter under my bed. Next, I envisioned one of my homemade, crystal-holding bandanas. It was stashed away in my nightstand drawer with a few others, leftover from the ones I had donated to the animal shelter.

"Great idea," I blurted, surprising the crew around me. "I'll be right back."

Mrs. Peterson asked Caroline if she could watch over Eddy while she prepared for the departure.

"Of course," assured Caroline, making her way into the kitchen to perform her duty.

∽

Anxious to see if a new crystal had appeared under my bed, I sped past Mom, who was talking animatedly with Amy on video chat at the kitchen table, and raced Marigold up the stairs to my room. As her wet, black nose sniffed under the bed next to my hand, I pulled the platter out. Sure enough, there it was: a new green crystal.

"Marigold, look here!" I said excitedly. "Do you know what it is?"

Marigold sniffed the smooth, pale-green stone as I picked it up off the velvet. As she inspected the treasure, I reached over, opened my nightstand drawer, and pulled out one of the crystal bandanas.

"Come on," I encouraged Marigold. "Let's borrow Mom's crystal book and see how this stone can help."

Marigold and I entered Mom's room, where I grabbed the tattered reference book from her tall wooden bookshelf. Together, we ran downstairs to Mom, who had just finished her chat.

"Do you mind, Mom?" I asked as I pulled up a chair and plunked the crystal book down in front of her. Curious about all the action, Mr. Magoo perched on the open door of her cage, and the finches peeped loudly. Marigold sat beside us, tail wagging.

"How can I help?" Mom asked.

"I just need to talk this out. A new crystal appeared to me when Mrs. Peterson agreed to take Eddy for emergency care in the city. Here it is." I handed Mom the stone, and she studied it for a moment.

I leafed through the yellowed pages of the crystal book until I found the section on green stones. "This is it!" I exclaimed, beaming as my eyes lighted upon the exact crystal.

"Seems like a match to me," Mom agreed. "Read what it says about jade's healing properties."

"It says right here," I began, running my finger across the page as I read, "that jade supports the body's own healing ability and is a powerful cleansing stone that enhances the flow and filtration of bodily organs."

"Does this seem fitting for what you sense about Eddy's condition?"

"It's definitely a match," I said. "I'm going to put the jade in the bandana so she can wear it to the clinic." With that I dropped the crystal into the pouch and folded the edge over so it wouldn't fall out.

Mom closed the crystal book. "You're all set then," she encouraged with a smile, but I was already halfway out the door.

⌘

Jake gently slid the cat carrier across the backseat of his mom's white car and shut the door as lightly as possible, not wanting to startle Ed. But Jake had been *too* gentle, and the door hadn't quite closed.

As I raced up to the car, I heard Eddy meowing through the opening. "I have something for her," I panted, now shoulder to shoulder with Caroline, who also stood beside the car. "It's a crystal bandana. See, I've secured a special stone inside its pocket."

Jake's expression grew suspicious as he took the orange bandana and inspected it. "This is unusual, Indigo. Where did you find it?"

"I made it myself," I answered. "Just wrap it around Eddy's neck and tie it, but leave it a smidgeon loose. I've done the research, and I'm confident the crystal inside will help Eddy while she's in the hands of the doctors."

"I'd hate to freak her out even more," Jake said warily. "You should've seen me trying to get her in this carrier! I'm afraid if I open the crate door, she'll jump right out."

"I'm not afraid," I said boldly. "Caroline and I will stand guard on either side of you."

Jake hesitated a moment, then reached for the car door handle. With the bandana in his left hand, Jake opened the door, reached inside, and unlocked the carrier. Caroline and I stood tall, holding our positions on either side of Jake. Standing on my tiptoes, I peered around Jake's shoulder to see Eddy, who stood tense yet quiet on the blue plastic floor.

"Before you open it, let her see the bandana," I suggested. "That way, when you put it on her, she won't be so surprised."

"Good idea," Jake agreed. As he pressed the orange fabric onto the metal cross-bared door, Eddy leaned forward to inspect the cloth.

"She seems to like it," observed Caroline.

"Yeah, I think I'll give it a try," Jake announced as he opened the door, reached around Ed's neck, and tied the bandana in place.

Once the carrier door had clicked into the locked position again, we all breathed a sigh of relief. "Nice job, Jake," I congratulated.

As we high-fived each other, we heard Mr. Peterson's truck turn into the driveway. Catching his attention from the porch, Mrs. Peterson shouted, "Honey, park on the street, will you? I need to rush Ed to the vet."

Getting into her car, Mrs. Peterson leaned across Jake, who was now in the passenger seat with his elbow resting on the open car door window. "Thanks for your help, guys."

Jake nodded along with his mom's expression of gratitude and added, "I'll let you know what happens."

As Caroline and I followed their car out to the street, we met Mr. Peterson dressed in his navy-blue fire department uniform. Looking all serious and concerned, he asked, "So Ed's *that* sick, huh?"

"Oh yeah," I answered.

"Well good thing you two were here this morning to help handle the situation," he replied. "I was called in to investigate another recycling dumpster fire. This is the second Sunday in a row someone has set fire to the dumpster behind the Moosehead Cafe. A witness said they saw a young kid—middle-school age—walking in the alley early this morning. It was still dark outside. A few hours later, I got the call that our squad had put out the flames. I'm particularly concerned because if it's a kid lighting the fires—"

"Oh no!" Caroline cried. "You don't think it's one of our classmates, do you?"

"I'm not sure who it is," Mr. Peterson replied quickly. "Our small town is lucky. We live in such a safe place, and this run of fires is completely out of character. Maybe you can keep your eyes and ears open, just in case you come across something that could help us find the culprit?"

"Will do, Mr. Peterson," I assured him. "With school starting tomorrow, I'm guessing there'll be lots of buzz about the fire, especially if a middle-schooler is involved."

"I bet you're right," Mr. Peterson agreed. "If you hear anything, let me know. Any information that aids the department's investigation will be helpful."

"I'm happy to help!" I said with total sincerity.

CHAPTER 27

MOM TO THE RESCUE

⟳ ～⟳⟲～ ⟲

All that talk of fire parched our throats, so when we got back from Jake's house, I went straight to the fridge.

"Iced peppermint sun tea or milk?" I asked Caroline.

"Iced peppermint *sun* tea?" Caroline queried, her nose crinkling.

I reached into the fridge and raised the glass pitcher for her to see. "With two teaspoons of sugar, it's real tasty. Mom heats the water in the sun with the teabags already in it rather than on the stove top."

"*Um*, sure," Caroline said, taking a seat at the table.

Setting the pitcher on the counter, I grabbed two glasses from the cupboard. Caroline stared out the window at Silvy, who was grazing in the pasture. Marigold stayed right near my feet, tracking my every step. If there was a crumb to be scarfed, she was on the job.

"What's on your mind?" I asked as I set our glasses down on the table. When she didn't look up, I sensed great sadness. I sat down across from her.

"I don't think I can keep this bracelet," she said, reaching for her leather band and placing her hand on the clasp. "I can't handle the things you handle. I see how you are—like this morning, for instance. If that's what your bracelet does to you, then I don't think I want mine."

I gulped, realizing I had no idea what to say. I knew the events of the morning had been odd, but . . .

Just then, Mom, dressed in a yellow short-sleeved shirt and denim capris, turned the corner from the living room into the hallway. As she entered the kitchen, I couldn't help but notice a beautiful, white light shining behind her, highlighting her entire body. It reminded me of the aura that surrounded me in my room when the pyramid had transformed into my golden platter. The sight of Mom's glow rendered me speechless.

"So how'd it go over there, girls?" Mom inquired as she reached the kitchen table. "Are the Petersons off to the emergency clinic with Eddy?"

"Yes, Mrs. Monroe," Caroline answered. "They left about ten minutes ago, hopefully in time for Eddy to get the care she needs."

Glancing first at Caroline, then at me, Mom said, "Seems there are some heavy hearts in this room. Are you girls okay? You've had quite the morning."

Seemingly shocked by my mom's keen sense of awareness, Caroline furrowed her eyebrows and looked my way. Sad that she might not like her bracelet, I shrugged my shoulders and looked down at the table. Within seconds, I felt Caroline's gaze lift and land on Mom. "Mrs.

Monroe, you know that Indigo gave me this very special gift, right?"

As Caroline raised her left wrist, Mom bent forward to marvel at the treasure. "Yes," she said, pulling out the chair next to her, then reached for Caroline's hand.

Relaxing her hand in Mom's, Caroline nodded. A damp glaze appeared across her eyes as tears pooled above her lower eyelids.

"Oh no, don't cry!" I pleaded from across the table. "I never meant for the bracelet to make you sad! Here, give it to me. If that's how this one makes you feel, something's seriously wrong with it." Then, sounding panicked, I pleaded, "Mom, quick, take it off!"

Still holding Caroline's hand, Mom turned and looked at me. "It's okay, Indigo. Don't worry. Nothing's wrong with it. Why don't I fill you girls in on some missing pieces, okay?"

I pulled my chair around beside Caroline and Mom, forming a close little triangle.

Folding her hands together and resting them on the table, Mom began, "First off, Caroline, the bracelet Indigo gave you was brought forth especially for you and your family. The same is true of Indigo's bracelet, although it has been passed down from generation to generation. It's specific to her and our family. Although your bracelet looks the same as Indigo's, yours will work for *you* in the way that's best for *you.*"

Caroline and I listened closely, hanging on every word. Mr. Magoo and the finches interjected with soft peeps.

"As Indigo can attest," Mom continued, "the bracelet can help you understand what makes you special and encourage you to listen to kind and loving wisdom. What you hear and see may not be the same as what Indigo hears and sees. Does that make sense?"

"You mean I won't have visions like Indigo?" Caroline asked. "I mean, see things that aren't actually in front of me?"

"I don't think so," Mom confessed. "But what I do know is that you'll become more aware of yourself and the qualities that come naturally to *you*—if you want to, that is. This is the most important piece of the puzzle. Nothing's going to happen when you wear that bracelet unless you want it to happen. But if you agree to . . . let's see how to put it . . . *work* with it, you may be surprised by what you discover about yourself."

"That's for sure," I blurted out. "Take this morning, for instance."

Mom covered her grin with her hand. "Yes, you may be surprised or confused, and maybe even startled, like Indigo here, but there's absolutely nothing to fear."

"That's true," I interjected again. "Being me, I've seen and experienced some *pretty weird things.*"

Caroline's head tilted in wonder, her eyes fixed on mine.

Before Caroline pressed me to elaborate on just how weird, Mom interrupted, "The choice is always yours and only yours, Caroline. Do you feel better?"

"I think so," she answered, still sounding somewhat bewildered. "You're saying it's up to me if I want to *work* with the bracelet."

"That's right," Mom reassured her. "Keep in mind, too, that it will work with you in a way that makes sense to *you*. Take Indigo here." I interjected a big smile. "She's sensitive, cares for animals, and digs her toes in the water at the Looking Pond to experience the heartbeat of nature."

Caroline wrinkled her nose. "That's *so* not me."

"Exactly. So, knowing what you know now, do you think you'll have the same experiences as Indigo?"

"Well," Caroline replied thoughtfully, "if I'm not drawn to animals, then I won't suddenly start caring for them the way Indigo does. Plus, Indigo always picks up on everything—she's *that* sensitive. Even before she had the bracelet, she could tell when I was having a bad day even before I realized it."

"That ability seems to run in our family," I chuckled, winking at Mom.

"Since I'm not naturally *that* sensitive," Caroline continued, turning her attention to me, "the bracelet won't make me start seeing the *things* you see."

Mom and I both smiled encouragingly.

"What you may notice," Mom explained, "are those gifts that come naturally to you, qualities about yourself that make you uniquely Caroline. It's funny how it's often easier for us to notice what makes other people special. You could both probably make a long list of things you appreciate about each other, but it might be harder to list the things you appreciate about yourself. "

"True," Caroline agreed. Then she confessed, "I really

don't know what comes—how'd you say it?—*naturally* to me or what makes me uniquely me."

"Oh, I know, I know," I interrupted waving like a zealous kid in the back of the class.

Mom and Caroline both laughed, then Mom said, "If *you* want to know what comes naturally to you, Caroline, don't be afraid to let the bracelet help you."

Simultaneously, Caroline and I took a deep breath. She looked over at me. "I did mention that I could sure use a bracelet like yours, Indigo. And look here, you gave me one of my very own."

I nodded happily, feeling my eyes moisten. Silence took over the room, and I watched my best friend stare at the infinity clasp between her right thumb and index finger.

"I'll let you guys get on with your morning," Mom said, getting up. "Tomorrow is a big day—your first day of middle school. Caroline, as I mentioned to your mom when I briefly told her about the bracelet's special qualities, you can ask Indigo if you have any questions. And, Indigo, if you wind up having questions, ask me for help."

Caroline wrinkled her brow a little. "You spoke with my mom?"

"Yes," Mom replied with a wink. "I called her on my cell phone from your driveway the day Indigo brought you your bracelet."

I looked at Mom adoringly. The mysterious light still glowed all around her, most especially outward from her back. "I'm sure I can answer *some* of Caroline's questions," I said, "but I'm also sure you've got a lot more answers than I do, Mom."

Mom gave me one of those mysterious smiles. "Remember, girls, you're never alone. There's *always* help around you. You just have to be brave enough to ask for it."

Mom walked out of the room, and Caroline turned to me. "Your mom is sooo cool."

I wholeheartedly agreed.

CHAPTER 28

A BARN VISIT

"Are you in here, Indigo?" Jake called.

I peered out of Silvy's stall, my cleaning rake still in my hand.

Jake hesitated as he stepped through the barn entrance, obviously wary of dirtying his white tennis shoes.

This was the first time Jake had *ever* set foot in our barn. I had just finished cleaning up and planned on bringing Silvy in from the pasture for the night. My barn boots were covered in muck, and my purple riding jeans were streaked with mud and dust, so it was pointless for me to attempt to get clean in a second. Nevertheless, I wiped my orange sweatshirt sleeve across my flushed face.

Venturing deeper into the barn despite the fact he'd been concerned about his shoes, Jake propped his elbows on the windowsill of Silvy's stall. "Your mom said I'd find you in here."

"I was beginning to get worried," I said, leaning on

the rake in the middle of the stall. "I stopped by your house a couple of hours ago, before Silvy and I rode to the Looking Pond, and no one was home."

"I know," Jake sighed. "It's been a long day. Mom and I just got back from—"

"Where's Eddy?" I interrupted.

"She's staying overnight at the clinic because she had to have emergency surgery. You were right, she was this close to dying." He held his fingers in the air to indicate a tiny space between his thumb and index finger.

I hastily exited Silvy's stall, still holding the rake. "Is she going to be all right?"

"The vet says as long as she continues to heal, as she's doing now, she'll make a full recovery."

"What was wrong?"

Jake nodded. "It was a bladder stone. I don't know much about them, but the gist of it is that the stone blocked a tube connected to her bladder. That's why she was in so much pain. Mom and I got to see her before we had to leave. She was pretty sleepy from the pain meds. She'll stay at the clinic until she's made a full recovery. . . . Eddy dodged a big one, Indigo."

"Yes, she did," I agreed.

Jake looked down at the ground and swung his right tennis shoe back and forth until he had knocked so much dirt and hay out of the way that he'd created a bald spot on the stone floor. After an awkward pause, I asked nervously, "Are you ready for school tomorrow?"

"I guess. Mom and I did some last-minute school shopping in the city today." Jake stopped swinging his leg and looked down at his new shoes, which were now thoroughly dusted with barn dirt. "We needed to distract ourselves while Eddy was in surgery. Mom bought a new pair, too."

"That's cool," I agreed. "Shopping does have a way of brightening the day."

"How about you? Are you ready for school?"

"Yeah, I'm ready. I have a new backpack waiting for me by the back door. And don't worry," I laughed, swinging my left boot along the dirt floor just like Jake. "I won't come to school wearing these old things."

Jake looked down at my boot and snickered. "That must have been a tough day for you."

"You better believe it," I confessed.

Jake reached into his jeans pocket. "I almost forgot. Here's that crystal you put in Ed's water dish."

As I took Mom's red carnelian from him with my free hand, I saw a vision of a red crystal on the velvet of my golden platter. I fell silent. When the quiet continued longer than Jake was comfortable with, he called out, "Indigo? Come in, Indigo!"

Snapping to attention, I responded, "Thanks for returning the crystal. I'd better go get Silvy and bring her in for the night."

Jake took a few steps backward, clearing his throat. "Thank *you* for everything. And, well . . ." He cleared his throat again. "I want to say I'm sorry for all those times I called you names and thought you were weird."

I gulped. The moment seemed totally unreal, so I kicked the rake I was holding and felt it jolt and vibrate in my hands. I set it against the wall. *Yes, this is really happening.*

"By the way," Jake added, "the staff said they would put the bandana on Eddy after the surgery. I told them that, as long as it wasn't causing her any trouble, it wasn't to come off her the whole time she stayed in the clinic."

I had known the crystal would help Eddy, but I was surprised that Jake felt so strongly about it, too. My heart grew real big, and out of nowhere, I unthinkingly threw my arms around him.

He sort of patted my back awkwardly and then stepped away, seeming embarrassed by the impromptu hug. When he turned to leave the barn, a sense of impending doom welled up in my stomach, like a stick of dynamite seconds away from exploding. Then, right before he walked away, he turned back and held out his hand for a handshake.

As we shook, he said, "I don't know what makes you do and say the things you do, but I trust you . . . and you can trust me to keep your secrets . . . Courageous Lioness."

We dropped our hands back to our sides, and then Jake turned to leave.

Things would be different between us in middle school.

A few moments later, after bringing Silvy into the barn for the night, I spied Mom in the living room as I rushed into the house. She'd snuggled up on the couch in an afghan knitted by my grandmother, holding a book in her hand. She called out for me as I passed.

"I'll be right there!" I shouted, rushing up the stairs to my room with Marigold at my heels.

Sure enough, as I expected we would, Marigold and I discovered a red carnelian resting on the platter under my bed. "Oh, wow," I gasped, picking up the stone and holding it out to her. "I have one of my very own now! Look at it, Marigold. Isn't it beautiful?"

Marigold sniffed the stone, then ran to my beaded door.

"I know," I agreed. "Let's show Mom."

We hurried back downstairs. Marigold lay down at Mom's feet while I sat on the cushioned edge of the couch. Setting her cup of raspberry tea on the windowsill, Mom placed her hand on my shoulder as she inquired, "What did Jake have to say?"

Overwhelmed by my new and confusing feelings for Jake, I simply sighed. "Ugh!"

CHAPTER 29

A "BRIGHT" FIRST DAY

When I stepped into the unfamiliar hallways of Avondale Middle School on Monday morning, I was totally unprepared for what I saw. Every last kid glowed like a brightly lit Christmas tree, mostly white but different colors and intensities, too. Squinting to shut out some of the light, I noticed familiar faces among the crowd in addition to new ones. I wasn't sure why this hadn't happened on the bus ride in, but I guessed it was because I was so deep in thought about the year ahead that I hadn't been paying attention.

I noticed with some alarm that Simone and Tess had made each other's acquaintance. It figured. Both girls had a hazy greenish-red glow that streaked away when they darted past. When Caroline bounded up to me, she had a bluish-white glow, and Jake, who flung his bangs toward me in acknowledgment, was beaming a kaleidoscope of colors all around him. Come to think of it, he did have quite the multicolored kind of personality.

The part of me that had experienced my own aura,

Mom's aura, and Eddy's aura wasn't surprised, but a bigger part of me felt alarmed. At home I could handle *seeing* things, but school was another story.

As I walked to my first class, the glare was so strong that I could hardly make out the room number. Once I found the class, I had a hard time finding my way to an empty desk. Finally taking a seat, I blinked my eyes into focus enough to see the teacher who stood at the front of the classroom. Unfortunately, she was glowing, too.

It wasn't long before I developed a splitting headache. In the lunchroom, I buried my head halfway inside my padded lunchbox. Caroline, who sat to my right glowing with such intensity, didn't know what to do with me. I briefly explained what was happening, but her first concern was, "This isn't going to happen to me, right?"

When I assured her that it wouldn't, she took a satisfied bite of her turkey sandwich. My lunch was spread out before me, but I didn't feel hungry. In fact, I sort of felt sick to my stomach.

I looked away and my eyes fell on the boy to my left. He didn't have any lunch and kept staring at my uneaten sandwich. When he noticed me looking at him, he said a little shakily, "Are you going to eat that?"

I shoved the sandwich his way. "Go for it," I said. Then I took a deep breath and dropped my head back into my lunchbox.

Right after lunch came wood shop class. I'd never worked with wood before. On a normal day, I'd be pretty excited to craft something of my very own, but this was turning out to be *no* normal day.

After outlining the class objectives, the teacher grouped us in pairs. My partner turned out to be the kid with my sandwich in his stomach—Drew. When we pulled our stools up to our table, I noticed a thin outline of white light around his body and a red glow flashing around his heart. I tried not to stare, but honestly, looking at him was a bit of a relief since he didn't light up the room like a fluorescent bulb. However, my relief was short-lived. I felt my eyes filling with tears of sadness.

When I checked inside myself, I wasn't aware of any particular sadness of my own. Sure, I was annoyed, frustrated, and in pain from my headache, but I wasn't sad. On the other hand, sitting next to Drew felt depressing. He didn't talk unless the teacher called on him, and his limited eye contact with me told me he wasn't available for conversation.

Twenty minutes into class, tears began to roll down my cheeks. Using my sleeve as a Kleenex, I brought my hair around the sides of my face to conceal my emotions and tried to think of funny jokes. All I came up with was the cheesy one Mom told at the karaoke contest. I also thought of Noel and how happy she'd been when Caroline and I performed our song at the contest. And then, of course, Sienna Glass, who I'd had so much silly fun with when I was little. But nothing, I mean NOTHING, I came up with lifted my spirits.

At that point, I saw a vision of the three giant-sized gray stones again, standing tall in a triangular formation. I'd seen them the day before at Jake's house. To distract myself from the sad feeling, I began counting the gray stones in my head, over and over, 1-2-3-1-2-3 . . . The more I counted, the better I felt. So I kept counting.

I'm not sure what happened in wood shop class after that, and I'm quite certain Drew got the feeling that now I was the one who wasn't available for conversation. Fortunately, the time passed quickly, and when the bell rang, I brought my full attention back into the room.

While I gathered my books off the table, the shop teacher walked over and rested his hand on my shoulder. When I jumped, he backed away, surprised. "Indigo Monroe, right?" he inquired.

"Yes, that's me. I'm sorry. I'm feeling a bit dazed."

"I can see that," he replied with a frown. "You seem to be in another world. Are you okay?"

"I have a bad headache, sir," I explained, watching his white aura flicker.

"Well," he insisted, "let me walk you down to the nurse. You might not know where she hides out yet." He smiled and offered to carry my books.

"Lead the way," I agreed. "But if you don't mind, I'll hold on to these." Hugging my texts and binder to my chest, I followed him to the nurse's station.

The nurse, who greeted me, seemed as concerned as my teacher. Looking into her big blue eyes, I assured her, "I'll be fine. It's just been one of those days—you know, the first day at a new school and all."

"I understand," she commiserated. "I remember my first day at middle school, too." She looked young enough for me to guess that it wasn't so long ago. "Are you feeling well enough to return to class?"

Glancing up at the clock, I realized that my last class of the day, Social Studies, was about to start. Checking in on my emotions, I found, to my surprise, that I felt fine. Other than my headache, I didn't feel sad, and all the counting had dried my tears. I nodded.

She flashed a little light in my eyes to check my pupils, as if I needed any more light coming my way. What she saw seemed to convince her it was safe to send me to class. I'd be a few minutes late, so she sent me with a note.

Since the halls were empty, navigating my way to my last class wasn't a problem. Even with all that was going on, I was aware that my schedule was pretty cool and so were my teachers. Caroline and I had lunch and a few morning classes together and Jake was in my gym class, which was right before lunch. So far, Tess and Simone weren't in any of my classes. What a relief! Truly, my only issue was all the dazzling visual input.

I handed my teacher the note when I entered class. Drew wandered in seconds after me, but he didn't have a note. His head was down and his books were loosely propped against his hip.

Oh, please don't sit next to me, I quietly begged. But the seat next to me happened to be the only one open.

Pretty soon, I found myself drawn to the red aura that beamed from the area around his heart. I became so mesmerized that my eyes tracked right to Drew's chest. Wherever the teacher was in the room, I didn't see her, and I didn't hear her. All I heard was the whisper inside myself saying, *"You can help."*

When I heard the whisper, I reached for my bracelet. Within seconds, I noticed deep sadness seep through me just like it had in shop class. Then the vision of the gray stones appeared in my mind's eye, and I again started counting silently . . . *one, two, three.*

Counting the stones broke my "Drew trance" and brought my attention to the front of the class, where the teacher was discussing the plan for the first semester. I kept counting. Though I couldn't concentrate on her words, I did notice something peculiar. Like many of the other people, she was surrounded by a pretty white light, but she also had a second light—a unique, oval yellow orb that beamed from her belly. Instantly, I knew it was a baby even though she was skinny and wasn't showing any sign of a bump.

As my shop teacher had done, she checked on me after class. Apparently I hadn't just been mouthing *one, two, three;* I had also been tapping the numbers out with my shoe.

"It's been a long day, hasn't it?" she stated more than questioned. "I always feel overwhelmed on the first day of school. Imagine trying to remember all these students' names—and standing up there all day." She reached behind to rub her lower back.

When she smiled, I instantly felt relaxed.

"My mom's a nurse. I've heard that women who are expecting a baby sometimes have back pain, so it's probably even more difficult for you to stand up there, being pregnant and all."

The words had come out so naturally, and I hadn't

thought about what I was saying before I said it. When her face whitened and she staggered back into her chair, I realized that maybe she didn't know. I gulped, afraid I'd said too much.

At that moment the second bell rang: This meant I had less than five minutes to get to my bus. Nevertheless, I inquired, "Are you all right?"

"I'm fine," she quickly assured me, but I wasn't convinced. "Run along now. You don't want to miss your ride home." She placed her hand on her stomach.

With no time left to grab my stuff from my locker, I raced out to the line of buses. The first bus began moving forward as I reached the curb. Scanning the black numbers above the doors of the buses behind it, my eyes locked on to bus number 33, the fourth in line. Dashing over to it, I found the door already closed, so I knocked. To my relief, the driver swung it open.

"Thank you," I said breathlessly as I grabbed hold of the metal handrail and leapt aboard.

"No problem," he replied. "But the sooner you arrive, the better. We've got a full ride this year."

He wasn't kidding. When I looked around, there was only one place left for me to sit. Drew removed his backpack from the seat and made way for me. But before I took my place, I started counting again. I couldn't bear feeling another ounce of sadness. School was supposed to be fun.

With all the bright silhouettes and rowdy chatter around me, the atmosphere in the bus was electric. The pain pulsed in my head. To drown out the chaos, I wrapped my arms around my ears and leaned forward toward the back of the seat in front of me, still counting, tapping my foot to the numbers.

When the bus squeaked to its first stop, I looked up to see that we were parked one block west of downtown and the Moosehead Cafe. Standing up without saying a word, Drew waited for me to turn my knees outward, clearing a path for his exit. "Oops, sorry," I said, realizing I was in his way.

"It's okay," he mumbled.

A bunch of kids got off the bus at Drew's stop.

When the bus pulled away, the kids remaining inside sat up in their seats like meerkats. *This is where the dumpster fires have been happening,* I noted to myself.

The bus buzzed with accusations toward the kids who'd just gotten off. "Look, her house is right next to the alley where the fire was!" someone shouted. Another called out, "I bet that kid did it! He's the one who got in trouble last year for beaning kids with pinecones."

As the bus approached the charred dumpster, several kids rushed over to my side to see the crime scene. Throwing my arms over my head, I tucked myself close into the metal wall. Seeing my reaction, Jake hauled a thousand-pound kid off my back and sat down next to me.

"Are you okay?" he asked. "This is crazy. Everyone thinks they know who the arsonist is."

"It's a madhouse," I agreed.

"So, how'd your first day go?"

"Horrible," I replied flatly. Wincing, I held my hand up to the right side of my head.

"What's wrong?"

"I have a splitting headache," I answered. "How about you—did you have fun?"

"It was pretty cool. Gym's my favorite class, and my locker is right next to the vending machines. Sorry about your headache."

At that moment, the most awkward image came into my mind: Jake and I were holding hands at the Looking Pond.

"What's with the goofy smile?" he asked, bringing me back to earth. "Are you *seeing* something again?"

I had no energy to stop the flow of my thoughts into words, and I responded, "Yeah, we—you and me—were holding hands at the Looking Pond."

Instantly, I gulped. Jake gulped, too. He looked at me, then looked away. Then, looking at me again, he scowled. "That's not cool. Are you a mind reader, too?"

Jake smacked the back of the green vinyl seat and got up in a huff.

If I'd read his mind, like he'd said, it meant he'd been thinking about holding my hand. I let that sink in for a moment. Then, realizing that he was now mad at me and the likelihood he'd ever want to hold my hand now was slim, I dropped my head against the seat in front of me and started counting.

Between counts, I heard the whisper: *"Look through the stones and step into the center."*

Shh, I commanded myself. *One, two, three . . .*

CHAPTER 30

ONE, TWO, THREE

When the bus coasted down the hill to our stop, I darted to the front. When the door opened, I jumped off and raced home, never once looking back.

Welcoming me at the back door, Mom asked, "How was your first day of sixth grade?"

Still counting, I didn't answer and headed straight to my room, where I lay belly down on my bed and buried my head under my pillow. A moment later, Marigold broke through my beaded door, with Mom on her heels. "What's going on, honey? Was it that bad?"

As Mom seated herself on my bed and began stroking my back in an attempt to comfort me, I answered "yes," whereupon she rubbed my neck and shoulders until I finally flipped over, only to draw in a deep breath and gasp, "I need to use the bathroom."

"Okay, honey, I'll be right here when you get back."

She must have heard me counting as I walked to and from the bathroom, because she asked, "Why all the counting?"

Sitting down next to her, I explained, "It keeps the

visions and sadness at bay." Mom kept quiet, so a few moments later, I asked, "Can you see the lights—the auras—around people, too?"

"Yes," she replied softly. "Remember, I told you that I could see yours? Are you seeing someone's aura?"

"Not someone—hundreds of someones!" I replied with agitation. "First, I saw my own, which was pretty cool. Then I saw one around you and then around Eddy yesterday. I could totally handle that. But today was *crazy.* An entire school of walking lightbulbs! And then, every time I sat next to this kid named Drew, I felt horribly sad. I even started crying in wood shop class."

"Oh, Indigo," Mom said sympathetically, "it sounds like you've had quite a day. But you know what? Now that you can see auras, you're ready to see what lies beyond. This supercharged sensitivity runs in the family. If you listen carefully and choose wisely and stay aware, I promise you'll learn to live with it—*and* appreciate it."

I looked at her doubtfully.

Mom raised her eyebrows and wrapped her arm around my shoulders. "You've become aware of your natural gifts as well as your surroundings. Combine all of this with your intuitive senses, and voila! You're awake! And when you're awake, you may find you'll be called to help others—like you did with Eddy."

Although Mom was trying to reassure me, I found it difficult to focus on what she was saying with my throbbing head and all the counting. Noticing how distracted I was, she ended with "If you need my help, all you have to do is ask."

"Okay," I replied wearily.

When the phone rang, Mom left my room to answer it. It was Dad calling to see how my first day went. I felt bad for not taking the phone when she called for me, but I was too beat and my head hurt too much to move.

"I'll call him later, I'm going to take a nap!" I yelled. My head throbbed even more from the volume of my voice.

Marigold jumped onto my bed and curled up at my feet. I counted 1-2-3 with each breath she took until I fell asleep.

⌒

The next morning at the bus stop, Jake didn't even say hello, which made for an awkward situation. Still, I needed to know how Eddy was doing and gathered up the nerve to ask.

His answer was short: "She's doing okay. She'll be at the clinic for a few more days at least." He didn't even look at me when he spoke.

If this was what "being awake" felt like—I mean knowing and seeing things that were going to get me into trouble—I didn't want any part of it. So that was that. I decided to commit myself to counting full time.

At lunch, Drew sat at the table with Caroline and me. The counting kept me from feeling the deep sadness and seeing the red light around his heart, but it didn't stop me from noticing he didn't have lunch again. So, before striking up a conversation with Caroline, I handed him my sandwich: turkey on wheat with lettuce and mayo. It was hard enough trying to talk and count—I didn't think I'd be able to eat, too.

"Thanks," he said bashfully.

"No problem," I replied.

When Caroline asked about Eddy and Jake, I stopped counting, but kept the numbers going by tapping on the table with my index finger. As I whispered to her about the vision I'd had of Jake and me holding hands, she gasped, evidently as shocked as Jake had been.

"See?" I exclaimed. "That's why I count! It's the only thing that works!"

Caroline watched my finger drumming up and down on the tabletop. "That keeps you from seeing visions?" she asked, her head bobbing to the beat.

I nodded.

"Your visions freak me out. I'm glad they're not my thing. But if anyone can learn to deal with them, it's you. I bet your mom could tell you how to turn them off or something. She really made me feel better about wearing the bracelet—and speaking of which . . ."

She held out her left hand. Dangling from the leather was a green ribbon tied in a knot around the band.

My eyes popped open. Caroline had her first symbol! I was beyond excited for her and actually stopped counting. "Do you want to tell me about it?" I asked.

She nodded eagerly. "It's a piece of string from the bunch of balloons my parents gave Noel and me yesterday for our first day of school," she explained. "Last night, I was doing my homework—"

I gasped. "Wait. We had homework?"

"Well, I did, in science. My teacher said she likes digging in right away."

So far I'd made it through the first part of the day without having missed any homework assignments. I didn't recall any homework being assigned in Social Studies, so I was probably in the clear. But if I didn't do something soon—aka ask Mom for help—I'd surely flunk out of sixth grade before it was even over.

"Anyway," Caroline continued, "sometimes, when I'm doing homework, I pretend I'm a teacher giving a lesson on the subject. I was reading about the scientific method when Noel wandered into my room, so I invited her to be one of my students. To make it fun, I grabbed the bunch of balloons and assigned one of the terms to each balloon. Like, for example, the orange balloon stood for *hypothesis*. When I defined the term, I handed Noel the orange balloon. By the time I was done, Noel was holding all the balloons. She had a big smile on her face, and I had organized and memorized the terms by color."

"Then what happened?"

"You know the drill," she replied. "I heard a whisper. At first I freaked out, but then I listened closely and realized it sounded just like me."

It had taken me a really long time to realize it was my own inner voice, and I was impressed that Caroline had figured it out so quickly. "You're so smart. That's one of the things I admire about you."

Caroline blushed and turned her head away to hide her embarrassment. "This whisper drew my attention to the fact I *am* really good at explaining things, if I must say so myself." A smile crossed her face, and she covered her mouth with her sandwich. "Or teaching things," she mumbled through the bread.

"You're the best at that," I agreed. "You can untangle any situation and straighten it out with just the right words."

After taking a swig of her water, she replied, "I never really realized it was a gift because it comes so easily to me, and it's fun. Anyway, the whisper guided me to cut a piece of ribbon from a balloon and tie it to my bracelet so that I could see it every day to remind me of the gift I have for teaching."

"Well, you've got it. Keep up the good work. And remember, if you need help, you just have to ask." I winked, then quickly returned to counting.

"Got it. Thanks!" she said and then gobbled up the rest of her sandwich.

The rest of the day continued with me in my counting daze. Fortunately, I had only two classes left, and I managed not to alarm my teachers the way I did the day before.

The bus ride home felt like déjà vu with everyone chattering on and on about the arsonist, convinced it had to be someone who got off at the stop one block west of Moosehead Cafe. Not about to accuse anyone when I didn't know who was guilty, I kept my head down on the seat in front of me and counted my way home.

As I ran from Jake and our bus stop, Dad pulled up beside me in his sports car. Rolling down the window, he greeted me enthusiastically, "Hey, stranger!"

"You scared me!" I gasped. "What are you doing here?"

"I'm having dinner with you and your mother tonight. Hop in. I'll drive you the rest of the way home."

Grabbing the sack of hot food from the floor of the passenger side, he placed it on the backseat. "I brought us take out from the Moosehead Café. Fried chicken and mashed potatoes!"

I wasn't very far from home, but I hopped in Dad's car anyway. Since the divorce, Dad had only eaten dinner at our house twice. This time, Mom had invited him to hear about my first two days of middle school. I stopped counting long enough to notice that he, too, glowed the way everyone else did. The golden light was real calming, and I wanted to admire it, but the numbers started rolling in my head again. It was when I counted through my chores before dinner that I started to worry I had become possessed by a bad habit.

I joined my parents at the kitchen table when it was time to eat, and normally I would have been so happy to tell them all about my day, but I sat there in silence.

"So I called Lucy's mom last night," Dad said, stabbing his fork into his mashed potatoes. "She said Lucy and Roots are doing great! He even sleeps in her bed with her. Isn't that sweet?"

"Oh, I know," I replied shortly. "We made sleepover plans for a few weeks from now." I went back to counting.

Dad put down his fork. "That will give you something to look forward to. So how's school?" he inquired, biting into a fried chicken leg.

I switched from saying the numbers in my head to tapping my index finger on the table, so I could reply. "School is okay."

Mom and Dad became focused on my dancing finger.

"Do you like your teachers?" Dad asked gently. "Your mom says you haven't mentioned anything about them."

Mom shifted in her chair.

I kept my answer short. "Yep, they're nice."

Mom and Dad exchanged a concerned glance; they were getting the idea that I didn't really feel like talking.

I picked at the fried chicken and counted, while they ate in uncomfortable silence. I could actually hear them swallowing their food, which interrupted my 1-2-3 flow. Finally, it became too much for me to keep sitting there. "Thanks for dinner," I said, "but I'm tired. Don't forget fishing, on Sunday, Dad. Doughnuts, Looking Pond. Time for bed," I mumbled.

I know they responded, but I didn't hear their words. I just dropped my plate into the sink with a harmless crash, then shuffled off to my room. Marigold didn't even follow me.

❧

When I awoke the next morning, Marigold was curled up on the floor by my bed, snoring. On my nightstand were three stacked chocolate chip cookies with a note tented on top: *Indigo, you are not alone. We are always here for you. If you need help, just ask. Love, Mom and Dad.*

Getting out of bed, I counted one, two, three on my way to the bathroom. I patted down my flyaway curls and brushed my teeth, all the while counting in threes. In fact, my entire morning routine adhered to the rhythm of one, two, three. When it was time for breakfast, I counted to the stairway, where I heard Mom say into the phone in a low voice, "It's time, Charlotte. We worked through the details last night. Everything is taken care of."

A moment later, Mom peeked out of her room. "Good morning, honey. Why don't you feed Silvy? I'll make you breakfast in just a second."

When I returned from the barn, Mom was standing at the stove flipping French toast with one hand and sipping a cup of coffee with the other. 1-2-3, I sat at the table.

Mom took a seat across from me. "Is all this counting getting in the way of concentrating at school?"

1-2-3. "Don't think so," I replied.

"Can you hear the whisper?" she asked.

Now that was an interesting question. 1-2-3. "I don't think so," I replied, and it suddenly occurred to me that maybe the counting not only canceled out the visions and lights but could also be drowning out my inner voice.

"I packed your lunch," Mom informed me.

1-2-3. "Need one more." 1-2-3. "Drew is hungry."

"What?" Mom asked, sounding perplexed.

1-2-3. "I can't explain."

Mom didn't push for more, and I appreciated that. She just quickly slapped together a second sandwich and wrapped it in foil.

1-2-3. "Thank you, Mom." 1-2-3. "See you later."

CHAPTER 31

HELP!

At school, I felt like I was teetering on the edge of a total breakdown. I just couldn't stop counting, even when I tried real hard not to. At lunchtime, I gave Drew the sandwich Mom had prepared for him and quickly ate my own in bites of three. Then, because Caroline wanted to study, we finished out our lunch period in the library. While I flipped through the pages of a book in sets of three, Caroline sat contently beside me, really reading.

Halfway through wood shop class, my teacher approached my worktable, where I sat beside Drew, and asked me to follow him out to the hall. I hopped up and followed him, leaving behind the pieces of wood I hadn't even started to assemble.

"Indigo," he said once we were outside the classroom, "I can see that you're still very distracted. If you're not focusing on safety first, you could smash, or worse yet saw off, one of your fingers. I'm going to have to escort you down to the office and call your mom. Just to be clear, I'm not mad. But I am really concerned about you."

Still counting in my head, I looked up at him and my

tears began to flow. Placing his hand on my shoulder, he guided me down the hallway.

We were about to turn into the office when Jake walked past and caught a glimpse of my watery eyes. He stopped in his tracks and watched as I entered the nurse's station.

Fifteen minutes later, Mom arrived. "Oh, honey," she whispered, kneeling in front of my chair.

"Please help me!" I cried.

"We're here for you, honey, all of us," she assured me, her voice cracking. "Let's go home and figure this out, okay?"

1-2-3. "Lunch box and backpack." 1-2-3. "In my locker." 1-2-3. "Need to get."

"Forget those things," Mom soothed. "We've got more important things to take care of than lunch boxes and backpacks."

Wrapping her arm around my shoulder, she walked me out of school toward the parent drop-off circle. I blinked three times to make sure my eyes weren't playing tricks on me. Leaning against my mom's car was none other than my aunt Charlotte. When she saw me, she held out her arms.

"Aunt Charlotte, hello!" I shouted, running into her embrace.

I rarely saw my mom's younger sister because she lived in Los Angeles, California, a plane ride away. She wasn't married and didn't have kids. I always thought her job as a police officer was the coolest. I hadn't seen Aunt Charlotte in over a year.

"Why are you—" I began to ask, wiping my drippy nose with my shirtsleeve. I couldn't add a fourth word because that would break my count.

"I'm here for you. You did ask for help, right?"

My mouth dropped open. "Yes . . . I . . . did. Just . . . back . . . there," I confessed, pointing in the direction of the school entrance.

⌒⌒

When we reached home, Mom put the teakettle on the stove and we took a seat on the couch in the living room. Aunt Charlotte's suitcase was open on the floor near the bookshelf. On the wooden coffee table by the couch were two golden platters with red velvet bundles lying on top of them. Beside the platters stood a tall white candle, secured in an antique silver candlestick.

When the kettle began to boil, Mom excused herself from the room. I watched her ponytail sway back and forth as she exited, then turned my gaze to Aunt Charlotte. Her red hair fell just below her shoulders, and her long-sleeved, turquoise shirt bore an image of a flying bird.

"I don't expect you to talk or tell me anything, okay?" Aunt Charlotte began. I lifted my eyes off the beautiful bird and gave her my full attention. "I know you're overwhelmed, and that's why your Mom and I are here to support you and fill in the missing pieces. Is that all right with you?"

I nodded three times, which sufficed for a "yes."

Mom entered the room with three cups of cinnamon tea, offering Aunt Charlotte and me a cup each before seating herself beside me. Reaching for the matchbox on the table, she lit the candle and then sat back with her legs pulled up into a comfortable cross. When Aunt Charlotte leaned back into the couch and sat the same way, I followed suit.

The candlelit room smelled like sweet spice. Mom and Aunt Charlotte both became real calm, almost mysterious. Then Mom began, "I know you're busy counting. It's hard to speak and count at the same time. Feel free to nod along or communicate with us in whatever way is most comfortable for you, okay?"

I nodded thrice.

"First, Aunt Charlotte and I are going to share a few personal experiences with you. Then we're going to sit quietly together for a while."

I again nodded thrice.

"You know that I once wore the bracelet you are wearing on your wrist. But did you know Aunt Charlotte once wore it, too?"

I shook my head back and forth three times, then quickly changed my answer with three vertical head bobs. *It kinda makes sense, I guess,* I thought.

"Well, she did," Mom said. "This bracelet has been worn by everyone on my mom's side of the family for hundreds of years. So because we've all worn this family bracelet, we've all had similar experiences. Since we are family, we tend to experience this bracelet in the same way. Now when I say that, I don't mean we are exactly alike, have the same gifts, and love the same things. Each of us is unique in our own special way. But just as we have similar physical features, so that, for better or worse, us ladies kind of look alike"—Aunt Charlotte chuckled and gave three nods—"we all had visions and saw light around people. Grandma experienced the same, and so did Great-grandma. I see visions and lights, too."

"As do I," Aunt Charlotte interjected with a smile.

Nodding three times, I felt tears well up in my eyes.

"When we wore the bracelet," Mom continued, "we became aware of ourselves, our gifts, and our surroundings. Awake to this way of being, our intuition increased and our ultra-keen senses saw visions and auras. At that point, it felt like we were called to action to help other people, which is why our visions were often unfamiliar and didn't relate to our lives specifically. Just like you, your aunt and I were overwhelmed."

"Called to action?" I sniffled.

"Oh, yes," Mom said, reaching over and smearing a tear off my cheek. "See, once you know and value your gifts, like for example the way you naturally love and care for animals, then use discernment in your surroundings while caring for animals, you are what Grandma used to call 'awake,' which means you're ready to serve others with your kind of care. Does that make sense?"

My head stood still. *Is there a nod for "kind of, not really"?*

Aunt Charlotte shifted her teacup into her other hand, then touched my leg with her warm fingers. "We don't expect you to totally understand. Just keep listening. As you know, things always have a way of working out."

I placed my hand over my aunt's as if to soak in her reassurance.

"We've all seen the three giant standing stones, right?" said Mom, nodding her head as she spoke. "And we all counted them right away when we saw them, right?"

Mom nodded thrice, followed by Charlotte, and lastly me.

Mom and Aunt Charlotte put their teacups down on the old wooden table and opened their red velvet bundles on their platters. Both reached into their stash, each drawing out three light gray stones. "Do you have these on *your* golden platter?" Mom asked.

Right then, I had a vision, which caused me to stop counting, though I didn't realize it at the time. Mesmerized by the beautiful collection in front of me, my mind's eye saw three gray stones on the platter under my bed. Placing my teacup on the table, I ran upstairs. Not missing a beat, Marigold followed right behind. Together, we discovered three gray river stones next to the red carnelian on the velvet of my golden platter.

"*Wise choice asking for help,*" said my inner voice.

Scooping up the stones, I ran downstairs and jumped back onto the couch between Mom and Aunt Charlotte. "Yes, here they are!" I announced, revealing three stones in my hand.

"Brilliant," Mom said, closing her fingers around her own precious stones. "Now, let's all hold our stones in our hand for a moment."

As we held our stones, Mom and Aunt Charlotte closed their eyes, and I joined them. I felt a little strange, while at the same time it felt natural to me.

"How do you feel?" my aunt inquired.

I listened for numbers in my head, but there was only silence. Opening one eye, I checked to see that the hand that wasn't holding the stones wasn't tapping out one, two, three. It wasn't. My body felt relaxed. In fact, I felt as calm as Mom and Aunt Charlotte looked.

"I feel a lot better, and I'm not counting," I announced, glad I could speak more than three words.

"That's wonderful. But as you've experienced, there's always more. When we hold the stones, we feel better, but can we hold the stones all the time, everywhere we go?"

Well, sure, I thought to myself, *it's a heck of a lot easier than counting all day.* Then, with a hint of gloom, I admitted, "I guess not."

"Right on," said Aunt Charlotte. "I'd be in a dangerous situation if I had to hold these stones while trying to put handcuffs on a criminal. And imagine your mom trying to lift a patient in their hospital bed with only one hand."

Mom giggled, and so did I.

"Now that you have your three stones," Mom explained, "you can *feel into* them, like we're doing now. If you make that choice, they'll show you the way to help and protection. Remember, it's always all up to you. You want to be certain that whatever you do is the wisest choice for *you*. If you're unsure for any reason, just place the stones back on your platter. Tools often rest in a secure place until we're ready to use them."

I rolled the stones around in my hands. I felt better than I had in days.

"I will be here until Friday night to help you out, along with your mom—that's two days," Aunt Charlotte added. "I'd stay longer, but the department is short staffed this weekend."

"I'm *really* glad you came," I said, not hinting at the disappointment I felt that she'd be leaving so soon.

With that, Mom and Aunt Charlotte led the way into silence, which was occasionally interrupted by slurps of tea. The candlelight flickered, highlighting our mysterious yet calm presence. At one point, I gazed into Aunt Charlotte's velvet bundle, captivated by her collection of gold and silver coins, together with a small cluster of crystals. I hadn't noticed any coins in Mom's bundle. I guessed that was because, although we were family, we were unique in our own ways.

Soon my eyelids began to droop, and I could feel my body sinking deeper into the cushions. "I'm sleepy," I confessed. "I think I'll lie down for a bit before dinner."

"We'll be right here," Mom and Aunt Charlotte replied in near unison.

Sometimes moms and aunts were right where you needed them to be.

CHAPTER 32

STONE TEMPLE

Before surrendering to sleep, I checked in with myself about the stones. No questions came to me, and I had no fear. I knew the stones were powerful because my counting had stopped, and I wanted to learn everything I could about them. But my excitement was no contest for my drowsiness, and within minutes I dozed off, my three gray stones clenched in my hand.

Forty-five minutes later, I awoke. Before my eyes were scenes from a most unusual dream. As I retraced the sleep story from beginning to end, I watched the code to a family secret mysteriously unveil itself.

My dream showed me a place in the woods behind the Looking Pond. If we were willing to follow a hidden path, Aunt Charlotte, Mom, and I would find a sacred temple—a place of protection. I jumped out of bed and leapt over Marigold curled up on the floor. "Come on, girl, we've got some investigating to do."

Marigold and I found Mom and Aunt Charlotte in the kitchen, chatting and cracking peanut shells.

"I had the craziest dream, somewhere behind the Looking Pond is a stone—"

"—temple," chorused Mom and Aunt Charlotte.

"I want to go," I declared. "Want to come, too? I could use your help finding the trail."

"We'd love to," Mom and Aunt Charlotte agreed, tossing peanut shells high in the air as if they were celebrating a momentous occasion.

Marigold, at her usual place at my side, wagged her tail, whacking the leg of our kitchen table in fast rhythm. "Yes, Marigold," I assured her, "you can come, too."

Soon we were on our way down Tree Canopy Trail. Filtering through the branches, the sun's rays wrapped us in warmth. I rode on Silvy's back, wearing my lucky purple jeans and orange sweatshirt. Mom pedaled beside me on her green bike with the white wicker basket, while Aunt Charlotte scooted alongside her, knees rotating in frog position on my old lavender bike with the flowery banana seat. Marigold was in heaven, running ahead of us, then circling back and around Silvy.

A gentle breeze blew through the canopy tunnel, and my long curls danced behind me to the rhythm of Silvy's steps. All three of us had placed our gray stones deep in the pockets of our jeans to keep them safe. We just knew we were supposed to bring them.

When we arrived at the weeping willow tree next to the Sitting Log, we dismounted. Rather than tether Silvy to the tree, I let him graze, knowing he wouldn't wander off. Then, instead of facing the Looking Pond as I usually did, I directed my eyes to the forest that lay behind us. I pointed. "I think it's that way," I announced. "Follow me," I said more quietly, sensing the place we were headed was indeed secret.

Where the grassy field met a line of trees, I looked down and saw a dirt trail. *Hmmm, I never noticed this before.* "This way!" I called to Mom and Aunt Charlotte.

Since Marigold was in uncharted territory, she followed behind, sniffing our every step. I led the pack, even though I was new to this part of the forest. After a couple of minutes, we came to a fork in the trail. Stopping, I placed my index finger on my lips and felt inside me for the right path to choose. "Left!" I said assuredly, and Mom and Aunt Charlotte nodded in agreement.

Veering left, we walked for a few more minutes until we came to a grassy clearing. There in the center stood three giant gray stones in a triangular formation—just like the ones I'd seen in my vision. I came to a halt and stared at the mammoth rocks. They were four times my mom's height and easily five times as wide. My heart thumped. When I gasped, I realized I'd finally arrived, not just to the place I saw in my dreams, but to a place that felt like home.

"This is it!" I cried.

"Stone Temple!" we all hollered in unison.

I approached one of the humongous stones, and I placed my hands on the smooth, cracked surface and whispered, "Hello."

I felt like I was being hugged. With my hands still on the stone, I leaned into it and rested my forehead on the cold surface. As my curls fell forward off my shoulder, I turned my head, delicately pressing my right ear against the stone. Within seconds, I heard, "Welcome. You are safe. Walk inside and stand among us, dear one."

I opened my arms and embraced the stone. Mom and Aunt Charlotte moved in close. The world around me vanished. The world inside me came to life.

The stones in my pocket vibrated. Glancing to my right, I saw Mom and Aunt Charlotte reach into their pockets, so I did the same.

Hand in hand, Mom and I walked to the center of the triangle. Aunt Charlotte followed, while Marigold stood guard outside the triangle of stones.

"They're like gentle giants," I said in wonder, swiping the small stones out of my pocket and clenching them tightly in my hand.

"If you choose, you can call on Stone Temple to protect you when your senses feel overwhelmed," Mom explained.

"I can't always run out here every time that happens," I protested.

"That's why we're here with you now," Aunt Charlotte chimed in. "Because you asked for our help, we can assist you in integrating the power of these stones into your awareness. That way, you don't have to count, you don't have to be here, and you don't even have to hold the three stones you were gifted."

I sighed with relief. "So what do we do next?"

"Look at the stone nearest you," Mom answered. "What do you see?"

I moved to face the stones, and Mom and Aunt Charlotte moved to face the other two stones.

I peered at the gray rock and followed the cracks until I saw three holes in a triangular formation indented there. I traced out the triangle and dipped my finger into each hole in turn. Suddenly, I remembered how I'd opened the pyramid door. I reached with my right hand for one of the stones.

"Wait," Mom instructed. "All at the same time. On the count of three, place one stone in the bottom right corner of the triangle, and we'll do the same here with our small stones. One . . . two . . . three!"

As we each fed the large stones one of our gifts, the right bottom hole drew in our offering and sealed it in place.

"Now, take your second stone and place it in the left bottom point," Mom instructed.

Aunt Charlotte counted, "One . . . two . . . three."

The hole drew in our offerings and sealed them in position.

Then it was my turn to count. Feeling confident now, I said, "One . . . two . . . three."

As we inserted our last offerings, the wind picked up, swirling around our feet and rising up through the center of the stones. Mom stepped back, turned around, and reached for my hand. Aunt Charlotte did the same. The wind spiraled faster and faster, moving up above us. Caught up in the swirling air, my hair spun in a fiery red tornado.

I squeezed their hands until I heard my whisper: "*You*

are safe and never alone. Just close your eyes long enough to see yourself among the stones. "

I closed my eyes until I saw a vision of myself standing in the center of the stones. Totally mindful, I felt safe and calm in all the mystical craziness around me. Even though I was actually standing with the stones, seeing myself among them in my mind's eye felt amazing.

When I opened my eyes, the stones were aglow. The soft yellow light emanating from their surfaces joined to create an orb of illumination that encircled us. Then, as the wind died down, silence filled the temple. Still maintaining her protective stance at the perimeter, Marigold interrupted the quiet with two barks.

I knew this was the moment to decide whether I wanted to accept this tool.

"The stones are here to serve you," Mom explained, "as they have served all of our family. We have a strong ability to see, hear, and feel things we can't touch. It's not always comfortable to see and know things other people may not know yet, so sometimes it's wise to invoke the stones' protection. It enables us to turn our sensitivity on and off, or up and down, giving us the freedom to work with it on our own terms."

Mom seemed to be voicing what I sort of understood deep down. I couldn't get rid of the visions and the light because they were part of me, like they were part of my mom and aunt. But I could turn them down if I needed to concentrate on other things, and amp them up if I needed the guidance they offered—like when I knew Eddy had to go to the vet right away. If I accepted this tool, I could adjust the intensity and see things like other people saw them.

I spoke all of these thoughts aloud to Aunt Charlotte and Mom to confirm I was on the right track.

"Exactly," they confirmed, and then Mom added, "Our senses are incredibly valuable and can assist us in how we use our gifts. So it's important to allow our seeing, hearing, and feeling ability to live in our lives, but they must do so gracefully."

"Without counting," I added with a grin, and Mom nodded.

"All that's left is to accept the tool, Indigo," Aunt Charlotte began, "by bringing the stones' protection into your awareness."

I somehow knew that this meant I should let go of their hands and that I had nothing to fear. Our hands unclasped, and I touched my bracelet. The whisper spoke: *"Touch the light and know you are never alone. All you have to do is ask for help and it will surround you."*

I walked confidently to the circle of light that illumined the perimeter of the stone triangle. Reaching into it, I saw my hand glow, just like it did the night the pyramid transformed into my platter. Next I saw a vision of myself standing inside the triangle among the stones. I blinked, intuitively understanding that it would connect me to the stone's protection whenever I needed it in an instant. Light traveled up my arm and exploded in a magnificent burst. When I looked back at Mom and Aunt Charlotte, they, too, were aglow, like twin suns.

After a few moments, I knew it was time to withdraw my hand. As I did so, the light vanished, and we were our normal selves again, standing quietly among the stones.

When we got back from Stone Temple, the three of us made breakfast for dinner—scrambled eggs and toast. Afterward, Aunt Charlotte, Mom, and I sipped chamomile tea and talked about school. I felt at peace knowing that all I had to do was mindfully blink my eyes and envision myself in Stone Temple to tune out all the lights and visions so that I could begin concentrating on sixth grade.

I shared with Mom and Aunt Charlotte how I felt around Drew. "The hardest part of my day has been when I have to sit next to him," I explained. "There's something about him that makes me feel sad. Then there's this red light around his chest. It's so distracting, I can hardly stop staring at it. Plus, he plunks himself right next to Caroline and me at lunchtime."

Mom looked thoughtful. "*Hmmm.* That's interesting. It seems like he wants to be near you."

"Maybe there's something there for you to see," Aunt Charlotte suggested. "When something keeps appearing in my life, I know it's important for me to look deeply into it. People, events, numbers, songs all have a way of reappearing, sometimes over and over, until we see them fully and completely. What's cool now is that you have access to Stone Temple. If you feel overwhelmed next to Drew, you can blink mindfully for protection and then look comfortably *through* the light."

"Ah ha," I said. "I can see through the light even if I call upon the stones."

"That's right," affirmed Mom. "Working with the stones offers you a safe, calm environment in which to see what you need to know. Being yourself, using discernment, and calling on the power of the stones for help means you're that much closer to experiencing the truth of a matter."

"Who knows, Indigo?" said Aunt Charlotte. "As you master your abilities, maybe you'll choose a career that allows you to serve others using all your senses."

"So true," Mom agreed, setting her cup down. "Your senses help you at work, Charlotte, which makes you a smart cop when you're out in the field. Can you imagine, Indigo, how Aunt Charlotte might allow her visions and insight to assist her on the job? She, too, uses Stone Temple as a tool, which means her ability comes to her in a way that works best for her when she's on the job."

"For example," Aunt Charlotte added, picking up on Mom's point, "if I see menacing light around someone, or sense fear, anger, or hatred from a criminal, I call upon tools within myself, my partner, and others for the support I need. And you, sis, your patients are lucky to have you on their side. I bet you can quickly sense when something's wrong, which helps them get the care they need."

"It's true. I've learned to use my gifts and intuitive abilities to serve others just like you, Charlotte." Smiling sweetly, Mom winked at her sister and looked at me. "It takes practice, Indigo, but I know that as you work with Stone Temple and continue to live the wisdom of the heirloom, you will be able to do the same if you choose."

"Well, I'm already crazy about animals," I said. "Maybe I'll be a veterinarian someday. Aunt Charlotte, you protect us as citizens. Mom, you care for patients. Maybe I'll help heal animals when they're sick."

Sipping my last drop of tea, I returned my thinking to the subject of school. "I'm pretty sure I'll actually listen to my teachers tomorrow and start doing my schoolwork."

Mom looked at me with a silly grin, which gave me the sense that she'd been secretly worried about my lack of attention to school. "I'm sure you will, honey," she reassured me.

∽

Before I crawled into bed that night, I pulled out my golden platter and marveled at the red carnelian. If I intended to be a veterinarian someday, I'd need to collect more healing crystals, since they were powerful tools. Together, the crystals and I could offer something magical to the animals we worked with.

As I lay in bed, I held our visit to Stone Temple close to my heart. With my hands clasped together on my bedspread, which was neatly tucked under my neck, I had a good feeling about the following day. I had already set out my long jean skirt, white button-down shirt, and black converse tennis shoes by my lounge chair.

With my body immersed in warm sheets, my eyes grew heavy. But before I drifted off to sleep, I raised my left wrist in front of me and studied the heirloom. I was thankful for my bracelet and all the help that encircled me.

CHAPTER 33

THE "DREW PUZZLE"

Morning came in a flash. It was Thursday, and I had three full days of lessons to catch up on. Consequently, the day started with a bunch of consecutive mindful blinks where I envisioned myself among the stones—that is, until just before I got off the bus, when the whisper reminded me that one blink would do.

This brought up a good question: When I blinked, how long would the stones' protection last? When I asked inside myself, I heard, *"As long as it needs to."*

In a way, that made sense. After all, the red carnelian had accomplished what it did for Ed and Roots in just the way that was needed, and I didn't have to do anything except make it available to them.

Since I had blinked over and over on the bus ride, I figured I was safe to enter school. Sure enough, as I walked through the halls, I didn't even need to squint. And once in class, my pencil worked feverishly transcribing the day's lessons and homework assignments.

When the lunch bell rang, I looked forward to seeing

Caroline, but when I got to our table, she wasn't there yet. It wasn't long before Drew entered the lunchroom. The second I saw him headed toward me, I blinked in a vision of the stones. However, when he sat down, I still saw the red light around his chest.

Okay, I can handle this, I told myself determinedly, *but no sadness!*

Acknowledging Drew with a friendly nod, I pushed the additional brown-bagged lunch I'd prepared toward him.

"Thank you," he said, staring down at the bag.

"No problem," I replied. "But I don't think I can do this every day. You're going to have to make your own peanut butter and banana sandwiches next week, okay?"

In that moment, a vision slid into view of Drew opening his refrigerator. Inside were a few measly items: a half-full jar of pickles, a container of mustard, and three cans of soda. Then I saw him slam the door shut.

Drew doesn't have enough food to bring for lunch? I thought. I gulped, then I revised my last statement. "I can bring you lunch for the next two weeks. But after that—"

Drew interrupted, "I don't expect you to make me lunch. It's the first week of school, and it's my own fault. I'm having a hard time getting up to catch the bus, let alone make lunch. I'm sure I'll have this morning school routine down soon enough."

I knew from the vision that what he'd said was a cover-up.

The next moment, I heard Caroline's voice beside me. "Hey, Indigo!"

I shifted my attention to her, while I simultaneously chewed on the insight I'd received about Drew. Half-immersed in a conversation with her about our English class, I still felt distracted by the vision of Drew's barren refrigerator. I wanted to understand more about him. I also wanted to know why, even with the stones' protection, I continued to sense things about him. It occurred to me that this might be what Aunt Charlotte meant when she said that certain things keep showing up until we see them through completely. It was also true that I neither felt overwhelmed by the vision nor desperately sad in Drew's presence. So if I continued to look, maybe I'd see whatever it was that wanted to be seen.

∽

As I settled into wood shop class, Drew set his books down at our table. I searched for the red light on his chest, eager to understand its significance. I knew that, if I wanted to know more, I needed to investigate before class started, so I could conduct myself in a safe manner once our woodworking got underway.

I looked directly into the red light, and two visions appeared in my mind's eye. The first was of Drew walking toward a man I guessed was his father. The man sat in a large, navy blue recliner in a dimly lit room, reading a newspaper. I watched as Drew approached, asked a question, and walked away with his head down when the man ignored him. For an instant, sadness filled my heart. The second vision was of Drew lying face down on his bed, his arms cradling his tear-stained face. Then my attention shifted to a picture on his dresser, and I noticed a pretty lady posed within the frame. *More pieces of the "Drew puzzle."*

Just then, the shop teacher introduced the day's lesson. With pencil in hand, I switched my attention to the front of the class. I was fully present and accounted for and ready to craft something cool.

I paid attention in Social Studies, too. It was only my second time there since I'd missed it the day before. My teacher told me she was glad to see me back at school and, how did she put it? "So attentive and wide-eyed."

After class, I made the bus with time to spare, and I got a good seat toward the back. This gave me the ability to see all the action on the bus. When it screeched to a halt at the downtown stop, one of the seventh graders actually hit Jake on the head as he passed by. His name was Michael. It surprised me because Jake wasn't the kind of person other kids picked on.

Drew, who was standing behind Michael as he waited to exit the bus, backed up, making room for Jake to retaliate. Jake just reached back and straightened his hair, then waved Drew forward. "I ought to give him a good whack, but it isn't worth it," Jake said.

Michael was on some special sort of rampage, it seemed, because next he yanked on the backpack of the kid in front of him. When the boy fell to his knees, Michael jumped over him and descended the steps to the street.

What a jerk, I thought.

Instantly, the bus began ringing with accusations. "I

bet it's Michael who's setting the recycle fires!" Simone said a few rows ahead of me to one of her minions.

"He's such a hothead, always looking to make trouble," the minion agreed.

Never imagining I'd side with Simone, I thought, *I bet they're right.*

As I looked out the bus window, I noticed that Drew kept to himself, head down, backpack slung over his shoulder. With each step toward home, his dark purple bag flopped about on his back; evidently, he had very few books packed inside. In a way, I empathized with him. From the visions I'd seen, it was clear that he, too, was having a rough week.

As the driver released the brakes and the bus began moving, I saw Michael chucking pebbles from the side of the road at one of the kids in my Social Studies class.

If anyone had the nerve to start a fire, it would be—

My thoughts were interrupted by a startling vision. I saw the back of a boy I didn't recognize, standing next to the recycle dumpster behind the Moosehead Cafe with a stack of newspapers under his arm. He put the papers down on the road, then pulled a box of matches from the back pocket of his jeans. Striking the match on the black sandpaper strip along the side of the box, he lit the corner of the topmost paper, watching as it caught fire. A moment later, he hoisted the stack of paper over his head and threw it into the green steel container.

Feeling stunned and a little frightened, I blinked to call up the stones' protection. For the next thirteen minutes, until the bus approached my stop, I stared out the window. Anxious to share my visions with my aunt and my mom, I began walking up the aisle before the bus even came to a halt. Jake, who had already stood up to exit the bus, looked back down the aisle and, seeing me approach, sat down in his seat to let me pass.

"Go ahead, Jake," I encouraged.

Staring into the tiny green crevices of the vinyl seat ahead of him, he insisted, "Ladies first."

It had been a few days since he had said a word to me, so this was a good start.

∽

Mom and Aunt Charlotte were seated at the kitchen table in anticipation of my arrival. "So, how'd it go?" Aunt Charlotte asked, and Mom echoed her question.

Marigold immediately followed up with a welcome-home pounce on my long jean skirt, nudging my hand for affection.

"I survived," I replied. "But I've got some puzzle work to do. I think I just saw a vision of the crime at the dumpster, as well as of the kid who committed it. I didn't see his face, but I saw enough to confirm that he's a boy around my age."

"Really?" Mom asked, intrigued.

"What's this about a crime?" Aunt Charlotte asked, becoming police-officer alert.

Mom clued Aunt Charlotte in about the fires, adding, "It seems someone saw a young boy vanish from the scene last Sunday."

"Mr. Peterson is investigating the fires," I added. "He was called in last Sunday morning after the second fire. In fact, he asked Caroline and me if we knew anything about the situation. At the time, we didn't. But we offered to help and promised to share any information we happened to learn once school resumed."

Mom and Aunt Charlotte looked at each other, then at me. Whereupon Mom asked, "You offered to *help?*"

"Sure."

An uncomfortable silence followed, so I took the opportunity to take my backpack off and join the two of them at the table.

Mom broke the quiet. "Do you want a cup of tea? We're drinking lavender-honey. It's quite scrumptious."

Following my nod of affirmation, Mom went to the kitchen cupboard. She returned a moment later with my favorite mug in hand, the one covered in multicolored wings. Picking up the carafe on the table, she poured me a cup as she remarked, "You offered to help Mr. Peterson, and today you had a vision of the crime scene?"

"Well, I didn't see who set the fires," I clarified, "but I think I know how they get started."

"In that case," Mom suggested, "let's back up and see if all the clues you've found solve the crime. By the way, did you feel better today? Were you able to focus in class and experience school like normal?"

"Yes, other than having visions, which I assume *are* normal?"

"They're normal for us," Aunt Charlotte confirmed with a crooked smile.

"I guess I could say it's normal for me, too, now. I had three visions, but I didn't feel overwhelmed by them, and the lights around my classmates weren't visible."

"Tell us about the visions in sequence," Mom said.

Pausing every once in a while to take a sip of the delicious tea, I recounted everything that I had seen and experienced that day. I ended with what happened on the bus (leaving out the part where Jake called me a lady) and how a few people accused Michael of being the arsonist.

"He's such a bully. I can't help but wonder if he's the one setting those fires."

"It's certainly possible," Mom speculated.

I looked across the table at my aunt. "What do you think? You're the cop."

"Let's see," she said, walking over to the counter to retrieve a pen and notepad. "You say that Drew doesn't have a lot of food in his refrigerator." She sat down again and wrote the name "Drew," followed by a less-than symbol, followed by the word "food." "You stated that Drew's dad was reading a newspaper." She wrote the word "Dad," then drew a line connecting it to the word "newspaper." "You also said that when Drew approached, his dad ignored him."

"That's right," I said, as I watched Aunt Charlotte scribble the word "unavailable" next to "Dad" and a line connecting the two words.

As I pondered the diagram, something clicked. Remembering how sad Drew had seemed when he'd walked away from his dad, I reached over to borrow the notebook and pen, writing the word "sad" above Drew's name and joining all the words and symbols together with lines. "But what about the picture of the pretty lady?" I questioned.

"What did you say Drew's last name is?" Mom asked.

"I didn't say. But it's Collagen, Drew Collagen."

Mom peered out the kitchen window into our backyard, and we all sat quietly for several moments. Finally, my birds chirped from their cages by the window, breaking the silence. Lying under the table, her chin resting on my black tennis shoe, Marigold sighed loudly.

Pushing her chair from the table, Mom announced, "I'll be right back."

Aunt Charlotte and I sipped tea, neither of us speaking. Though she looked entirely comfortable with the silence, I found myself feeling a little anxious and telling myself there must be *something* we could talk about.

When Mom returned, she reached for the notepad. "May I?"

"Of course," I said, handing her the pen. Drawing another line from Drew's name, she attached the word "Mom" and wrote, "deceased."

"What?" I exclaimed.

"I thought that last name sounded familiar," she explained, "so I checked the obituaries online. Drew's family lived in the next town over. When his mom died six months ago, I guess he and his father moved into the apartment above the pharmacy near Moosehead Cafe."

"How did you recognize the name?"

"From work. I can't discuss information about patients in the hospital. Let's just say that right before some people die, they aren't in the best of health." Mom looked down at the notepad, as Aunt Charlotte slurped a mouthful of tea.

"So that picture is of his mom?" I said. "How sad."

Mom connected the words "deceased" and "sad."

"Indigo," said Aunt Charlotte, "what did you say the boy lit on fire?"

"News—" I stopped mid-word. "Oh, no," I exclaimed. "It can't be!" I whisked the pen and paper clear across the table.

"I know it's hard to imagine," said my aunt, "but if I've learned anything in this life, it's that anything is possible."

"But he's really nice! I mean, he's nothing like Michael. He's as quiet as a mouse and wouldn't hurt a fly."

"I'm sure he's a good kid, but he's obviously hurting, according to your visions. Sometimes when people hurt, they get angry. And when they get angry . . ."

I reached for the notepad, wrote the word "angry," connected it to the word "sad," and connected that chain to the word "newspaper."

"He sets his dad's newspapers on fire," I concluded.

CHAPTER 34

THE VITAL TRUTH

_~

Tearing off the first page of the notepad, Mom placed it near the tea carafe. "The next step is tricky, Indigo, but nothing you can't handle."

I knew the drill: "Things always have a way of working out."

Using a blank page in the notebook, Mom wrote down three statements, one below the other.

The first read: "Live the love you feel inside, not the fear that makes you hide."

The second said: "Be aware of your surroundings and use discernment."

The third was: "Help is all around you, just ask."

Picking up the notepad and handing it to me, she inquired, "What comes to mind when you read these statements?"

Touching the leather bracelet on my wrist, I silently reread the sentences. As I heard the whisper respond to each, I spoke the words out loud. As I listened to my voice, goose bumps rose on my forearms. "Be courageous—be *me.* Choose wisely. To be brave sometimes means asking for help."

"Yes," Mom and Aunt Charlotte chorused, reaching across the table with their left hands, placing them on my left wrist. With their hands connected to our family bracelet, Mom said, "If you proceed with what you know about Drew, using the wisdom you just shared with us, you'll be safe and of service to Drew and your community."

"Your mom is right on," Aunt Charlotte confirmed. "From personal experience, I can add that when I'm this way, I'm at my best. It not only makes me a smart woman—it makes me a better cop."

Having lived with the bracelet for months, I understood what Mom and Aunt Charlotte were saying. "I'm still not sure what to do next," I confessed. "What do I do with the information from the visions? Who's going to believe me when I tell them I had a vision of the crime scene? Has this ever happened to you?" I asked my aunt.

She rolled her eyes dramatically. "All. The. Time."

"So how do you handle the situation?" I pressed.

"I tell the *vital* truth."

"I don't understand. What do you mean?"

"You see what other people see," she explained, "and you also see *more*. If you want to relate to others who don't see *more* like you do, tell the truth in a way they can understand. In this instance, how might you share what you know by telling the vital truth?"

"First off, I don't even know who to tell."

Mom jumped in. "That one's easy, honey. Who's connected to all your visions?"

"Drew."

"All right, then. Like Aunt Charlotte says, when something keeps showing up, pay attention and look all the way through it."

"You mean start by talking to Drew?" I gaped at them. "Are you kidding me? I'm going to tell him I had a vision of him standing at his refrigerator, and I know he doesn't have food to make his lunch?"

"Do you think Drew would understand if you tell him about your visions?" Aunt Charlotte asked.

"Probably not."

"Then how else could you share the truth, just giving him the most vital pieces?"

"I don't know," I sighed. With my eyes glued to the edge of the kitchen table, I felt my heart begin to race. "You guys are the trained professionals. Help me."

With contagious enthusiasm, Mom and Aunt Charlotte tag-teamed me. They each took turns telling me about visions they'd had and how they were able to modify that into the vital truth so that others could relate to and benefit from the information. They also told me about times when they'd shared too much, and how for some people, the nitty-gritty details sparked fear, suspicion, and even anger. I really appreciated their honesty.

Next we did some role-playing. Aunt Charlotte pretended to be the fire marshal, which helped me plan my vital-truth answers to any questions Mr. Peterson might ask when I phoned him to see if he would be home the following afternoon. All I had to tell him was that I wanted to discuss the dumpster fires and might bring a friend who could provide information for his investigation. Then, Mom played Drew, and I planned out what I'd say to him as well.

When I voiced a concern that Drew might not turn himself in, Mom said, "If he doesn't choose to ride home with you, you'll meet with Mr. Peterson without him. If you want, we can go with you. All you have to do is tell the vital truth. So, what might that sound like?"

"If Drew confesses to me at school, it wouldn't feel right to rat on him and share what he tells me in private, so I guess I could say that I suspect a fellow classmate might have something to do with the dumpster fires? And if he asks me why I suspect it, I guess I could say it's personal?"

"That works," said Mom.

So, over all, the coaching session went great, and I learned a lot. With Mom's nursing skills, Aunt Charlotte's police experience, and my visions in play, I must confess our plan was genius. I made the call to Mr. Peterson. He'd be home. I felt the butterflies jumping around in my belly, but I knew all the planning and talking to Drew and Mr. Peterson was a wise choice.

The next morning, Silvy whinnied from the barn. "I know, I'm coming," I assured him. Pulling up the long sleeves of my button-down shirt, I raised my bandana skirt, then my feet one at a time into my boots.

Pushing aside the barn door, I announced cheerily,

"Good morning, Silvy. I see you." Silvy gazed into the walkway, his eyes meeting mine, anxious for his morning feed.

"It's going to be an adventurous Friday, Silvy," I said. "Wish me luck." After opening his stall door, I pulled myself against his neck. As we connected, he leaned in, rubbing his cheek on my shirt.

While I was filling Silvy's feed and freshwater bins, Marigold ran into the barn and barked twice. "Thanks, Marigold," I yelled from inside Silvy's stall. "I'll be right there."

Pulling the wooden door shut behind me, I yanked off my boots and put on my sneakers. "Good dog," I said, patting her on the head. "I'll see ya after school, okay, girl?"

Running down our driveway to the bus stop, I shouted back at Marigold over my shoulder. "You're lucky. You get to spend the day with Aunt Charlotte. She's leaving tonight, you know."

Again, Jake and I stood at the bus stop in silence. We had been *so* close to becoming friends and then I had to blurt out that vision I had of him holding my hand. I wanted to kick myself. When the bus arrived, I found a seat in the back while it rolled on toward the next stop. Jake followed me down the aisle and sat catty-corner from me. When he looked back at me and flashed me a smile, I waved.

After learning about the "vital truth," I realized I would have kept the vision of us holding hands to myself had I known better. The vital truth there was that he wanted to hold my hand, which was something I had to know but not something I needed to share.

"Ed's home," he said. "Figured you'd want to know."

"I'm so glad," I said, but before I could express further excitement, he flipped his bangs and turned back toward the front.

As I entered the school grounds, I blinked a few times to invoke the stone's protection, and then I made my way to Caroline's locker, where she was unloading the contents of her backpack.

"Hi," I said cheerily, and she responded with even more cheer by pulling me in for a hug. The bracelet really seemed to be helping her. I knew it was difficult for her to ride the bus back and forth with Tess every day, but she really seemed to be holding up well.

"I have a strange favor to ask you," I said.

"Coming from you," Caroline said with a laugh, "I wouldn't expect you to ask me a *normal* favor."

I chuckled. How right she was. I explained that I needed to speak with Drew privately at lunchtime and asked her if she'd mind giving us some space so he wouldn't suspect anything was amiss. I also told her that when I knew more, I'd tell her everything. For now, this was something I needed to do on my own.

"No problem," she said with the sort of understanding only a best friend can offer. "We have all day to hang out at my house tomorrow. And Noel can't wait for our karaoke session!"

"I can't wait either," I agreed. "I'm going to ask Noel to teach me the sign for the word *truth.*"

᳁

"Where's your friend?" Drew asked when I arrived at our lunch table that afternoon.

"She had work to do in the library," I told him. Plopping down my lunch, then Drew's, I said, "I changed it up this morning; it's turkey and cheese. Are you okay with that?"

"Yeah," he said, clearly delighted.

We sat quietly while I got up the nerve to speak my truth. "Something tells me that maybe you don't have a lot of food in your home."

Drew took a bite of his sandwich and stared at the table in front of us.

I persisted, "I see you scarf down that sandwich, and I can tell you're real hungry. You also don't say much, which tells me there's something heavy on your mind. Are you all right?"

Drew took another bite before setting his sandwich on the empty brown bag beside him. Rubbing his hands together under the table, he turned to look at me. "My dad's real sad," he admitted quietly. "Ever since my mom died a few months back, he can't seem to get on with his life. All he does is sit in his chair and read the stupid paper. I mean, really, who reads the newspaper anymore? And I can't remember the last time he went grocery shopping. He buys take-out from the Moosehead Cafe all the time."

"I'm sorry to hear about your mom," I said. "I can't imagine what it must be like."

Taking another bite from his sandwich, Drew seemed to zone out again.

"Drew," I announced, "I know you lit the recycle dumpster on fire."

Drew almost choked on the food in his mouth. Coughing it loose, he took a drink from the bottle of water I had put in his lunch.

Mom and I never bought bottled water unless we had to; with all the plastic bottles bobbing in oceans and filling up landfills, we preferred to use metal carafes with tightly sealed lids. But since Mom knew I was making lunch for two this week, she'd picked up a small pack for Drew.

When Drew remained silent, I spoke again, "I'm worried you're going to get hurt, or buildings will catch on fire and someone else could get hurt. Then what, huh?"

Turning to face me, he said, "So you're the one who saw me running away last Sunday?"

"Not exactly," I said, my voice trembling and my heart pounding. "But I know you light your dad's newspapers on fire and throw them into the dumpster."

I was relieved when Drew didn't ask how I knew. Had he asked, I would have explained that I knew in my own way, which was honest but didn't tell the *whole* story. Telling Drew I'd had a vision would freak him out, like it did Jake.

"So now what?" Drew finally asked, a note of desperation in his voice. Taking a last bite of sandwich, he grabbed his brown lunch bag and fiercely crumpled it up into a paper ball. "Are you going to tell on me?"

"I haven't yet, have I?" I asked. "I was hoping you

would meet with the fire marshal and tell him what happened. That way, they won't worry about who is setting the fires, and you can figure out a safer way to deal with your anger."

"A safer way to deal with your anger" were Aunt Charlotte's words. As a policewoman, she'd said she'd seen many kids destroy property and commit petty crimes because they were very unhappy. Even though I didn't think Drew meant to destroy the dumpster, I knew he was angry and was going to find himself in a world of trouble if he didn't get help.

"The fire marshal is my neighbor," I explained. "He's a nice man and is concerned about the kid who's responsible for the fires. I think, if you visit with him yourself, you'll find him to be understanding."

"Are you kidding me?" he yelped. "He'll probably put me in jail!"

"As a matter of fact," I replied calmly, "I talked about this with my Aunt Charlotte, who's a cop in California."

Slamming his hand onto his forehead, Drew groaned.

"Don't worry—I know what you're thinking," I assured him. "Just trust me. I asked her advice on the matter, knowing full well there's nothing she can do to punish you. She said that, in most cases, kids who get caught lighting fires take fire-safety classes and perform community service. You might have to meet with a counselor as well. The way I see it, that would be a good thing, don't you think?"

"What if I don't meet with the fire marshal? Will you tell him anyway?"

"Yes, I will," I said firmly. "I offered to help him a week ago before I knew you were responsible, and I must keep my word."

Drew refused to look at me.

"Do you think you can ride home with me on the bus?" I pressed. "I know Mr. Peterson is off work this afternoon. We could walk over to his house from my bus stop and sit down for a chat."

Drew didn't answer.

"Look, I promise, you'll really like the man. He's not scary, and he's real helpful. He changed a flat tire for me and my mom once, and even let me borrow his fishing rod at the Looking Pond. We caught the biggest bass that day. Do you like to fish?"

Drew cleared his throat and turned toward me. "So, there's good fishing in that pond, eh? I heard a rumor about that. It was a bass, you say?"

"It was twenty-three inches long, can you believe it? We threw it back though. It gives us something exciting to fish for on the weekends. We call him Whoop. You know, like, 'whoop-whoop, we're so excited'?"

Drew turned his head to the side and looked at me funny.

"Mr. Peterson is an excellent fisherman. I bet if you wanted to go to the Looking Pond someday, he'd take you. He's that kind of guy."

"I'll have to call home and get permission to get off at your stop," Drew mumbled. "What do I tell my dad?"

"Tell him the truth. You're going to meet with our neighbor, Mr. Peterson, who happens to know a lot about the great fishing at the Looking Pond. I'm sure Mr. Peterson will help you figure out how to talk with your dad about the fires if you ask him."

"How will I get home?"

"If your dad can't pick you up, my mom could drive you home on our way to the airport. My aunt is flying back to California this evening."

When the lunch bell rang, Drew stood up. Turning to face me, he said, "Fine. I'll leave a message for my dad. He won't care if I'm home or not anyway. See you on the bus."

As Drew walked away, his head lowered, I let out a huge sigh of relief.

"See ya later!" I called out.

CHAPTER 35

THE FIRE MARSHAL

D rew and I sat together on the bus. Jake kept his distance but kept eyeing us after he noticed that Drew didn't get off at his own stop. When the bus stopped on our block, Jake hopped off after us, then dashed ahead. He kept looking back, probably wondering why we were heading toward his house. He disappeared inside his front door well before we reached the front porch steps.

"Come on, Drew," I coaxed. "Mr. Peterson won't bite, I promise."

I rang the bell.

When the front door opened, Mr. Peterson greeted us. He motioned for us to come on in. "Hi, Indigo," he said. "I've been expecting you. And who's this?"

"This is my friend Drew," I answered. "I told him all about the Looking Pond and the bass we caught that day. He's new to town, and he likes to fish. I thought maybe you could take him with you and Jake someday."

"That would be fun," Mr. Peterson said, leading us into the kitchen. "Would you guys like something to drink?"

"Sure," I replied, "I'd love a glass of water."

"How about you, Drew?" Mr. Peterson asked.

"Water would be fine, thank you, sir," he replied with a squeak in his voice.

When Eddy walked into the kitchen, I immediately commented on how good she looked. She still had a bandage on the shaved part of her belly, but I could sense that she was on the mend by the soft white aura that surrounded her.

"Thanks to you," Mr. Peterson replied. "Jake speaks very highly of how you came to Eddy's rescue. He's upstairs right now. I'm sure he'll come down a little later."

I smiled, a little embarrassed. Caring for animals came so naturally to me that it didn't seem like a big deal. Lowering my hand and rubbing my fingers together to lure Eddy my way, I watched as she first brushed up against Mr. Peterson's leg, then pranced toward my hand. Ducking her head under my fingers, she pushed up against them, pressing me to pet her soft calico fur. "I'm so happy you're better," I cooed.

Drew took a sip of his water as he watched the cat and me, then set the glass back on the table with a loud *knock!* When I glanced up, he cleared his throat and looked away. No doubt he felt awkward. I would have, too, if I didn't know what a cool guy Mr. Peterson was.

"Fishing isn't the only thing Drew wants to talk to you about," I began. "He has something to share with you. Last Sunday, you asked if I knew anything about the dumpster fires. I didn't know anything then, but I learned that Drew knows all about them. Drew, why don't you take it from here?"

Drew looked nervously at me, then at Mr. Peterson. Clearing his throat again, he proceeded to reveal the truth. "It was me, Mr. Peterson. I mean, I lit my dad's papers on fire, then threw them in the dumpster. I didn't mean for the dumpster to go up in flames, although it makes sense that it would."

Loud footsteps pounded on the stairs, and a moment later, Jake appeared in the entrance to the kitchen.

Jumping up from the table, I grabbed Jake by the arm and led him onto the front porch. "Your dad's preoccupied at the moment," I explained.

"What the heck, Indigo? What's that Drew kid doing in my house?"

"It's a private matter," I said firmly. "We need to give them some space."

"He's a pretty strange kid, you know."

"He may not be the happiest kid you've ever met," I said defensively, "but he has some personal business to take care of with your dad."

"What's so personal about it?"

"I can't say, or it wouldn't be personal now would it?"

"Oh, come on," Jake snapped. "I have a right to know why he's sitting at my kitchen table, don't you think?"

"Not if it's a personal matter," I shot back, "unless either Drew or your dad want to tell you about it later."

"Why are *you* involved? I know he sits next to you every day at lunch. Are you guys going out or something?"

"Uh, no," I gasped, "but I've gotten to know him enough to know he's having a hard time right now."

Jake's face fell. "Yeah, I heard he lost his mother to cancer last February."

"Where'd you hear that?" I demanded.

"On the bus, when the kids were whispering about who the arsonist might be. I think that kid Michael said Drew's dad is a real piece of work. Since Drew's mom died, all his dad does now is walk back and forth between their apartment and the Moosehead Cafe."

As I slid my back down the pillar and sat on the porch floor, Jake gestured to the wicker rocking chair next to the front door. "Sit here," he invited.

"No, thanks," I replied. "I kinda like it down here."

As Jake took a seat in the rocker, I decided now was a good time to try to repair our new friendship. "I'm sorry I said anything about my vision of us holding hands the other day."

Jake squirmed a little. "I know you can sense things, like you did with Eddy and the smoke and the Pop-Tarts and other stuff." He paused for a minute and his face grew red. "Maybe I *was* thinking about holding your hand, but it's not like I even meant to think about it or anything . . ."

My heart began thumping. Glancing down at my bracelet, I fiddled with the infinity clasp. I didn't know what to say, and fortunately, I didn't have to say anything because Mr. Peterson and Drew came outside just then.

When I saw Mr. Peterson's hand resting on Drew's right shoulder and both seemed relaxed, I hopped to my feet. "So is it all cleared up?"

Both Drew and Mr. Peterson said yes at the same time. Drew gave me a slight smile.

Jake stood up, looking perplexed, but he somehow seemed to know that it was his dad's official business, and it had nothing to do with him.

"Well, we've got to go," I announced. "My aunt has a plane to catch and we've got to get Drew home."

I tugged at Drew's shirt and pulled him down the porch steps. "Bye, Jake! Thanks, Mr. Peterson!" I called over my shoulder.

"Thank *you*, Indigo," Mr. Peterson called back.

⁓

The four of us sat uncomfortably quiet in the car. While I fiddled with my bracelet, Drew stared out the backseat window, bouncing his left leg up and down just enough to catch my eye every darned second. Mom and Aunt Charlotte held their gaze on the road, turning their heads on occasion to flash secret-like smiles to each other. It was as if they knew, without me even telling them, that everything had worked out as planned with Drew and Mr. Peterson.

Several minutes into the drive, Aunt Charlotte ventured, "Drew, was Mr. Peterson understanding?"

Drew gulped, his leg now bouncing faster, his hands clenched in his lap. "Yes, ma'am, Mr. Peterson was kind. He'll have to notify the police, but he thinks I'll only have to take fire-safety classes, do some community service, and meet with a counselor. He said he'll come to my house tonight and help me talk with my dad. He even offered to take me *and* my dad fishing at the Looking Pond some weekend."

"What time is he coming to your house, Drew?" Mom inquired.

"He offered to bring us dinner tonight. So around suppertime, I guess."

"Is your dad expecting you right away? If not, I don't have to drop you home now. You're welcome to ride with us to the airport."

"That sounds good, Mrs. Monroe. Thanks, I'll ride with you all if that's okay."

"Perfect," Mom said, gently hitting the steering wheel with her left hand in excitement. "How about a round of chocolate shakes from the drive-through? We have time for that don't we, sis?"

"We always have time for chocolate, right, guys?" Aunt Charlotte draped her arm around the back of mom's seat, looking back at Drew and me.

Drew and I nodded "yes," like bobble heads on a bumpy road.

When we arrived at the airport, I hugged Aunt Charlotte tight. "I'm going to really miss you," I said.

"You're quite the gal, Indigo Monroe. Keep up the good work, okay? I'm very proud of you."

I squeezed her once more, then reluctantly let go. Mom had already said her goodbyes and stood by the car waving as Aunt Charlotte wheeled her red suitcase through the sliding doors. Drew sat inside the car, slurping every last puddle of chocolate from the bottom of his cup.

Placing my left hand above my eyes to shield them, I peered into the airport terminal. Countless lights surrounding travelers reflected off the large glass windows, so I blinked in the stones' protection, causing them to dim pleasantly.

As I watched my aunt disappearing into the crowd, to my surprise I noticed a shimmering white light across her back that was swinging up and down with her every step. *Hmmm*, I thought, as I remembered seeing a similar light on Mom's back earlier in the week. The light wasn't overwhelming. It was beautiful.

Like Aunt Charlotte said, "If something keeps showing up, look into it fully." So I did. I looked at the light intensely.

When Mom opened the driver-side door and took her seat, I knocked on the passenger window, motioning to her to roll it down. "Did you see that?" I whispered.

Mom smiled. "You mean the wings?" Then she winked and rolled up the window. Shocked, I stared at her through the glass. As I got into the car, I turned to her. When she placed her index finger over her lips, I nodded "okay."

When we pulled up at Drew's apartment near the pharmacy entrance, I noticed that he grabbed the inside handle of the car door and held it tightly, as if he were fighting the inevitable. Unfortunately, he would have to face his dad and tell the truth. He might even have to be brave enough to ask for help.

Mom pointed to the rearview mirror. "That's Mr. Peterson's truck, right?"

Drew and I looked behind us. "Yep, that's it all right," I said. "Good timing, eh?"

Releasing the door handle, Drew breathed a sigh of relief. "Thank you, Mrs. Monroe. Indigo, I'll see you at school on Monday."

I felt really good about how the day had turned out. From the way Mom looked at me, I could tell she was really proud. On the way home, I filled her in on how it went at lunch with Drew and how he had arrived at his decision to meet with Mr. Peterson. It turned out that our plan had worked perfectly.

Then Mom told me that she wouldn't have dropped Drew off at home if Mr. Peterson hadn't been there. Drew deserved to have a trained professional by his side when his dad learned the news, she explained. If Drew's dad got really angry at him, Mr. Peterson could calm things down. "Safety first," she added.

I didn't fully understand why it wouldn't be safe for Drew to be alone with his dad, but then Mom explained that sometimes anger catches on fire, and fire can be dangerous. (We all knew that!) She reassured me that Mr. Peterson would connect Drew with all kinds of help so that he could feel less angry and make better choices.

"I hope his dad gets help, too." I added. "Drew needs food in his refrigerator."

CHAPTER 36

A GOOD LISTENER

I pressed the white button and "poof," Noel stood before me in the front doorway, arms outstretched. Dropping to my knees in one of my newest Monroe Originals—a long bright paisley skirt—I swooped her up for a hug.

"Come on in," Caroline said from behind.

Once inside, Noel poked my leg. I looked down. She pointed her index finger at her mouth, and then at me.

"She's signing the word *truth* for you," Caroline explained with a giggle. "I told her you wanted to learn it."

A huge smile lit up my face. "Thank you, Noel!"

I tried signing the word, and she nodded approvingly.

Caroline signed to Noel, patted her on the back, and Noel signed, "See you later," and then she scampered off. I blew her a kiss.

"I asked her to give us some privacy for a little while," Caroline said. "I told her we have big-girl things to catch up on."

A few minutes later, my best friend and I sprawled ourselves out on her bedroom floor. As we lay face-to-face, my long curls hung over my shoulders brushing Caroline's purple carpet. When the red flare of my hair started to annoy me, I removed a yellow elastic tie from my wrist and pulled my curls up into a ponytail.

With her chin in cupped hands, her head propped up by her forearms, Caroline listened closely as I filled her in on the past week, uttering an "uh-huh" with each break in my story. I trusted Caroline completely and knew she'd keep all my personal experiences a secret.

"So once you asked for help from the stones, the lights went away?" she pressed.

"They definitely dimmed so that I wasn't overwhelmed. But there are also lights that appear even when I blink in the stones. According to my aunt, those are the ones I ought to pay close attention to, look all the way through, since they may be there for a reason."

"Wow, that's pretty cool," Caroline said. "You've got to feel so relieved."

"I do," I assured her.

"So what was that whole thing with Drew about? Why did you need to talk with him alone at lunch yesterday?"

Realizing I'd said I would fill her in today, but also aware that some of the details of what I saw were private, I didn't know how to answer. How could I *not* share everything with my best friend? I didn't want her feel I didn't trust her.

When I fell silent, Caroline prompted, "Indigo?"

I recited what I heard inside me: "That part's personal, Caroline."

"Okay, I understand," she said, smiling reassuringly. Then, suddenly, it felt as if the two of us had stepped outside time. When something flickered behind me, I turned my head around. There, hovering over my back was the same shimmering light I'd seen on Aunt Charlotte's and Mom's backs.

I blinked. The white light became even more intense, so I held my gaze just enough to remember what Mom told me at the airport. Imagining *myself* with wings, I examined the light closely.

Caroline stared past me. Entranced in a bracelet break, I knew she wouldn't be fazed by what was going on with me. So even though I was totally amazed and wanted to yell, "I'm going have them, too!" I kept my mouth shut.

Yes, Caroline was my best friend and the best listener ever, but what I saw was for me to see and needed to remain private—at least for now. Plus, Caroline seemed pleasantly preoccupied with something way beyond me.

As soon as her attention came back into the room, Caroline asked boldly, "May I have your hair tie?"

Whisking it off my ponytail, I placed it in her hand. "Take it," I urged with excitement. "It's yours!"

"Thanks, Indigo," she said. Then, unhooking her bracelet, she strung the loop through the leather and motioned to me to refasten the infinity clasp.

"Do you want to tell me what you saw?" I asked, thrilled to witness her receive her second symbol.

"I don't *see* like you do," she replied thoughtfully, causing me to feel a little embarrassed and fall silent. Still caught in her own world for the moment, she sat up and fiddled with her new symbol on the bracelet, evidently trying to understand what she had experienced.

"What did that feather on your bracelet represent again?" she asked after a while.

"My love for animals and how I want to help them all the time."

"That's perfect. You're so good with them."

Seeing as I'd just held back personal information from her, I wasn't expecting her to share what she had clearly come to realize. But ever so softly, she said, "I'm a good listener."

I grinned ear to ear. "Yes . . . you . . . are."

CHAPTER 37

JUST ANOTHER DAY

The following morning, I nearly jumped out of my skin when I saw Jake through the screen of my back door, his hands cupped around his eyes to shade the quickly rising sun. Behind him was Luke.

"Indigo," he said, "sorry to bother you, but . . ."

"No worries," I said, opening the screen door. "I was just about to get ready for my fishing date with my dad."

Luke shifted nervously, and Marigold locked her eyes on him. She was bound and determined to put herself between me and this stranger.

"Marigold, move away," I commanded, grabbing her collar and pulling her from the door. "It's okay, I go to school with him."

"We're fine out here," Jake assured me, falling back, so I let the door close behind me. Together we sat on my back porch steps. Luke had never been at my house before, and I was really curious why the boys had come over.

"While we were getting our fishing gear together, I was telling Luke about how you helped Ed," Jake began, his voice a little shaky, "and he got to thinking. He has a few questions for you about his horse, Gypsy."

I stared open-mouthed at Jake, thinking, *Did you tell Luke everything about that day?*

When Jake went on to explain, "Oh, and just so we're clear, Luke knows you have a gift when it comes to animals," I felt myself relax. Then, winking at me, he added, "A gift I can't even *begin* to tell him about."

I sighed with relief.

While Luke told me all about Gypsy, I listened intently. As he spoke, I had visions of Gypsy that gave me an idea of what might be bothering her. "Have your parents contacted your veterinarian yet?" I asked.

"The vet is scheduled to visit next week," he assured me. "But I thought you might know how I could help her in the meantime. I just can't stand seeing her so unsettled."

"I know how you feel," I said. "Did you guys just get a new horse?"

Luke glanced at Jake. "Did you tell her about Max, Jake?"

"Nope." Jake smiled.

Turning back to me, Luke explained, "Max arrived at our barn last week."

"And is his stall right next to Gypsy's?" I asked.

"It is."

"Is there another stall across from Gypsy that Max could have?"

"Actually, there's an open stall right across from her. Why?"

"You might try putting Max in that stall. I think Gypsy would prefer that."

"Well, that's easy enough," Luke professed.

"I suspect that if Gypsy can see more of Max, she'll feel more settled. But do make sure your vet checks her out." As I spoke these words, I suddenly had a vision of a beautiful pink and green crystal on the velvet that lined the golden platter under my bed. I stared away and fell silent, but not long enough for the boys to notice.

"Thanks for your help," Jake said, getting up off the steps.

We all stood.

"Yeah, thanks for the advice," Luke added. "That settles it—no fishin' for me today! I'm gonna go switch the stalls now, and I'll let you guys know how it plays out."

I had a feeling it would work out well for Luke and his horses.

As soon as they left, I raced to my room to look under the bed. Sure enough, on top of the red velvet was a pink and green stone. I grabbed the crystal book from my nightstand and discovered that it was a watermelon tourmaline. As I read about the stone's healing properties, I wasn't surprised to discover that they included "an ability to stabilize one's nerves." I sensed it was a great crystal for helping stressed animals.

I had one more bandana left in the drawer in my nightstand, so I dropped the crystal in the bandana pouch and stuffed the whole thing in my pocket. I made a mental note to make more bandanas so I'd have more for times like these.

An hour or so later, rocks crunched as Dad drove into our driveway. As he stepped out of his car and held up the bag of doughnuts, I grabbed the tackle box and Thermos from the back porch stairs and held them up, too. It was our special fishy way of greeting each other.

In the garage, we loaded Mom's bike with gear. While I rode horseback, Dad bounced along on the old cushiony seat of Mom's bike. It had been two weeks since we'd fished.

Mom had filled Dad in on what had been going on with me. She'd shared with me that when she suggested bringing my aunt in for a visit, he'd insisted on paying for the plane ticket. I thought that was great.

As we made our way to the Looking Pond, I told him about my experience at Stone Temple. He didn't zone out the way he used to when Mom and I talked about Sienna Glass. In fact, he listened closely. I didn't mention the shimmering light on my back, not even to Mom. For now, it felt personal, like when I'd first gotten the pyramid. Besides, I hadn't seen it since yesterday in Caroline's room.

When I finally stopped talking, Dad gave me a long stare, then said, "You know, even though I may not understand how your gifts work, I'm here to help if you need anything."

After all we'd been through, I knew Dad meant what he said.

Arriving at the weeping willow tree, I saw that Jake and his dad were parked on the edge of the pond. Two others were with them. Jumping down from Silvy, I was delighted to see that one of them was Drew, accompanied by a man I guessed was his dad. They were seated next to Mr. Peterson and Jake, each with fishing rods in hand.

"Is that Mr. Peterson?" asked Dad, still straddling Mom's bike.

"Yep. And he brought my classmate Drew and his father to fish with them.

Once Jake spotted us, he waved Dad and me over to join them. Anxious to see if they'd caught anything, we grabbed our goods and hustled in their direction.

"Anyone caught Whoop yet?" I whispered, eyeing the fishermen.

Dad stood behind me waiting for an introduction.

Surprisingly, Drew chimed in first. "Nope, but we've had a few bites." He swung his arm back and threw out another cast. "Dad, this is Indigo," he added.

"Nice to meet you," I said, leaning in to shake his hand. "And this is my dad, Mr. Monroe."

Dad set down our gear and stepped forward, clearly jacked about carrying on a conversation with the guys about all things fishing. While they bonded, I saw a shimmering white light around Drew's chest. Surprised by the change in color, I sat down beside him on the bank. Drew sat next to his dad, who sat next to Jake, who sat next to Mr. Peterson. Dad plopped down on the opposite end and shook hands with Mr. Peterson. They'd known each other a very long time.

Drew slowly reeled in his hook. "Yes, perfect son, nice and easy," said Mr. Collagen. Drew's aura brightened instantly from the attention.

Knowing Drew would make another cast, I ducked down low and waited. "I won't hook you," Drew announced, swinging his rod up and over my side and throwing out another cast.

Sitting up the second I heard his fishing line whiz by, I said, "I knew you wouldn't." But maybe I hadn't been so sure.

Dangling my feet on the water's edge, I looked by the weeping willow tree at Silvy. There he was, totally happy, grazing under the morning sun. When my eyes bounced back around, Dad was holding out my rod, waving it to catch my attention. "Here, honey, it's ready to go."

Seeing that he'd baited the hook and everything, I waved it forward. Mr. Peterson passed it to Jake, who passed it to Mr. Collagen, who passed it to Drew, who paused before handing it off to me with his free hand.

"I won't be needing any more lunches," he said under his breath with a smile.

Smiling back at him, I watched as the white light around his chest began to expand. Sensing that was a good sign, I simply nodded and reached for my fishing rod.

Taking it all in, the birds singing, the leaves rustling in the wind, Dad's laughter, and Drew's light heart, I set my rod aside.

"How's it going over here?" asked Jake, making his way to our side of the fishing crew.

I reached into the front pocket of my purple jeans and pulled out the crystal bandana.

"Give this to Luke," I said, handing him the bandana as he sat down beside me. "Tell him I thought it might help calm Gypsy. There's a watermelon tourmaline inside the crystal pouch, just like the bandana I gave to Eddy. Although Gypsy's too big to wear it, Luke can tie it to the back of her harness so it's resting on her head and neck. Tell him to tie it tight—maybe double or even triple tie it. Okay? I'm sure he'll think it's a bit strange, but what the heck. He asked for help, and this is the kind of help I'm good at."

Jake smiled as he tucked the bandana into his pocket. He hesitated for a second and then he reached for my hand. My heart began to pound. Glad I wasn't all wormy from the bait, I met him halfway. When our hands clasped, he squeezed a little, his hand lingered, and then he let go. I blushed. He quickly stood up then and walked back toward his dad.

I smiled real wide inside and my heart felt so big that it would burst. And it wasn't because Jake had just actually held my hand, like he really did *like* me. It was because it felt like everything was just fitting into place.

I sure had come a long way since Mom had given me our heirloom. I'd learned so many things about myself, and even without all the magical experiences that surrounded me—from Sienna Glass to the crystals to the transforming pyramid to the auras to Stone Temple to the visions—I felt like anything I set my mind to was possible if I listened carefully and chose wisely.

Suddenly, I tingled all over, and a brilliant white light surrounded me. I peeked over at the others who were all absorbed in their fishing and one another, so I knew no one else noticed that I was having a moment. Besides, I knew they couldn't see what I saw. Feeling totally calm and capable, I didn't blink in the stone's protection. I wanted to see everything all the way through.

On my back, I felt a strange sensation of something unwrapping and then unfolding. When I glanced over my shoulder, what I saw and felt took my breath away: A set of beautiful white wings splayed open, spreading outward, wider than my shoulders and higher than my head.

With *my* wings now fully grown, it hit me: a deep knowing that I could fly—that everyone of us could fly, no matter who we are or what gifts we possess. When we grow our wings, *anything* is possible.

"Indigo," Drew called. When I didn't respond, he pushed on my knee with his free hand. I turned toward him, and he held up my bracelet. "Isn't this yours?"

I nodded in appreciation and reached out for the heirloom. When it was safely in my hands, I said a silent thank you to the bracelet for helping me all these months and for blowing that mystery—who am I?—out of the water.

I slipped the bracelet in my pocket for safekeeping, and I rejoined the hunt for Whoop with a cast that flew so far past all the guys' bobbers that they turned and looked at me with goggly eyes. Grinning just a little, I shrugged like it was no big deal, nudged forward to the edge of the bank, and tucked my wings in close.

Within moments I felt a fierce tug on my line and the bobber plunged deep into the water. When I yanked my rod back to set the hook, the guys jumped to their feet.

"Whoop, whoop, whoop!" they cheered, and I joined in—the loudest whooper of them all.

GRATITUDE

I am grateful to Brian, my husband, who provides, protects, and holds pure and loving space for me to grow; Sophia Delaney and Emma Louise, who inspire me to grow; my mom, dad, sister, and brother, who make me grow; Ali, Lynn, and Juls, who "tell it to me straight" as I grow; and my grandma, Beanie, who showed me I *can* grow up to be a ninety-eight-year-old superhero *and* live on planet earth.

I am also grateful to John K., Shonagh, Alisa, Diana, Julie, Laurie, Susan, Laurel, Odin, and John L. Our gatherings remain invaluable to me.

A heartfelt thank-you to Shirley Moulton, Carol Lawrence, Stacy Toten, Shefali Tsabary, Annie Burnside, Cathy Cassani Adams, David Ord, Lisa McCourt, Carol Rosenberg, Gary Rosenberg, Erin Taylor, and Lynnda Pollio. Our connections have been a source of great comfort along the way.

Alexandra Hambright Solomon, I am forever grateful for your faith, support, and encouragement.

Last, I am grateful for the child in me who knows. You are honest, patient, and wise. A bundle of joy. A Master within. I. Love. You.

ABOUT THE AUTHOR

ALEXANDRA FOLZ has a master's degree in nursing from University of Michigan. She is a writer, mother, and intuitive. She currently works as a team leader and member liaison for www.BuildingConnectedCommunities.com and is an intuitive counselor, meditation facilitator, and volunteer for hospice.

Alexandra is passionate about expanding awareness, honoring her inner voice, and pushing through fears while sharing her gifts with others. One thing Alexandra loves most is collaborating, bringing innovative ideas to life by celebrating and engaging with other people's natural abilities. Alexandra's book, *The Heirloom,* is living proof that collaboration and support by many create magical works of art.

Alexandra currently lives in Washington State with her husband and two daughters.

To learn more, visit www.alexandrafolz.com. Also, please visit http://zazushouse.org/. This parrot sanctuary represents the heart of what Alexandra values and is the home to her beloved friend Beeba, an African grey parrot.

CPSIA information can be obtained
at www.ICGtesting.com
Printed in the USA
LVOW13s2016200117

521683LV00003B/12/P